The Summer You Slept On Glass

D A DEANS
Paper-Owl-Press
New Jersey

ISBN-13: 978-0-9916183-0-9 (Paperback 2nd Edition)

Permission granted to print the lyrics to: *When Dreams Feel Real* by Bobi Mizimakoski.

Publication Date: 2014
Printed in the United States of America
Imprint Name: Paper-Owl-Press, Paramus, NJ
PaperOwlPress8@gmail.com

"Eat in a circle."
"No silly, save the best for last."

To my rock, without your love and support,
this could never be.

Endless love,.

The Summer You Slept
On Glass

PRELUDE

IN THE KITCHEN, HANNA STYVERS found her twelve-year-old son being his usual self, eating cereal out of the box and swigging milk from the carton.

"Johnny Styvers," she firmly stated, holding back her impatience for proper etiquette, "you do realize if you put the cereal and milk into a bowl, you will produce the exact same effect?"

"Yeah, but don't cha know—I'm saving the planet?"

"Saving the planet?" she injected. "How so?"

"Keepin' it green—no washing, get it? No wastin' water, detergent, paper towels." He smiled, showing teeth an orthodontist would hate.

His mother, Hanna, shook her head. There was some validity to his train of thought. Contemplating her next choice of words, she studied him in his element and saw the manifestation of the man who helped create this masterpiece, as he had his father's strong presence and slim physique. Relaxing some, she felt blessed her son also had a mix of her blue eyes, brown wavy hair, and a shared inner sensitivity of commitment to causes. *One day he will be the perfect catch for some young girl,* she thought. Glancing at the kitchen clock, it pushed her forward to finish what she started. Little did she realize that life, like milk, could curdle before an apparent expiration date.

"Jay, I think the milk and cereal have taken enough

hits." She now spoke, somewhat agitated. "It's bedtime."

"Come on, Mom, I'll be thirteen in two months. Jeez, Seth's little brother, Brian, he has a curfew later than me. Wrong I tell ya!"

With puckered lips, she intensely looked to him with deep contemplation. "I'm going to give you something you must swear to guard with your life." She looked into his eyes as if an alien had embedded software into her CPU.

"What?" he asked, frustrated she changed the subject of a later bedtime.

From her pocket, she took out a key chain of a swan, with a single key. Taking off the key, she handed it to him.

"So what's it to?" Johnny asked. This was so out of place for his mother.

"It's to a box with secret information in it— important information, kind of like treasure."

He studied the unique key, and his eyes lit up. "Treasure you say?"

"Yes," she said, "family treasure."

"It's a special key, ain't it, Mom? He looked hard at it. "An' it's important to you?"

"Very," she whispered.

With a soldier's protective eye, he looked to her, "I'll guard this with my life, Mom."

"Jay, in the near future, we will dig up the buried treasure," she said, watching his face glowing with curiosity. "But right now, you, my dear, need to get some sleep. Tomorrow is a big day."

"Yeah, Park View is gonna cream Rolling Hills," he said with boldness, as it triggered thoughts of how she blew off his new bedtime question. Lethargically he continued as if each word that followed held the weight of a cement slab. "I know. I need my energy for the game. Can't build a house to stand the test of time if ya don't have a solid foundation with each story following the blueprint." He rolled his eyes. What exactly that meant he wasn't sure. But his father built houses, and his mother, well, she was always just saying stuff like that.

"Now, go get some sleep, mister. Tomorrow is another day, and we can agree on a new curfew then." She smiled. "Have you talked to Seth? Is he ready for the big game?"

He felt his ears grin. "Yup, we're brothers. SBDs, ya know:, Secret Brothers of the Domain."

"There's no doubt in that, considering how peculiar you two are. If I didn't know the truth, I'd say you both shared the same brain waves in the womb." She gave a slight chuckle.

"Yeah," he said, "we do sound alike, but that's cool."

"Now, don't forget your prayers and your guardian angel." She paused. "I love you, Jay."

Johnny walked past the living room, "Love you too, Mom, night. Night, Dad."

"Good night, Son," his father called from the living room, "and brush your teeth."

"No problem. Got it done, Dad."

Hanna Styvers gathered her things. Phone in ear she popped her head around the corner and peeked into the living room. Her husband, Joe, was in his usual place after a hard day of construction; in his easy chair, watching the weather channel on TV.

"Nekos, I need to see you," she whispered into the phone. "I have it. Yes, it's in a safe spot. Meet you? All right...yes, tonight...I understand...yes, I know where that is." She picked up her keys.

"Where ya going?" a voice from the living room chair rang out.

Selective hearing, she thought. *It is a gift.* She closed her eyes and sighed. "I have to go out. I'll be back in about an hour."

"You're not meetin' him, are ya?" his strong voice carried up the stairs to the corner of the landing where grown-up conversations were overheard.

She sighed. "Why don't you just trust me? I have to do this." *The less everyone knows at this point the better,* she thought.

"You're putting everything we have on the line here. Let it go, Hanna."

"You don't understand, Joe."

"You never knew her. You have no idea what kind of person she was or what kind of people you're dealing with here."

"She was my real mother, and like it or not, I am part of this whole mess. It has to be told, Joe," as she flicked her finger toward the front door, "and all indications are I might have family out there."

Loud and quick, his mouth shot like a pneumatic nail gun. "What about Johnny? What about your son? Have you thought about that?"

"Yes, and I don't want him to grow up to think his mother had no backbone and just let things be. And if you don't quiet down, he won't do well tomorrow. Tomorrow is a big day,"

"Take care of your precious ghost chase during the day, Hanna; don't go out tonight."

"I have to do this, Joe." Joe pushed the volume of the television up a level, as Hanna followed suit, with the sound of the front door closing behind her.

Up on the second floor landing, Johnny tiptoed back to his room and pulled the covers over his head. Whatever just happened was his fault, and he just knew it. He heard his name, and he had to be the cause of whatever it was. "Hey, God, please don't let my night light go out tonight and help me figure out what made my parents so mad at me cuz I'm not sure what I did. And God, wish Seth and me luck in the game tomorrow. Maybe ya could help us win? Night, God."

* * *

Hanna hastened down the side of the house to the backyard where the box lay hidden, then continued down the grassy knoll to the willow tree where she dug a hole earlier in the day.

There she stopped to sit on the bench Joe had made for her. She sat and placed the last clue into the wooden box—the swan key chain minus the key she had just given to Johnny. Studying the swan one last time, it seemed to come alive, looking vibrant as it appeared to swim in its clear Lucite frame. Showing off its hand-carved feathers alluring as the white tips of a French manicure, it surveyed its surroundings with a radiant, topaz eye. The box she placed it in was unlike any other with an unusual lock and key. She knew the key chain and box were both handmade by a master artisan. This was the last clue she hoped would connect her with a family lost and bring justice to a town called Rolling Hills. She knew the risks to take down this dragon, and it enraged her to find this had gone on for so long. But with every reign, there was a beginning and an end. It was now time to right the atrocity that befell her lineage, well before her existence, by the biological mother she never knew. Closing the box, she locked it with the sister key to the one she had given to Johnny.

Looking up, the evening stars seemed to sparkle with auspicious light as she sat with a vision of arms entwined. Her hand caressed the wood of the bench where she and Joe sat many a night to gaze upon the heavens—two souls who once shared each other's dreams. Lingering on thoughts of days gone by, her focus slowly unraveled with a snapping sound up by the house. Hidden, she stretched to look. Nothing. Only the glow of a flickering porch light. Straining to see the watch on her wrist, time again pushed her to move along. Behind the willow tree, under the wishing rock, she buried the box in silence.

Scurrying up, past the side of the house to the street, she opened the car door and looked up to see a dim light from Johnny's bedroom window. She smiled, remembering how she also needed to keep the light on at night back when she was a child. From behind, a voice startled her, placing a sturdy hand on her shoulder. "Hanna Styvers?"

1

SITTING HIGH UPON THE STEPS of 284 Ewing Avenue, Johnny Styvers had forgotten how good Mother Nature could be, feeling his forearms soak up the penetrating rays of warmth. Like a reptile, he was building strength for a new day, and he was enjoying the subtle stillness of the neighborhood.

As he sat, a light breeze nudged his weary eyes to monitor the movement on the sidewalk below. A familiar figure sauntered past him as if he were a rock, impervious to mother earth's emotions. Recognizing that familiar gait, one step lagging a nanosecond behind the other, Johnny's blood surged while his senses sparked a short circuit in his brain that churned and muddled the muck, deep within his solar plexus. Today, the sight of Seth brought up a deep connection Johnny hadn't felt in years. The life before his mother disappeared, a friend who never left his side, until he severed all ties, all contact with his past, a past that couldn't continue until his mother returned home.

"Yo, Kogan, where've ya been, buddy?" Johnny blurted out, glued to his perch with one leg stretched long, the other bent.

Seth Kogan turned toward the sound. A soft wind followed his eyes up the steps to rustle back the wavy brown locks of his once good friend. For a moment, he expected to see Mr. Styvers, Johnny's dad, with Johnny's deeper, more commanding tone of his voice.

"Hey, Johnny," Seth replied, squinting to find his former friend's eyes. *Yeah, it was him, eyes the color of blue ice, almond shaped, neatly spaced,* he thought. *The eyes—the one thing that never changed on the face as it aged.*

Johnny smiled. His perfect teeth reflected the sunlight, sharpening his flawless features even more. Out of nowhere, as if they both inhaled simultaneously, the surprising smell of roses from their youth permeated the air.

"How have you been, John?" Seth intensely studied his boyhood friend dressed in jeans and a black T-shirt, plugging a dark band's name to a leather strap on his left wrist. He watched him light up a cigarette, inhale, and crack his jaw, as if sending out smoke signals, warning of an impending war. "Picked up an expensive habit, huh?" Seth asked.

"Pretty good. Why do ya walk by the house an' never ring the bell? Yo, where's the race?" Johnny paused, then questioned again, "Where ya been, bro?" He asked as if it was yesterday and they were still twelve years old, at a time when they were inseparable and lived their lives in the Styvers's backyard, down by the willow tree. The tree, where they forged an alliance with a blood brothers oath.

"Hey, I've been around," Seth retorted, "but if my memory serves me well, I recall you sort of went your own way. So, I think my answer should be, 'where the hell have you been, mate?'"

Johnny shot back, "So when did short, stubby hair become the rant? Are ya some athlete/preppy geek now?" He eyed Seth's button down shirt with what looked like a pen in the pocket. Before Seth could speak, he added "And yo, what's with the colored hair?"

"It's naturally dirty blond, if you remember, and when did long, hippie hair become you?" Seth bantered back rolling his fingers into a ball, keeping his eyes on the target.

They stared each other down, waiting for an invisible voice to push them past reasoning. Seth moved up the steps, raising his arm back, fist in hand. Wavering, a crooked smile emerged, and he gave his once old friend an arm-wrestle handshake and hug.

"Yo, wanna hang?" Johnny grinned back.

Hesitation was the name of the game. "Um, sure." The sunlight forced Seth's eyes away from the object around Johnny's neck. It was the key—the key Johnny's mom had given him the night she had vanished before their friendship had broken apart, before the grown-ups decided to look up the word *hell* in the dictionary and let it run amuck. Now, he could see the key held tight to Johnny's chest by a hemp rope, one that matched the color of his hair. *Interesting,* Seth thought, *after all these years, he still had it, the key his mother gave him and he swore to protect* He logged this tidbit of information into his memory bank. Looking somber, he asked, "So, what you been up to?"

"Workin', pumpin' gas at the Pump & Save."

"Oh, the Pump & Save," Seth replied. For some reason, his dad didn't allow him to go to that gas station, something about shady gasoline. "Yeah, having a job's good." Not that Seth had one. His dad stressed school. Plenty of time to work, he'd say. His dad had his own thoughts about what road Seth's life was going to take. A job with some extra cash would come in handy, considering the allowance he received each week. Just enough for—nothing. He couldn't complain. His dad bought him a sweet Acura with a stick shift, sunroof, and power everything. The only thing he had to do was get good grades, go to college, and come out with a master's degree. That's all. No pressure, though pumping gas sounded like a nice derailment. He looked hard at Johnny. "You still go to that school over in Harrier?"

"When it suits me, I'm like a king over there. Yo, it's good to make the rules. So, how 'bout tonight? We on or what?" Johnny pressed.

Seth wondered. Thoughts of their childhood friendship gathered through his veins. *Maybe Johnny needed to reminisce about back in the day when they were inseparable, and were bonded together by an oath—calling themselves, "The Secret Brothers of the Domain". Then the only questions they had to answer were what do you want to do now and who's sleeping over whose house?* Standing on Johnny's steps, a feeling came over Seth as if they came from different schools, mixed with an urge to rekindle what once was. *Why, after all these years did Johnny say hi?* He had walked past Johnny's house more times than he could count over the last five years. *What was different about today? Or was anything different since they last spoke?*

"Sure, John," Seth said. "Call me later." He wrote his cell phone number on a piece of scrap paper he pulled out of his pocket. "Is your house phone still the same?"

"Wouldn't dream of havin' it changed. Later." Johnny turned and walked into the house.

2

ARRIVING AT HIS FRONT DOOR, Seth felt eyes upon him from Johnny's home. No sooner did he step inside he heard a voice from within. "Seth, is that you?"

"Yeah, Mom."

"Did they call about your car?"

"No, Mom, not yet, Mom. They told me it would be done later today, Mom."

He walked into the bedroom to find Agent Kogan folding laundry. She gave him a warm smile. "I see you were talking to Johnny Styvers."

No surprise there. He breathed in, closed his eyes, and rolled them in pain. After Johnny's mom disappeared, his mother decided to become the sight and sound of Ewing Avenue. Sometimes it was a good thing, but most times, it was just plain annoying. She should have worked for the FBI or the CIA, instead of raising him and his little brother, Brian. She would have been perfect for the job— average height, average looks, and all the things that kept her in that unmemorable category.

"Yeah, we're going to hang out tonight," he replied, waited for the guillotine to drop. She seemed to revel in putting the kibosh on new things, especially any interactions with Mr. Styvers or Johnny since the night of the incident.

"That's good," she said. "He could use a stable

person in his life, and you, my son, have it together." She continued folding the laundry.

Seth contemplated his reply, while raising an eyebrow. Agent Kogan was working overtime. No way was she going to get the upper hand.

"You know," she said, without making eye contact, "you could help him."

Ah, there was a means to her madness! Maybe she was losing her touch because she was so off base. But he wondered, why the change of heart? Clueless, he thought, just clueless. "But what if he takes me to the dark side, Mom?"

"Don't be silly. You are more powerful than you know," she said with a wink.

"So, you don't care that Johnny gets into a lot of trouble? Word on the street says he was involved with that mess over in Harrier," he prodded.

"Honey, I've realized that Johnny right now is adrift at sea. What he needs is a lifeboat." She hesitated. "Maybe you are that boat? I couldn't imagine a son not having a mother."

Seth backed up. "I don't know, Mom; I haven't seen or talked to the guy since we were, like, twelve. This is the first time in years. So, for old time's sake, we're just going to hang out tonight, that's all." *Just because she seemed suddenly to have a soft spot for Johnny didn't mean he had to be the designated messenger from God.*

"Well, that's fine, dear; just don't forget to look deep. That is where you will always find answers."

Now he was really getting perturbed. "We have nothing in common, all right? It's for old time's sake so stop making a big deal of it." Agitated, Seth walked out of the interrogation room and hastened to the kitchen. "What happened to the Sun Chips that were on top of the refrigerator?" he yelled out.

"I don't know, Seth. If they're gone, they're gone,"

she sang in a high voice.

His fingers tightened around the refrigerator door. He opened it and stared into the cold empty space. That's what he needed, space. His mom could just pop his brain and ruin many decent conversations.

"Seth, Seth! Move out of the way, I'm starving!" Brian huffed, rolling his weight in front of his tall, lean brother to take control of the refrigerator door.

"Bri, you have enough heifer meat to last you till spring. Go to the gym or something; you're only supposed to sweat when you work out."

"Shut up, Seth. I haven't eaten since breakfast, and for your information, I ran home."

"You? Run? Ha! Do you even know what *run* means?" Seth taunted, like a deranged circus clown.

"Seth, do I have to come in there and take away some privileges?" a voice injected from the interrogation room. "And Brian, why did you skip lunch? What did you do with your lunch money?" They looked at each other. Agent Kogan did have the house bugged.

Seth put Brian in a headlock and, with pressure, his fist pushed down on the brown toothpicks of hair on his little brother's head "See, you little crapper, you, deciding to be in the heifer family is going to get me in trouble. You skipped lunch? Nice story, bro. Lose some weight, man. You don't need lunch because it seems by the look of your stubby nails you've got it covered."

"What?" Brian squeaked out to reply. His wrinkled face a cold tint of blue with each second of oxygen loss.

Seth loosened his grip. With a heavy whisper, Seth got right up in Brian's space. "Jerk face, stay out of my room, you hear—or you'll need waders for where you'll be going." Letting go, he pushed Brian out of his way. "Stop using that sticky hair crap; it does nothing for you."

Brian looked sheepish as his brother strode out of the kitchen. He never had an instant comeback. Only about an hour later would his brain give him the perfect reply. Even his own mind tortured him. *How could he ace tests and then not be able to speak up? Most importantly, how the hell did Seth know he was in his room? He didn't touch a thing—at least not this time.* He then realized Seth was getting back at him for snooping in his room a few weeks ago. *Seth had to be the one who put his lacrosse teammate, Larry Jones, up to torturing him.* It wouldn't look right being bullyragged by your own brother in public, especially at school. *How else would Larry know how to hit him where it hurt the most?* Humiliation, then the theft right before lunch, leaving him with only a penny to his name—a token of good will.

Grabbing a Yoo-hoo, Brian closed the refrigerator door, ignoring his mother, and proceeded to his room. At his desk, he opened the drawer. There was his sanctuary: Sun Chips, sour cream and onion flavored, and a box of Twinkies. He fired up his computer, double sanctuary. Today, like every other day of his life, he had gone out into the battlefield, and his body armor had saved him once more. He feared soon the enemy would find its weakness. He contemplated how many more blows his armor could take before the cracks would appear.

In his room, on his computer, was the one place Brian could find solace. If it weren't for his computer, the Internet, and the lock on his door, Brian was sure he would have gone mad long ago.

Grabbing the bag of chips, he signed on to the Internet and waited for his blog site to load. Many people had blogs. It seemed most of the world had one, and right now he needed to write and get things out. Later, he would demolish those thoughts in his online, fantasy war game.

He scoured the profiles. He had heard some guys talking in class about Johnny Styvers and his Internet blog. First try, got it. He wondered, *how Johnny could write such personal stuff for all to see.*

3

KATIE PAOLA WASN'T SURE WHAT to do. She felt her hands tremble as her aquamarine eyes stared in animation at the screen. One little click of the mouse, and her words would be sent. *What was so terrifying about that?* This guy, Johnny, wrote in his blog, and she felt he was speaking to her. She contemplated her own words that she wrote back to him, while her heart pumped sharply. Running her shaking fingers through her wavy brown hair, she continued staring at what she wrote. *Would he even care? Was she intruding? Golden rule: don't talk to anyone online you didn't know.* It was against everything she heard or learned, concerning safety on the Internet. But this was different— a blog site, detached, like a pen pal from another country. She didn't want to meet anyone and no one wanted to meet her, so what was the big deal? If she never crossed that invisible line, she would be safe.

The psychic's warning bellowed in her brain. *What about the dreams, which sometimes revealed the future of others?* She wished it would reveal her own. She remembered how she laughed with nervous energy, giving the psychic her swan key chain—the one that got the psychic all up in a tizzy. Then, the warning. All that hocus-pocus about frightful things to come. It was all crap. Her two swan key chains, her mother's and hers were her only solace since that disturbing night she learned of her mother's death. Now she and her daughter Dadia were connected by these swans. *How dare the psychic say it those unsettling revelations?*

From the window, a warm September breeze swirled around her, softly pushing the papers on her desk, nudging her back to the present. She was sick of being afraid—sick of warnings about some made-up person the psychic called Darius or Darien. She was sick of living in the dark, the shadows. *Hiding? Why? From what?* Her mind screamed as she threw out all things negative and focused on the positive. She would write and have her own blog with the screen name "Stella" to honor her mother. Maybe it would spark a sixth sense about her life.

Static electricity flowed from her fingertips as Katie felt the mouse jump, sending Stella's words into oblivion on the internet to someone named Johnny. Not knowing if she was wrong to do so, she read this boy named Johnny's words again.

> "Yeah, I'm sitting here, mind runnin' for like forever. Back, a senior, finally, in that damn school over in Harrier. Don't know why I bother. Who gives two craps? The ol' man doesn't. My life is…well…never gonna do anything good. I know he thinks Yo— loser. I'm just like him. My anger—getting worse—spiraling. I hate this! I see things too, in the dark an' it scares the hell outta me.
>
> The kids at the Harrier school are losers, all—the whole crew, and at the end of the day, they make us sit in this room and do— yo get this, nothin'! Ha, I guess I do belong there, got kicked outta everywhere else an' I can't see where any of this is gonna get me. I can't stand school—any excuse to leave.
>
> Man…take the other day, up late, miss my ride an' decide to start walkin'—why?

Don't know—happen upon this ol' guy standing on a ladder, cuttin' branches out some tree. Blood drippin' down the guy's arm. I figure he's bent on gittin' it done. So I go ova, to help the ol' man out, ya know, what any respectable guy would do for another half bent on hell. He wanted to pay me. Damn could a used the dough, but crap, he looked, well, I refuse an' walk. I get to school late an' I'm hassled. Being a few seconds late is more important. They don't give a rat's—well, you know.

So what I need is to get outta this damn house for good...but can't. Chained here. Saw Seth today, gonna hang. I haven't talked to him or his bro Brian in eons—*sigh* he's changed. We had a SBD oath once. Does an oath matter anymore?

Can't concentrate—don't care. Is there anyone out there that does? Loser is in my vocabulary—an' skin deep in trouble. Yo, haven't slept more than 3 hours in the last two days, mind racing, but never getting past the gate. My so-called ol' man—he knows who I am, he tells me every day when he looks at me."

As she finished reading his words, he immediately replied. It was the first time in her life she had so much to say, as distant thoughts of the psychic's warning dissipated into the darkness. With wild abandonment, she wrote back and forth and continued to read other blogs until she connected with another named Brian. Without thoughts of where her boldness would take her or the path her actions and words would eventually lead, she continued to type throughout the night.

4

SETH, BEING THE OLDER KOGAN brother was supposed to be on Brian's side—an ally, defender, supporter, a Secret Brother of the Domain, that pact they made with Johnny so many years ago. But no, Seth was more of an enemy now, like the ones he fought every day in school and on his computer. He was starting to wonder. *Was Kogan blood thicker than the powers that be?*

Brian's mind reeled as hours passed, as he played his Massive Multiplayer Online Role-Playing Game on his computer. Here he could build an allegiance with others while he built armies to defend his homeland. War took strategy, planning, and time. He never felt alone as he always had his comrades in arms keeping him occupied late into the night. Over the past summer, the twilight hours were spent staring at a computer screen, resulting in late-afternoon wake-ups. But summer habits had to die now that September rolled in. Early morning classes and sleeping clashed, and all attempts to change these patterns seem to be futile.

He looked out his bedroom into the darkness of the night. The dim glow from the streetlight and Johnny Styvers's bedroom window gave way to the notion that his mind was not the only thing up tonight. Then again, Johnny's light was always on. Even when they were small, Johnny, in defense, would say, "Hey, I never sleep, so why turn them off?" Seth always said Johnny got spooked by ghosts flying around his room and then he would laugh. Johnny would just stare him down and then go on to ignore the comment.

At two in the morning, at least half the world was asleep. He could stay up; the honor roll was just something that happened to him though he didn't understand what the big deal was. *Who needs sleep?* he thought. He could pass any test, eyes shut. Anyway, he had to pass his own tests by genius alone, for now he had to spend his time writing reports and doing homework for that jerk, Larry.

Larry Jones was a popular senior at Park View High. He had a typical, athletic physique and always dressed the part of being too macho for his own good. He played with his hair more than any guy should, and for some reason, it was acceptable. Captain of the lacrosse team the girls just went crazy for him. *Why?* Brian couldn't understand, for as far as he was concerned, Larry never really treated girls well. But they would just keep coming back for more. Maybe it was that scar under his right eye. Larry told this story of how one summer at Shepherd Lake he single-handedly saved a girl from being beaten up by her estranged boyfriend. The scar was one of moral honor, a code Larry said he lived by. *Funny how his words never seem to coincide with any of his actions,* Brian thought. Seth played lacrosse with Larry, and somehow he, Brian Kogan, became Larry Jones's lackey the moment he stepped into his freshman year. Today was the worst. He walked into the cafeteria and headed for the food line. Larry was eyeing him, and he felt Larry's posse was close behind.

"Kogan, so where's the money?" Larry taunted.

"Money?" Brian asked.

Larry stepped right into his face. His henchman, Frank Halley, came upon Brian from behind. Larry gave a quick glance around, then grabbed Brian's collar, "I know what you do with your mommy's girly stuff, and you wouldn't want it to get out around school, now would you?"

Brian was stunned. *What did he know? Not what Seth kept teasing him about, was it?* Brian kept silent, and he emptied out his pockets.

"I'll tell you this, Kogan," shoving a notebook into Brian's chest, "today's your lucky day, worm. You get to do my homework, and maybe, just maybe, I'll have mercy on you. Now be a good ghostwriter, type my name on it, and make sure it's A+ quality. Tomorrow morning, you'll be waiting for me by the cafeteria doors, before the first ring of the bell."

Back to reality. Brian thought about what went down at lunch. *Be exposed by Larry? His money confiscated? More days without lunch?* He wouldn't survive. There was nothing he could do—only concede. Completing Larry's work, he still needed to do his own writing. It was a long night already, and the hands on the clock again motioned that they had already seen the breaking of a new day. Finally, deep thoughts flowed onto the keyboard as the bedroom door flew open with a bang.

"Bri, buddy…what the hell's up, man?" His loving older brother staggered in.

"Seth, get out of here, and thanks, you're going to wake mom and dad, you jerk," he replied in a hushed voice. Seth held on to the back of Brian's chair, trying to regain his composure. Brian grimaced.

"Writing in that stupid journal again? You're such a loser, Bri. Hey, who's you writing to? Who's S-T-E-L-L-A?" He sputtered his words. "A new girly friend?" Seth spit out in a sarcastic and downgrading tone.

"You know, Seth, when a door is shut, it means *knock* before entering, and thanks, now dad's going to blame me for the hole in the wall! Jerk."

"Aw, little brother, you worry too much! Ef dad, ef you—ha, ef the world!" Seth replied, laughing and stumbling, and proceeded to fall to the floor.

Brian spoke in disgust, "And what's with the

cursing?" He couldn't imagine sharing a room with Seth. He knew a guy at school that had to share his bedroom with his brother. *The horror of it all,* he thought. Brian already lived in his own horror story; he didn't need more aversion than he already had. It was bad enough that he had to be at the same school this year with Seth, a senior, and he just an incoming freshman. He wasn't sure why Seth had sided with Larry Jones and had spoken crap about him. *Did he know Larry had him doing his homework now? And these were supposed to be the best years of his life? Yeah, right.* Larry was just compounding the pressure he already had. *How many more rocks disguised as tomatoes could he take?* The smell of Captain Morgan from Seth's breath reached the hairs in his nostrils. Enough was enough, he still had more work to do.

"What do you want, Seth?"

Seth put his finger up to his mouth. "Shh."

"Hey, what the hell's your problem?" *Why did God give him a brother like Seth?* "So, I see you're drinking now—with whom, Seth?" he asked in a low tone.

"Yeah, man, you shoulda been with us tonight, little bro. What an awesome time we had!"

"Yeah right, Seth, and who is us? You and Larry? Uh, could you just leave?"

"Larry? Nah, it was me and…Hey, you should come next time."

"What, so I can be you proverbial voodoo doll like when we were kids? You do remember, don't you? You and Johnny? Always trying to ditch me? No thanks."

Seth found his footing and eyed Brian's computer screen. Squinting to focus, he swayed back and forth in an attempt to keep his balance. "So what are ya writing on that stupid blog site? You're such a loser," he said, slurring his words. "Bri Bri, get a frickin' life, man."

In the lowest, deepest voice Brian could muster, he said, "Come on…be Q-U-I-E-T!" He locked his computer and rolled his eyes. *Oh, my God, he could never share a room with him. It would be absolute torture!* He was already looking down the edge of a cliff. One small poke in the back would send him into oblivion. To top it off, Seth was Mr. Clean, with nothing ever out of place. If something would be amiss, his bizarre alter ego would go on the fritz, blaming Brian for taking something, moving something, or hiding something. As if that was his reason for life—to move his big brother's stuff around. The real problem was that Seth had a photographic memory. He remembered stupid stuff, like what was on his dresser two weeks ago and was now missing or who changed the channel of the TV in his room. But Seth couldn't remember his homework from the night before, money for lunch, or if he had to pick Brian up from the mall. Brian couldn't imagine having to deal with all that, and then being in the same room too. Now Seth was trying to read his now blank screen and Brian was losing patience.

"Seth, just get out. Go to sleep."

"Bri, stop being a sissy girl and let's see what you're up to," Seth retorted.

Seth was poking him in the back, and he again was standing on the edge of that cliff. There was only one thing left to do: standing up he pushed his chair into his brother, knocking him off kilter. Doing so, he caught a glimpse out his bedroom window—a silhouette under the streetlight, staggering toward the Styvers's backyard.

"Come on, Seth, I'll help you find your room. Lacrosse stars don't get toasted like this, only wannabes." Grabbing hold of his lean brother, Brian put his shoulder under Seth's and put his arm around his brother's back. Seth put his arm around his little brother and steadied himself as they maneuvered to Seth's room. With a deep sigh, Brian laid him down on the bed. "By the way, what DID you do tonight?"

Seth just mumbled.

Brian scolded him. "And I thought dad told you

never to hang out with Johnny, you know, how he changed after his mother disappeared."

Seth ignored him. "Johnny, yeah, he's such the man. Did he ever tell ya about the weird stuff he sees?"

"No, Seth, I haven't talked to Johnny since we were small, when his mom insisted you guys let me be in your ridiculous secret club, remember? I thought we were Brothers of the Domain, but now I seem to recall you both were always trying to ditch me."

"Nah, ain't true, Bri, ain't true, but tonight…man, we were at the Fast N Easy Convenience Store, you know, the one over on…what's that street?"

"Russell Avenue?"

"Yeah, that's the place. Well, we're online to buy some crap, and these two guys walk in, he looks at them and just freaks out."

"Well, I'm sure he was drunk, Seth."

"No, he just freaked and left the store without paying! I say to the clerk—big muscular guy—'I got it. I got it,' and paid for his crap with mine. When I get outside, he's skitzing out in the car, tells me to shut the hell up and just drive. Weird, man…but ya just gotta love him." Seth stopped. Then silence.

Brian hoped he fell asleep. *Good,* Brian thought.

Then that annoying sound started up again. "About two hours later, he says the guy's eyes just started to melt right in front of him. I say, "W-O-A-H, K-O-O-L.""

"And he wasn't on anything? Sure, Seth. And what's with drinking and driving? I'm no snitch, but—"

"You don't know jack, Brian. Maybe if ya got your head outa that computer, you'd know we're not stupid. We came home from the Fast N Easy and then walked, jerk face. Don't ya ever walk around town? Nah—you don't."

"Whatever, night Seth."

"But freaky, man, the guy, Johnny said, was melting. And guess who it was? Mr. Jacobs from dad's work. I think he thought I was just being a Good Samaritan or something." Seth laughed then abruptly stopped. "Bri," he said in a solemn tone, "I think I'm gonna be sick, man."

"Lucky for me you have your own bathroom. Night, Seth." Brian quietly closed the door.

The faint sound of sawing wood in the distance soothed Brian Kogan's agitation, and he was able to return to a state of tranquility. Hearing the grandfather clock chime from the floor below—once, twice, three times—he knew he should be getting to sleep. It was amazing his parents slept through the racket Seth made, and now he was up for the duration. Thoughts kept going back to school. *Why was he so quick with testing and just knew all the answers?* That was the great part. But the other side of his genius held him sitting in class, waiting for the others to finish, and it bored him to death.

Thank God he had a love for music—music of the heavier sound—and found himself writing his feelings in the form of lyrics in the idleness of waiting. He dreamed of being in a band one day that would use his lyrics. While waited his life away, he filled it with lyrics so deep about what others took as just disturbing subjects, but they didn't understand. Some of his classmates would get a glimpse and be like, "Whoa, interesting, Bri, got some pent up thoughts in there buddy," but he just ignored them. They knew nothing about the soul he possessed, as he would look to them with contempt then ignore their existence. *They didn't understand or want to understand who he was, so screw them.*

With time, his writing flowed more and more to the hours at home and out onto his computer late into the darkness when sleeping souls dreamed. Tonight was no different from any other. He had to write tonight.

5

NOT COMPREHENDING WHY, THE VOICE in Joe Styvers's head urged him to the back door taunting and playing with his mind. *Yes*, he now remembered. *Where the hell is that good-for-nothin' boy?* Making his way down the hallway to the moonlit kitchen, his footing faltered, throwing his massive hand to the sheetrock. Steadying his extra weight gained from lack of desire, he felt his way down the dimly lit wall. Hard labor and regret seemed to disintegrate his soul, though his strength of ten oxen still prevailed. Flicking on the back porch light, he leaned up against the door molding. The light illuminated the stubble on his face. One, two, three times he heard the clock squawk. Pushing the bushy brows on his face toward the ground, he tried to remember why he was standing there in the first place. The sound of the wind kicking up through the screen door whispered his name, the same way his beautiful wife, Hanna, did. His wife who one night never returned home – to leave him and his son Johnny animated in a horrible dream they never woke up from. He hated nights like this, forcing days of old down his throat. With empty bottle in hand, he wiped his nose with his forearm, grumbled, then proceeded to bark out into the darkness spraying spit through the screen door.

"Whoo's out there? Show ya self-f-f."

The night air spoke in reply, rustling the branches of the willow tree along the backside of the property, only to jolt his memory again of *her*. There they would sit under the willow tree, hand in hand, to gaze upon the wonderment of the universe. But the universe taunted and tricked him and sent his wife on a wild goose chase. Hanna Styvers, the love of his life, became obsessed with this silly quest to find answers. Then *he* popped into the picture, and there was talk in town. Hanna, his love, didn't need to search for anything. He and Johnny were her family, her flesh and blood. Good people, honest people. *Why did she have to go digging up the past? Let the dead sleep,* he thought.

When his wife, Hanna, started her ghost hunt, he would secretly take his son, Johnny, to the pistol range to teach him how to respect, handle, and shoot a.38 caliber handgun. There, men taught their young men to honor and respect what a gun stood for—a power in the palm of the hand to be feared with reverence. For without reverence in this power, it could become life's deadliest demon. This was what men taught men, though he remembered one man felt this teaching flowed to daughters as well.

Joe smirked. He could hear that cute little blonde praise herself with every shot she fired. *Damn, she was a natural.* The kick of the gun never fazed her. Her father reveled in the fact she was dubbed junior sharpshooter of the club, and he rubbed it in everyone's face just like the fact he lived in a mansion over in Mountain Crest. *What was the guy's name?* Blinking, he took a swig from the empty bottle, *Welling something? Wittenberg? Wentworth?* Then remembering his tough, little man, smiling every time this guy's daughter showed up. Nowadays, he wasn't sure what a smile looked like on Johnny's face. Target shooting was Joe's specialty, for once upon a time, he was a sharpshooter. Once upon a time, he had trophies to prove it. Now the only tangible thing he had to show for his skills was a shaky grip and a tarnished medal of gold. A harsh wind out the back door distracted his thoughts, and bellowed through the branches of the trees.

"Ya better get off my property, or I'll come out there." He spit into the darkness.

Leaning into the wooden screen door, the rickety latch gave way throwing Joe's overweight mass out onto the porch. Flat out on the wood flooring he lay, dressed only in a T-shirt and pajama pants, once again swearing into the blackness beyond the dim glow of light.

"Sons a bitch!"

Around the corner of the house, a tall, wavy-haired shadow appeared. "It's just me," Johnny grumbled, eyes fixated on his dark life.

Johnny walked up the back steps watching his father do a balancing act with the porch railing. Trying his hardest to ignore all comments, he passed right by his father. Flinging open the half-broken porch door—it bounced repeatedly behind him. He just had one of the best nights of his life in years. Who would have thought meeting behind the strip mall back in the woods would be so much fun? Tonight was exceptional because Tori showed up, and Tori Halley was damn hot. Dreaming of her tonight was the only thing he wanted to do, but now he had to contend with his father's crap. *Why couldn't his ol' man be sleeping on the couch like usual? No, he had to be awake and of course, hammered.*

His father stumbled back into the house. "Don't cha just walk away from me, boy. Work called lookin' for ya. And ya'd better have that money, or I'm sellin' the house."

"You're not selling this house." Johnny spoke under his breath, sorting through the mail on the table by the front door.

"What ya say?" his father asked. "Ya no good piece of..." Joe stopped. Silence. The night air took over, invoking broken words of faith. "It's your damn mother's fault, leavin' us the way she did," he said in disgust.

"I heard ya. Don't you dare say that!" Johnny turned toward his him. "Ya don't know crap. She was the only good thing in this house!"

"Stop wastin' ya time boy. She was a good-for-nothing tramp. When you gonna realize that she's neva gonna send for ya, an' she's neva comin' back. Neva. So stop foolin' ya'self."

"Shut up, Dad."

"Your kind, trouble, good-fa-nothin' trouble ya are."

"Yo, just shut the hell up," Johnny replied, turning his back to his father. He felt his muscles seethe, constrict, and contract, from his forehead to his fingers, right down into the floorboards. It was back and trying to take control. *No, no…remember what Stella said…control, John.*

"Don't cha go disrespectin' me boy, an' ya betta look at me when I'm talkin." Johnny felt his father's massive outline inching close, staggering toward him, forearms tightening.

Control yourself, John; no pain tonight. Remember what Stella said. Eyes focused, he bolted up the flight of stairs, reaching the landing unscathed and in one piece.

The banister giggled from below. "Ya damn ingrate! Get back down here, boy!"

"You're a fool, Dad," Johnny retorted from the safety of the landing, knowing work-battered knees from years of construction kept his father from further pursuit.

"What ya say to me, boy?"

"I'd like to get a pool, Dad." You could hear a mouse fart. Round one: Johnny Styvers versus The Beast. Wit and control won the round. The only backlash came with a retreat of shuffling feet, then stillness from below. Through the rage that wanted to annihilate something—anything—a small smirk emerged. Somehow, tonight he felt in some sort of control. It helped that the guy who called himself dad was in the company of Mr. Daniels. And Jack was working overtime tonight, or Johnny would be eight feet under, choking on dirt.

Sliding into his room with a quick twist of the lock, he sighed, happy his ol' man was too inebriated to remember to yell about leaving his light on. That was an everyday ritual. There was no extra money lying around to waste on electricity, and most times he was lucky to find a small morsel that might be food in the fridge. But the light in his room had to stay lit. It just had to.

Putting on his headset, Johnny's agitation found a second wind. Music flowed through his body as he signed onto his computer. Seth's dad worked for a computer company. Every year the Kogan boys got new computers, and today Seth gave Johnny his old one and set it up for him. It beat going down to the gaming center to write in his journal. That cost money; this was free. Seth told his dad he would donate the old computer to a worthy cause. Yeah, Johnny Styvers was his worthy cause. This one had a wireless board. Seth set it up where he could get online through the Kogan router. If Seth's dad had the time to check his home configurations, he'd be pissed. His dad for some reason just hated him.

"Seth, I love ya, man!" he shouted, and logged into his blog and started to write, with music raging in his head.

> "Yo, somethin' bad gonna happen one day. Anger, hate— that just builds. My head is pounding. It just wells up inside like a creeping cancer. Freaky things happen only I seem to see, and I can't control it! Stella, I need to talk, now. That slug calls himself a father, right. I know, yo, I need more control, but how? Most times my friends have to pull me off a guy for just lookin' the wrong way, an' by then he's pummeled. (Well, only happened twice) an' both times I ran so fast, yo, it scared the crap outta me—but man, I hate it."

> My ol' man, I think I was like 13, first episode, the summer he took me to Shepherd Lake, just my dad and me. I was in the woods, ya know, lookin' at the nature, an' this kid walks up behind me and just cold

cocks me. I just went berserk. The wuss, crying, begging, saying, stop, please stop…and I couldn't…hey, he started it. I just kept on pounding him till his face was covered like raspberry jelly…I can't even remember what he looked like cuz all I saw was… nothing. Then, realizing my hands were soaked I jerked back, my throat started to close up, my body, in a vice squeezin' out my innards. My eyes filled up like buckets— Yo, I ran…I was so scared, confused, disoriented about what just went down. At the water—had to wash it all off my hands. I swear, it wouldn't come off, drippin', thick an sticky. Soaked, I run over to my dad…crying about what just went down…and ya know what the ol' man says?

"Good goin' son, teach em a lesson, ya showed em! Stop crying like a sissy. There's nothin' to cry about, he got what he deserved!"

I was crying because I was scared out of my eva lovin' mind—cuz I couldn't control myself and thinking, *Oh my God…Oh, my frickin' God…what the hell did I do?* And he's patting me on the back saying good goin'. So, tell me…. why am I so afraid…? And right now, I don't know—I don't know what!"

Johnny scanned his buddy list looking for Stella or Seth. One other soul was on tonight: Brian. No use in talking to him; he wouldn't have a clue of what he went through on a day-to-day basis. Brian had the perfect life, perfect family, great brother, and brains for school. He could be anything he wanted in life and had everything at his fingertips. There was no way Brian would ever understand.

6

NOW MS. PAOLA, COME ON, you need to come with me shopping! I need to get some new outfits, and only you have the best taste," Ashley insisted, as they stepped off the school bus on their way to the Wentworth Estate.

"Hum…which mall tonight, Ash?" Dadia asked, "The Galleria?" Every Friday it was a different indoor mall. Three different malls, then a night off, it seemed.

"Yeah," Ashley said with excitement, "How'd ya know?" A small smirk emerged, realizing that under that long, auburn hair and behind those big, brown eyes, Dadia Paola was smarter than she anticipated.

"Ash, do we have to? I'm so sick of the mall. I thought we could maybe go to the movies tonight. Go see a romantic comedy. You know I love them." Dadia wondered if Ashley would want to do anything other than go to the mall.

"But tonight we'll shop, I swear. I just got my allowance for the month, and I'm loaded. Come on, just shopping; no flirting, I promise."

Dadia looked skeptical. Ashley was not in need of a new wardrobe or another Fendi bag. She knew for Ashley it was: find boys, flirt, and get phone numbers. *Been there, seen what happens.* This was Ashley's mode of operation every Friday night, and Dadia was getting sick of it. *What the hell did she do with all those numbers, anyway?* As far as Dadia was concerned, most of the guys at the mall were just looking for one thing…and they were all jerks.

Ever since they met over the summer, it seemed they did more and more of this Friday-night mall thing. It was becoming a ritual, and she had to start thinking in advance how she could get out of going. She hadn't made any other friends since moving to Mountain Crest, and summer was a hard time to meet other kids. And then when school started, Ashley would grab onto her the second she started to talk to other girls, and before Dadia knew it, it was just her and Ashley. *Did Ashley scare them away, or was there something wrong with her?* She had known Ashley for a month before school started, and Ashley acted as if they were friends since birth. Dadia never had a friendship like that. She was an only child, and her mother moved them from town to town, making it difficult to connect with people. However, at school she kept getting the sense that kids were talking about Ashley, and gossip was something that turned Dadia's skin red. She did manage to become friendly with Julie and Stephanie, but it seemed to fizzle out. And she just couldn't figure out why.

Ashley, on the other hand, was smooth with those who walked the other side of the street. At first when guys crowded around her, it made Dadia feel good, but then a creeping smell would fill the air—a smell of deceit and a fakeness reminding her of restaurant food embedded into clothing.

"Do you promise we will shop?" Dadia asked, biting her lower lip.

"Now, Ms Dadia, oh yes, I promise," Ashley replied.

"Well, OK then," Dadia replied in a "seeing-is-believing" tone.

Ashley grabbed Dadia's arm. "Come on now, girlfriend. Let's go get something to snack on; I'm starved." Ashley spoke with glee proceeding up the long driveway to her home estate.

* * *

Park View Galleria was in the top ten status of being one of the largest indoor malls in the United States. Any store, any item you wanted you could find at the Galleria. The mall housed a hotel, ice rink, twenty movie theaters, bowling alley, chapel, hair salons, food court, upscale restaurants, kiosks, clothing/specialty shops, and a large gaming center, and in the center of the mall, a Ferris wheel. It was so large the state gave the mall its own zip code.

Walking into the east-side entrance of the mall, the corners of Ashley's mouth started to curl upward, and her eyes sparkled. Dadia caught the change in her friend's body attitude and knew what she was thinking.

"Ashleeee…," Dadia glanced at her. *Here we go again.*

"No, no, Dod, I promise! Hey, let's get something to eat first. I'm famished!"

"Ash, we just ate an hour and a half ago; you can't be hungry again," Dadia protested.

"You of all people should know I'm always hungry." Ashley laughed, stepping onto the escalator going down to the food court. "I think I must have a tape worm or something to keep this awesome shape I've got." She gave Dadia a look. "So, what do ya say, the usual?"

"Yeah, Vito's Pizza for you, and Sukki's chicken teriyaki for me, see you at the usual table." Dadia smiled. Reaching the table first, Dadia sat down and scanned the food court. Ashley was nowhere in sight. Looking over toward Vito's Pizza, she wondered if she had a last minute change of heart, and decided on some other food vendor. Minutes seemed like hours. Dadia's food was getting cold, but to eat alone, well, that was just weird.

"Da-di-aa! I'm feeling good tonight." Ashley cried out

popping up behind her, and there she stood in an audacious pose. She was a Wentworth, and Wentworth's did as they pleased.

"Ashley, what? Where? When did you change your clothes?" Dadia looked shocked. Ashley swirled around before sitting down across from her, "Got this sweet outfit last night. Like it? I know, I know, it's a micro mini, and yeah, it's cut a little low on top. But hey, it looks damn good on me, and the blue—doesn't it just accentuate my beautiful, blond hair? Ya do have to agree now."

"Um, yeah, ah, it does, Ash…that blue…and your hair…that's a real attention getter, but hey, I thought we were going to shop."

"We are, Ms. Dadia. We are."

"So, did you stuff the clothes you wore here in your bag?" Dadia asked, bewildered, looking at Ashley's Prada bag, the size of a quarter.

"Nah, no room, I threw them out."

"You what?"

"Yeah, Dod. What else would I do with them? I'll just buy some new stuff tonight. We're here to shop, aren't we?" With a devious grin, and a flick of her long blond hair, her features screamed out—I'm here!

7

"FRIDAY NIGHT. FOOD COURT. GALLERIA. YO."

"John, you got to be kidding. This is your idea of fun?" Seth blurted out in a laugh.

"Hey, don't knock it until ya see what shows up," Johnny said, looking sinister.

"Really," Seth replied. He wasn't sure why he was hanging out more and more with Johnny. Maybe it was some sort of retaliation toward his father or that stupid Brothers-of-the-Domain oath he made as a kid. In any event, hanging with Johnny guaranteed a good time.

"Game time at ten o'clock; check out the talent."

Seth looked to see what was in his buddy's sights. "Damn, look at that, two hot skirts."

"The one on the left—she's for me."

"No way, Seth. She's in my sights. Hands off."

"Hey, let's just see who gets her number first."

"OK, here's the plan." As they worked out their details, Johnny glanced over to where the girls were eating. "Damn, man, look over there…ya little bro hanging out with my nemesis, Larry Jones."

Seth looked over to see. "What the hell?"

"Hey, wait, they're talking to them! Come on, Seth, follow my lead; tonight you're my wing man." Seth followed Johnny, sizing up what the total plan of attack would be. They made their way through the food court, maneuvering in and out of tables and chairs, making sure they came up behind the two boys.

* * *

"Sup, Ashley?" Larry asked. Brian stood behind him. "Where've you been?"

"L-A-R-R-Y, long time no see." Ashley smiled with a wink. Larry could feel his heart pulsing. He stroked his hair back with his fingers. He was all set. He looked to the girl sitting next to her.

"So, where've you been hiding your friend?"

"Umm, this is Dadia." Dadia looked up with a quick acknowledgement, then went right back to her teriyaki.

With the sweetest voice he could muster, Larry sang out, "H-E-L-L-O, Dadia. Maybe you'd like to go to the races one night with me."

Needles shot from Ashley's eyes to Larry's delight. Dadia looked up past Larry, only to catch the brilliant green eyes of the boy who stood in the background behind him. Something in his eyes sparkled; she could swear it. She fell into a deep trance.

Ashley caught her eyeing him. "Hey, Dod—what cha lookin' at?" She laughed trying to get Dadia to see what she was laughing at and join in.

Embarrassed, Dadia quickly shot back a piercing look.

Larry sensed he was losing control of the conversation. "Hey, I'm Larry. Do you go to school with Ashley?" He looked at Dadia as if he were looking in the mirror and gave her a tease of his pearly whites. Dadia continued ignoring him, keeping her eyes fixed on Ashley. *Here we go again. So where did you find this one?*

"So, Larry, who's ya friends? Oh, I'm sorry, ya friend," Ashley nonchalantly asked, referring to the boy Dadia seemed so intensified on.

"My lackey, Brian."

"Hi," Brian said, ignoring Ashley altogether, his eyes watching Dadia. Dadia looked up to acknowledge him. Again their eyes connected, and both quickly looked away.

"Well, Brian, ya don't seem the type of friend I'd expect Larry to be hanging out with," Ashley said.

Brian's eyebrows pointed toward his nose, and his brain functions came back into the Galleria.

"What's that supposed to mean?" Brian gave her a sharp, questioning look.

"Oh, nothing, I've just never seen ya around, that's all," Ashley replied, tossing her hair, refusing to look away first.

"Hey, little bro!" A shout came from behind Brian, followed by a slap on the back. "What's up?"

As disembodied spirits, Seth and Johnny walked right through Brian and Larry, only to reveal their souls at the girls' table. Johnny beamed at Seth while he maneuvered into the seat next to Dadia only to ignore her.

"Larry," Johnny said, leaning toward Dadia with his arm up, "What's shaking man?" Larry looked at him with hesitation.

Johnny immediately lowered his arm around Dadia with a slight touch and release and looked to her, "Yo, I'm sorry…are ya in the wrong place?"

Dadia bit her lower lip. "What do you mean?"

"Well, the only place anyone's ever this quiet is in the library." He sweetly grinned at her.

"Yes, *you* could get me to go to the library," Seth injected himself into the conversation.

"And if ya worked there, I might even take out a book," Johnny continued, never letting go of his smooth style.

"So what's up, John?" Larry muttered sarcastically. "Your mom, she still AWOL?"

Johnny immediately shot Larry a look that wanted to brutalize him, only to release his unaffected voice as he looked to the girls. "So, who are these two beautiful women sitting here?"

Ashley's eyes gleamed. The stage was set, and she maneuvered herself into the part of leading lady. Dadia could be her understudy—like she needed one. It was show time.

"I'm Ashley," she cut in, "and this is Dadia....ya know, the library could be really fun...especially the one in Harrier. With all those floors, a girl and a guy could get...lost." She winked. "And if I worked there, it'd be my job ta check ya out,'" Ashley raised her eyebrows ever so slightly.

Larry was getting frustrated. He had to think fast—faster than Johnny or Seth—and take over this conversation. Tonight's anticipated plan had gone awry.

8

BRIAN KOGAN LOOKED IN DISBELIEF. There they were, Johnny and big brother Seth barging in on Larry Jones's conversation with these two girls. He was supposed to be next in line though a meek "hi" was all he got out. *Damn it.* He looked over to Larry. Larry's hair looked like it was wilting. Determined that this time intimidation by Johnny or his brother would take a back seat, he had to be bold. *Yeah, right.* He was younger; they were older. His vocabulary went as far as "hi", and they, on the other hand, were smooth like the spiral of a perfect football throw. Now Larry was no slacker when it came to girls; neither was Seth. But Seth owed him big time. If Seth screwed it up for him tonight, he would kick the living crap out of him—this time he'd at least try.

Brian managed to focus and keep his cool. In actuality, if it weren't for Larry, he wouldn't even be at the mall. Doing Larry's homework was now not enough. Now he somehow had become Larry's dog on a leash, to be at Larry's side and bark when Larry beckoned him.

Thoughts raced when he realized he had just met up with the most amazing girl he'd ever seen in his whole life. *And her name was…Oh, my God, what the hell was her name?* Panic, sweat, and fear of a red face being discovered lit up his eyes. All the excitement of meeting her pulled him away from the one thing he needed to do; listen. At least five times, someone said her name. *Listen up, jerk; you are not leaving here tonight without getting her name! And a cell phone number too!* Panic set in.

Out of nowhere, Brian blurted out, "So!" he looked at Dadia. All conversation stopped in the noisy food court. He froze like a perpetuating arctic chill that penetrated right through his eyes, piercing into his brain like an icepick. This made it impossible to move or at least come back with something humorous or intelligent to say. His mind encrusted in ice, his breathing labored; he felt his lungs collapse. He had to do something—something. If there were a God, He had forsaken him. *Help me! I'm dying here!*

Larry saw the pain in Brian's eyes. He was the only one allowed to dish out pain, and Johnny and Seth moved in without provocation. That settled it. He would side with his lackey. He and Johnny had their differences in the past, leaving him circumspect of Johnny's intentions. He would take control, but Dadia opened her mouth first.

"So…I'm sorry. I didn't get your name. You said it was…?" Dadia looked right at Brian.

Relief, anxiety, bewilderment, came all in one breath. He managed to find his voice. "Brian, Brian Kogan."

Seth and Johnny looked to one another. Johnny knew Brian didn't have a chance in hell and gave Seth his look of "no problem," but Seth never took anything for face value.

"Hey, little brother," Seth interrupted, "what are you doing here? There's a mall curfew for kids your age." He winked.

"Well," said Dadia, "Brian here seems to be the only one who should be allowed out tonight."

Ashley took over. "Larry, you never told me about your two friends here. You holding out on me?" She continued to dominate. "And you're Johnny. That's funny; Larry never mentioned you. Did anyone ever tell you, you have the nicest eyes? And um, who's your friend?" she asked, not moving her sight off Johnny. Larry in his cool, calm, outer appearance watched her, while the veins in his body surged with discontent.

"I'm Seth." Seth eyed her while she seemed to acknowledge his name, instead of his being. She felt him immediately wonder what was up. She threw him a small glance with the shake of her head. Her long hair flicked over her shoulder, and she cocked her head sideways. Seth registered a small tat or mole behind her ear. Small enough for most to miss, but he never missed anything. With a big smile, Ashley put to rest any inkling of thought, at least for the moment.

"Brian, come on, pull up a chair," Larry spoke in haste, sitting next to Ashley, pointing for Brian to sit down.

Oh, my God, Brian thought. He felt the palms of his hands sweating. *Did someone turn up the heat in the food court?* He kept trying to find the right moment to cut in, to say something witty, intelligent. Everyone else seemed to throw banter back and forth. Looking at Dadia, he couldn't hear a word anyone was saying. The world stopped, and a light radiated around her face, an angelic hue. He felt his knees buckling with the sounds of sweetness her voice sang out. Attempting to look nonchalant, he kept trying to pry himself away from her by glancing at everyone else, though it didn't matter. No one even realized he was alive. For a fleeting moment, he wondered why Larry invited him tonight, but thoughts went right back to, *What can I say to enter this conversation?* Catching Dadia look up, grin, and then laugh, he decided to make a last minute effort be a part of the group.

"Yeah, that was *so* funny!" he belted out. The minute his words left his lips, he realized she wasn't laughing.

With a sarcastic chuckle, she said, "Yeah, right."

Everyone looked to him with spotlights glaring, blinding him into oblivion. His heart, now exposed, sinking like the *SS Andrea Doria,* told him he had just said the most asinine thing anyone on earth could ever say. He was devastated. Amid the laughter and taunting jokes, his presence was out of the shadows. He had taken that step into the light to find out what he had already known; loser, drone, never going to be the one to get the girl. He was going to die a monk up in the mountains of Kilimanjaro. He was a circus clown with no makeup. It was futile. He could do nothing to stop them, and his mind blanked out. They made surrendering seem almost acceptable. Brian, the video game warrior, was losing the battle. The laughter of the masses had won, again.

"Little Bri, Seth's right; you don't get out much, do ya?" laughed Johnny while Seth looked on shaking his head.

The torture continued, and Dadia had seen enough. "Ashley," she said, cutting in over the brutal lashing the boys were giving Brian. "Are we going to do what we came here for?" She spoke in a firm tone, on the verge of disgust. Ashley was eating up the boys' banter, ignoring her plea.

"Excuse me," Dadia spoke in a harsh tone. She stood, pushed her chair back, and proceeded to walk away.

"Dod, where are you going?" Ashley halfheartedly looked up. She could see the back of Dadia walking away without any acknowledgement. "I'd better go after her," she said.

"Yo, let her go," Johnny cut in with his best stay-with-me smile. With a gentle hand, he held her arm. She felt a tingle when he touched her and she looked down at his strong, masculine hand. His gentle control emitted bold strength that held her attention.

"Yeah, let her go. She's just upset we're talking to the most beautiful girl in the Galleria," Seth interjected.

Johnny gingerly pulled her back into her seat. "She'll never have what you got," he whispered.

Feeling his vibe, Seth had his back. It was two against Larry. Ashley scanned the table, realizing she was in the center of three hot boys, demanding—and getting—their full attention. Dadia was the best.

"Well, sure, Dadia can take care of herself. Actually, she just wanted to shop anyway." She threw out her most alluring smile. "So, do ya guys live in Park View like Larry here? Dadia and I are from Mountain Crest." Larry just looked at her in silence.

"No way, you live in Mountain Crest? Not that town where the Crags live?" Seth asked.

"Yeah, that's the town. They don't bother us; they're like hermits. They live up on the crest of the mountain somewhere and pretty much keep to themselves."

Oh, my God! She said her name! Dadia, yes! Brian fused it into his brain, sitting there, calculating in disbelief what just transpired, and watching the first angel he had ever seen disappear. *They didn't even care she walked away, oh, maybe for one second?* Now they were back to whatever the hell they were doing. *Did she even exist to them? Was Dadia really friends with this girl? How could she abandon her like that?* The feeling he knew so well, of being the ghost of the party, shot through him again. He could flop on the table and wriggle around, and no one would even notice.

Realization set in and a glow of warmth consumed Brian's being. For the first time in his life, he was ecstatic. *They don't even know I'm here!* As the three guys vied for Ashley's attention, he decided to make his break. Larry had just taken the stage, focusing the spotlight on Ashley, and the three boys started to get into a battle for control. Backing up slowly, he was a stealth fighter pilot in enemy airspace. He glided away from the table as they continued with their intense talk. When his stride was out of view, his mind focused on the quest at hand. Quickening his pace in and out of the steps of lethargic people, his anxiety rose sharply. He had to find her—the girl of his dreams, the angel that just disappeared, into a deep sea of Friday night shoppers.

9

BRIAN KOGAN'S IMPATIENCE HEIGHTENED WITH every step, scanning through the layers of human faces. *Where could she be? Where? How could she have disappeared so fast?* His mind raced. Reaching the end of the corridor, he stood next to the wall, looking left then right watching shoppers whisk by. *Which way?* His heart throbbed. *To the right, yes the right...right is natural.* Ten steps down the corridor something held his feet smack to the floor. A shopper from behind bumped him. "Hey! Watch it, buddy!" the man shouted, continuing with disgust.

Sorry, Brian thought. The voice in his head brought him back to her...*turn around her right is her left.* He changed his direction, and slowed his pace trying to maneuver through the busy mall scanning with invisible, Dadia-vision goggles into every girl store he passed.

It was futile. He was never going to find her. She just dissolved like ice on a hot day. *Maybe if he went back to the food court he could get something out of her friend, Ashley? No, it was apparent she would never concede.* Feeling mental exhaustion, his eyes became blurry as he caught a restroom sign overhead. Needing to stop, compose himself, he made the turn toward the bathrooms. In the distance, a figure turned the corner toward the women's room. *Yes, it had to be...he had found her!* He could swear it on his grandmother's grave. Bolting into the men's room and over to the sink, he splashed water on his face, regained his composure, and decided to wait outside of the restroom doors near the water fountains. The voice in his head kept telling him, *Girls take a long time in the restroom. I'm sure she's still in there. Just wait, Brian; just wait.* Energy rising, he paced back and forth, finding a bounce in his legs. *What would he say when she came out? What excuse...why he was there?* Each time the women's door opened, he nonchalantly took a drink from the fountain. He was filling up like a balloon. Then the door opened, and she emerged, weary eyes scanning the floor.

This is stupid, he said to himself, *No lies, just truth.* "Hey, I've been looking for you."

Dadia raised her head in surprise. He looked at her chestnut brown eyes and felt an old boulder lift from his shoulders. He now understood. It was normal he liked those little Precious Moments dolls his mother collected. He was infatuated with them. Art did imitate life, but at the moment, this work of art showed signs of puffiness. He knew right away what she was feeling—how the inconsiderate tablemates in the food court had affected her.

"Why are you looking for me?" she said in a soft, hopeless voice. He melted, and that enraged him.

"It just made me so mad the way they treated you back there. It just pissed me off how Johnny got right in your face, and it seemed your girlfriend, well—." Catching himself, he abruptly stopped. He couldn't believe he was talking to her with such ease. Twenty minutes ago, he couldn't even muster a hello, but now his mind seemed clear and focused. "Um, your friend, Ashley, she's a piece of work," he added, softening his voice.

"Yeah," Dadia replied. She then became silent and awkwardness became a wall between them.

"Hey, would you like to get something to drink?" His brain was working overtime.

"Oh, I don't know. The last place I want to be is back at the food court."

"No, no, I was thinking more like that little café on the other side of the mall. Not a soul our age would be caught dead in there!" He grinned.

Well, I guess," she replied.

Fear and excitement, exuberance and utopia all rolled up in one emotion soared through Brian's soul as he walked beside her. Taming a wild grin rising, he forced control over it to be solemn, noticing she was still upset. Walking toward the café the fear of speech skipped through his head, and awkward steps became more and more noticeable.

Relief came at the entrance of the café. The host sat them in a booth away from the imaginary prying eyes of the mall. Fidgeting with the menu, he was sure she was also feeling that awkwardness once more. Just when he thought she would excuse herself and walk away for the second time, she spoke.

"I'm so sorry. It was very nice of you to look for me." Gently she bit the middle of her lower lip then looked around the café.

"No problem," he said with a big smile. "So, do you come to the Galleria often?"

Dadia looked right into his eyes then to the side. "Well, only with Ashley. It seems she likes to mall hop."

The waitress appeared out of nowhere and stood staring at them. Clearing her throat, her voice squeaked, "Are you two sweet young'uns ready to order?" The waitress confirmed with her question why no kids ever came into the café.

Brian hoped his eyes didn't give it away. He had just spent all of his money at the food court, and his eight-dollar food tray at this very moment probably found the mouth of the trash container.

Focusing, he remembered the special twenty-dollar bill folded into the form of a triangle football he kept stashed in his wallet. His grandmother had given him this token gift after football season the last year he played. She had spunk and loved the game. His grandma and he played the table football game, folding a piece of paper into the form of a triangle and flicking it through thumb and pointer finger goal posts. It was her favorite game, and he always laughed at that fact. She surprised him at the end of the season by making the football out of a twenty-dollar bill and putting it into a card for him. She told him to keep it as a remembrance of the fabulous season he had just finished. Because of his size, he was an exceptional defensive lineman, but before the next season started, his grandmother died. He had lost her and just didn't have the same thirst for the game and no desire to play again. He swore to himself that he would keep the twenty-dollar football forever, for many different reasons.

Now he was sitting across from this angel with no money in his wallet. He would never even consider the idea of asking her to pay or even borrow the money from her. He was the one who asked her, so he would pay even if it meant using his grandmother's gift. Deep down in his heart, he knew she would understand.

"So, why did your friend say that mean thing about your brother's friend? That his mom had left him? That she is AWOL?" Dadia asked.

Brian was taken back, "Oh Johnny? Well, Larry is just a mean jerk. He and Johnny, they have never gotten along." Brian paused. "Well, she went out one night and never returned."

"Oh my god, that is awful," Dadia replied.

The waitress stood, tapping her foot. Her eyes moved from Brian to Dadia. She raised her pencil-thin eyebrows and pursed her red-lined lips.

"What would you like?" Brian asked Dadia.

"Um, just a Diet Coke, please."

"And you, sir?"

"I think I'll just have a Coke, large, please."

"OK," the waitress slowly said. Her face revealed a "no tip" at this table look. "You do understand there is a ten-dollar minimum here?"

"Yes," he blurted out, "that's all right." He looked at Dadia with a smile. "We'll just have the sodas, thanks." *Twenty dollars would cover that,* he thought.

Before he could speak, the waitress was back with their drinks. She took each drink off the tray, eyeing Brian. She placed each one with the speed of a snail in front of them. The same went for the straws, then the napkins. It felt as if she were a helicopter, hovering over them like an annoying fly, bouncing from each piece of food to the next purposely touching every item one might put into his or her mouth. No matter how hard a person tried, the fly would laugh, taunting him or her to get rid of it. And in one's mind, there was only one possible solution. Brian stared her down, hoping she was more human than fly, and would just go away.

Relieved that the waitress had finally vanished, he looked to Dadia again. They both realized they had mental telepathy to find, each under their breath, were laughing. *There* is *a God,* he said to himself.

His silent utopia shattered at the sound of her purse ringing. He watched her fumble around, pulling items out of her bag and onto the bench seat, until she found it. *Damn,* he thought, *please do not let it be Ashley.*

Pulling the phone up to her left ear, she mindlessly stared into her soda, while she listened with complete concentration. "Thank you, thank you so much," she said. Looking up, she closed her phone and attempted to put all of her belongings back into her bag.

"I'm so sorry. I have to go."

"Go, where? Why?" he felt dejected.

"It's been sweet of you." Her hands fumbled searching through her overstuffed bag. "Here, some money for the soda."

"No, no, I got this, but can I see you again?"

In haste, she spoke, "Oh, yes, but I have to go. I'm so sorry. Thank you for the soda." She fled out the café doors.

He sat, not moving, dumbfounded in a fog. "Oh, no!" he exclaimed, leaping up.

"Excuse me, sir!" The host stepped in front of him.

"I know, I'm going to pay, but I can't let her go yet."

"I'm sorry—no pay, no leave." The host eyed him.

"I promise I will be right back to settle the tab," he pleaded with the host.

"Sir, do I need to call mall security?" The man put his body right in Brian's face.

"No, no," Brian said, stepping back, pulling out his wallet, and fidgeting to retrieve his grandmother's gift. With awkward flair, he opened it up, to show the host it was real money. "This should be more than enough to cover it, OK, man?" He pushed it into the host's chest and ran out the entrance doors, only to lose her again to the sea of lethargic Neanderthals. Nevertheless, she had said yes to see him again!

Like a creeping addiction, it came in disguise, until he felt the synapses and a knife blade twist into his heart. *Where did she live? What was her last name? Her phone number?* He got nothing, nada, nil. Standing alone, the universe forged forward. He was invisible to the human eye, and his heart bled to black.

"Hey." A gentle hand touched his shoulder. He turned, only to find it was just the waitress from the café.

"Oh." His face drooped.

"First, thanks for the tip. You restore my faith in youth. Second, the booths are cleaned between customers, and I think your girlfriend dropped this on the seat." She placed a swan key chain into his empty hand.

"Thank you." The corners of his mouth curled with a slight upward twist at the idea of Dadia as his girlfriend. "I'll certainly make sure she gets this," he replied, praying to God that he would.

10

MOUNTAIN CREST CAFETERIA WAS YOUR typical high school eatery, dressed in white cement walls, dull tile flooring, and a football field of bare folding tables with metal chairs. Behind one wall of cement housed the kitchen and staff that prepared the usual, boring lunches, under the mask of healthy eating.

Dadia Paola sat at her usual table and breathed a sigh of relief to see her so-called friend, Ashley Wentworth, was nowhere to be found. She wanted to keep it that way, at least for today. Ashley pissed her off Friday night. She expected her to: 1) follow after her when she stormed out of the food court, 2) call her later that night to make sure she got home safely or at least be concerned why she was so mad, and 3) over the weekend find out if she were still alive and breathing! Now it was Monday, and none of that had transpired.

Sitting alone, Dadia decided to look in her bag for her swan key chain. It was a special trinket from her mom, and for some unknown reason, it gave her a feeling of comfort when she held it in her hand. Made of clear Lucite in the shape of a pyramid with the top cut off, she could look through the bottom half to see a three-dimensional, sparkling white swan with a brilliant topaz eye embedded into it. Just rubbing it with her thumb and forefinger in a back and forth motion soothed her edginess. It was her healing stone, like the stones sold at vacation gift shops.

She knew they were just stones, but the thought of its being magical was enticing. She didn't care if it were a placebo; for her it worked.

Wanting peacefulness, she reached into her bag that held life's most precious items while her mind toiled with the thoughts of finding some new friends. Unsettled, her eyes widened. *Oh, my God, where is it? There is no way I could have lost it.* Panic set in. *Think carefully...*Last time she was in her bag. *Think! Oh, my God, Friday night, the Galleria, three times, buy food, in the bathroom, and...the café! Yes!* She practically dumped everything out to find her phone. *Maybe, they found it, or...that guy, maybe he saw it, found it...that boy...Brian!* In the distance, she glanced up. Stephanie was walking toward her, lunch tray in hand.

Trying to keep calm, convincing herself it was just at home, Dadia would ask Stephanie to join her for lunch. Then after school, Dadia would walk into her bedroom and find it on the night table where she left it many times before, but now she needed to concentrate on making a new friend. She had invited Stephanie a few times in the past to join both her and Ashley at the table, but Stephanie would glance at Ashley and decline. Today, sitting alone, maybe Stephanie would say yes to the invite.

"Stephanie!" she called out with a tone of excitement.

Stephanie looked over at her with curiosity. "Hi, Dadia, what's up?"

"Hey, would you like to have lunch with me?"

"Um, I don't know. I'm supposed to eat with Julie." Her eyes scanned the cafeteria.

"That's all right," Dadia retorted, in a shallow voice.

"Where's Ashley? Is she sick today?"

"No, I just thought it would be nice to eat together. We've never gotten to know each other, but that's all right."

Stephanie continued her search, finding Julie a few tables away. "Hey, why don't you join us? Julie's right over there," she said, pointing with her eyes.

Dadia looked over to where Julie was sitting. Julie smiled at her. Dadia picked her tray up and proceeded to follow Stephanie.

"Hi Dadia," Julie said, as she sat down. "Nice of you to join us." Her eyes passed over to Stephanie. Stephanie returned the look.

"Hi, Julie," Dadia replied; now thinking this was a mistake. Stephanie was always very friendly, but Julie—she was another story.

"Hey, I heard some awesome, good time happened Friday night at the Galleria with some hot guys from Park View," Julie blurted out.

Dadia looked at her with questioning eyes. "I have no idea what you're talking about. What did you hear?" Stephanie looked at Dadia.

A voice from behind Dadia spoke, "I'll tell ya what they heard, and they're wishing they had been there." It was Ashley, eyeing Julie.

Dadia kept her eyes from acknowledging anything Ashley said.

"Dadia, we need to talk."

Damn it. She hoped if she stayed quiet, Ashley would blow by like the night freight train in Harrier. Ashley stood there, not budging. Finally, silence made her look up to notice Ashley's eyes liquefy over, and Dadia's appetite diminished. "I'm sorry, Steph, Julie." Leaving her tray at the table, she followed Ashley out of the cafeteria doors.

Dadia and Ashley made their way down the corridor to the commons area. *It's not right, not fair. This friendship was going south,* Dadia thought. She was the victim here, but Ashley was somehow making her feel like crap. Sure, Ashley was upset. Dadia was sure it had nothing to do with her, but Dadia was still mad at her.

Through the commons into the courtyard she followed Ashley like a drone. They sat down beyond the sound of chatter, and Dadia waited for Ashley to speak first. She'd be damned to be the one to start a conversation. She still wanted an apology.

"Dadia, why did ya leave me at the Galleria Friday night?" she spurted out, as tears flowed down her cheeks.

"Oh, my God, Ash, what happened?"

"I was so upset ya left, and those guys, they tried to convince me—they said you'd come back! So—that's why I didn't run after you. But cha didn't come back."

"They didn't hurt you or anything, did they?"

"No, But I felt so bad. We were supposed to be at the mall for shopping!"

"Yeah, I know," Dadia said with trepidation.

"So why didn't ya come back?"

"Well, I was so mad at you, and then that boy, Brian, found me."

"No way, you mean big boy?"

"Hey, he was really sweet and made me feel better."

"I thought that stupid key chain was the only thing that could make ya feel better," she said with an intriguing look. "Wait, you *like* him!"

"Nooo, he was just nice, and I was upset. And besides he bought me a soda!"

"Now wait, he bought you a soda?"

"Anyways, I'm still mad at you, and I think I lost my key chain, maybe even at the Galleria—I don't know!"

"Aw, Come on', Dod, we're best friends. I'm sorry; maybe that really big, um, really nice boy found it." Ashley put her arms around her. "Come on, let's go back inside. The bells gonna ring. I'm sure ya key chain will show up."

"I suppose," Dadia replied. "Hey, clue me in, so, um, what is 'going to the races,' anyway?"

"Who told ya about that?"

"That boy who was with Brian—you know, the one that came over and said hello to you first? He said it to me."

"Oh, Larry. Well…" She cupped her hand to Dadia's ear and whispered. "When ya hook up, silly, we call it 'the races.' We watch the submarines race, get it?" She laughed.

"Oh," Dadia said, feeling embarrassed.

"Hey, Dod, I almost forgot, I invited those guys to a party Saturday night. You're gonna be there with me. I'll tell 'em to invite that kid—you know, the one that was sooo nice to ya," she said, with her eyes and mouth open wide making a funny face. Maybe he knows about ya key chain. Gotta go!" Ashley disappeared around the corner toward the cafeteria.

A spirited look overcame Dadia as she walked to class with thoughts kept hidden.

* * *

"Hey Julie," Ashley quickened her step to catch up.

"What, Ash?" Julie looked agitated.

"I'm sorry about before. I was just, upset. Personal stuff, ya know."

"Whatever, Ashley."

"Hey, there's a party Saturday night, and I just thought you and Stephanie would like to come. The guys from Park View—the ones from the Galleria—will be there. So, what do ya say? I really want both of you to come. Actually, I told Seth & Johnny about you, and they both seem really interested."

"Well, I'd have to ask Stephanie…"

"Sure, let me know." Ashley stopped, turned to go in the other direction. "Hey, Julie, don't cha go worryin' about Dadia."

"What do you mean?" Julie stopped.

"Stephanie will always be your best friend. Dadia won't take her away. Ya know, how Dadia can…well, forget I said it. I'll give ya the details on Saturday about the party. Bye!" Ashley turned and disappeared with the wave of students.

This was going to be the party of the year. Julie felt excited, but for a second, she wondered what was up.

11

"MR. KOGAN, WHAT WOULD YOU SAY the answer to question four might be?" Mr. Manteria asked his Park View High School class with his eyes and hand directing their attention to Brian. Brian was swimming in a daze. His elbows perched on the desk with one hand holding up his chin, while the other twirled what looked like a key chain.

"Uh, E equals MC squared," Brian replied.

Laughter and snide remarks filled the air.

"Mr. Kogan, I assure you, you are not in your physics class. Now if you could get your head out of the clouds, dreaming about Einstein, the class will attempt to bring you back to the reality of dark art in America. I am assuming that you must be an expert on the subject, because you seem to be bored to death." Mr. Manteria held stern as if Titan himself were speaking. "Please hand over whatever that is you are twirling in your hand."

Brian immediately put the enigmatic swan key chain in his pocket and sat up straight. "I'm sorry, Mr. Manteria. It won't happen again."

With a half-cocked smile and a sinister laugh, Mr. Manteria walked down the aisle to stop at Tori Halley's desk. Putting his hand on her shoulder, he continued, "Tori, dear, would you please answer question number four?" He threw her a wink and a smile.

Tori centered her body, coiled her long red hair with her index finger, and pushed her shoulders back, glancing to Brian.

"The answer," she said, hesitating, "Mr. Manteria, is, of course, yes."

Brian could feel his face catch fire with the smell of burning flesh and his ears start to sting. He glared at the back of her head. *Mr. Manteria is a maggot,* he thought, *sucking up to Tori Halley. Who leads us guys on like lost puppies. Prey on our good nature. Then we do everything you want, and what do we get? You, laughing at us behind our backs while planning with care and accuracy our slow demise. I hear what you say. I now see what you do.*

Brian moved his eyes around the room, unspoken, his heart fell to silence. *Tori…you splattered my blood on the wall and then bled my heart dry. How can you sit there, and laugh at me as if I were nothing? How can you live with yourself, playing on the souls of others? Yes, Tori, you're the makings of an atomic bomb, what a mushroom cloud leaves behind.*

"Now class, if we could all be astute like Tori here, we could reach a higher level of IQ. Thank you, Tori."

Brian's mind red flagged. "Astute?" He mouthed aloud. He couldn't believe the maggots coming out of the man's mouth. *Tori Halley? Astute? Yeah, right, just like her moron brother, Frank.* What the hell was in Mr. Manteria's brain? He must have cracked his head, for any form of knowledge in there had escaped.

Awakened by the sound of the period bell, light banter erupted. Brian hustled out of Mr. Manteria's room then sauntered down the hallway with key chain in hand. He watched smiling faces going past him, ignoring his existence. He walked around popular guys kissing popular girls at lockers and the hallway voices became static in the air. Making his way to his next class, he caught sight of Larry at his locker.

"Larry!"

"Kogan, you got that paper?"

"Um, yeah, it'll be done tomorrow." Looking down at the key chain with a yearning, he hesitated, and then spoke.

"By the way, that girl, Ashley, and Dadia...the ones we met at the mall Friday night...you're good friends with Ashley, right?"

"Yeah, and what happened to you?" In his locker, he looked at himself in the mirror and fussed with his hair. "You really missed out, Bri. No party invite for you."

"Party? What party?"

"Ashley invited us to a party Saturday night. I don't know, Bri. Ashley wasn't too sweet on you. She blamed you for making her friend leave."

"What? Me?"

"Y-E-A-H, you."

"Were Seth and Johnny invited too?"

"Uh, yeah..." he said, as his eyes looked sideways, and his lips flat lined.

The late bell rang, and the hallway cleared, leaving only the sound of classroom doors closing.

"I'm late, worm. You'd better get that paper to me by tomorrow morning, ya hear?" Larry glanced up and down the hall then gave a quick, hard punch to Brian's arm before disappeared down the corridor.

Bewildered, Brian stood in the hallway, rubbing his upper arm. He focused on the key chain once more. He couldn't believe what he had just heard.

A voice from behind him bellowed, "Mr. Kogan, now I find you after the late bell standing in the hallway." In astonishment and on the verge of rage, Mr. Manteria blurted out, "Where did you get that key chain?"

Shocked as if he were just caught with an illegal substance, Brian jammed it back into his pocket.

"Um, it's my mother's," he replied.

"Let me see that," his teacher insisted.

"Like you said, Mr. M., I'm late." Brian felt a chill as he bolted down the corridor past Mr. Smith, the librarian, to feel Mr. Manteria's eyes splatter his spine like a Thompson AK 47.

12

"YES, HE SAW IT TODAY. THE SWAN."

"Are you sure? Where?" he asked.

"In the town of Park View, in the strangest place, and most intriguing…on a boy, at the high school."

"On a boy?" he questioned.

"Yes, and it seems it belongs to his mother."

"Could it be her?" Excitement emitted from his voice.

"Interesting, but I doubt it," the voice said. "He's a freshman—smart, but quiet. When spoken to, he has an attitude. He's possibly a troublemaker."

"Hmm…very intriguing."

"He has an older brother."

"A brother, you say? We must know more. Find out all you can. This must be kept under wraps. No one must know that there is any interest at all in the key chain. I will be in touch."

"I will find out what I can. His mother couldn't be Hanna Styvers, after all these years, could it?"

"Well, anything is possible but not probable."

13

"YO SETH, MY MAN, WHAT UP?" Johnny yelled from his front porch. "Your ol' man buys you a car and what do ya do but—walk."

"Hey, the car's in the shop, again," Seth replied, looking up. "We hanging out tonight?"

"Nah, starting a new job working at the Fast N Easy Convenience Store."

"What happened to pumping gas?"

"Eh, they fired my ass. It seems I wasn't showin' up or something," Johnny said with a laugh. "I think there was some miscommunication going on."

"I guess," Seth said, laughing, "that would hinder that work security thing. So, you're working at the famous Fast N Easy, eh?"

"Famous?" Johnny asked.

"Oh yeah, Tori and Frank Halley's dad owns a whole chain of them, rolling in the cash flow."

Johnny's eyes widened. "Oh, I see. I had no idea. If he's got dough, he doesn't show it."

"I guess Tori and Mrs. Halley spend it all. Where do you think Tori gets all that money from?" Seth agreed with a nod. "Hey, after you get out tonight, we could hang."

"Yeah, I guess. I'm outta there at nine."

"No problem, I'll meet you in the back, and then we'll go from there."

"Sounds like a plan, bro. By the way, ya remember

Ashley from the mall—the party she invited us to? She wants us to invite your little brother."

"Oh no – you're kidding, she wants to invite Brian?" Seth looked uneasy.

"That was my cut. Seems either her friend may be sweet on him, or she just liked razzing him."

"I don't know if that's such a good idea, man."

"Well, I guess some things never change, huh? Just passin' on the invite."

"Hey, you don't have to work that night, do you?"

"Nah, I don't do Saturday nights." Johnny stood up and walked to the front door. "I gotta get to work, man. Later."

"Later, John." Seth wondered what was up with the invite and contemplated telling Brian. It was best to keep this party thing in his back pocket. Saturday was still a long way away.

Reaching his front door, Seth looked back over to the Styvers's home. Pain engulfed his chest at the sight of the Styvers's window boxes. There they were, paint cracking, peeling, fading to gray. Helpless, in a state of disarray, they were unable to hide their age or neglect.

His mind wandered back in time, remembering how Mrs. Styvers diligently tended to her flower boxes with overflowing bright red flowers. She was his second mom, always looking out for him and Johnny. Johnny would sometimes razz him, saying that his mom liked Seth more than himself, and sometimes he felt guilty indulging in that thought. She was caring, warm, and always seemed to know what they thought before they spoke. Any problem they had, she always gave 110 percent to help. She just looked at what was happening, and together, they knew a solution was on the horizon.

He hated himself for thinking he loved her more than Agent Kogan, because she just had a gentle way of caring. Somewhere below his ribs, he felt a painful gap as the past crept into his present.

Years ago, he and Johnny were inseparable and swore an oath to the Brothers of the Domain that they would be there for each other, no matter what. They called themselves the Secret Brothers of the Domain. Some of the kids on the block would call them the SBDs (silent but deadly), Even his little brother was in on the oath, though Johnny and he protested. Mrs. Styvers insisted, so they allowed him to say the secret oath, down by the willow tree behind the Styvers's home.

As Seth stood there wondering what happened to those days, he saw himself back playing kickball in front of the Styvers's home. How they would race up the porch steps to see Johnny's mom sitting in a chair, reading a book. The instant she would see them she would smile and get them anything their hearts desired from the kitchen. Most times, somehow she knew they were coming and baked their favorite chocolate chip cookies with a Hershey's kiss in the middle. They would swear that she heard them talking about cookies earlier in the day. She'd always hand them out and say, "Baked with love!" Seth smiled with fondness as the memories whirled around, filling his soul.

Then it happened—that night she disappeared. He asked Johnny what happened to his mom, and without provocation, Johnny became violent—ranting, raving, throwing things, and saying to shut the hell up about it. That was the beginning of the end. It scared the crap out of Seth, and he never had the nerve to ask again. His parents all of a sudden refused to speak to Joe Styvers, and he and his brother were forbidden to have anything to do with Johnny.

Johnny then slowly, methodically removed himself from everyone he knew, while anger seeped into every aspect of his life. Occasionally, from a distance, Seth would see a spark of his old friend, here and there in school. Back then, he wanted to secretly keep to his oath of the Brothers, but that dissipated when they saw less and less of each other. Eventually, Johnny was transferred to a school over in Harrier, for those who had troubles.

He wondered if he could now, today, keep a promise he made so long ago. *Did a childhood pact even matter anymore?* After five years, it felt good they were reconnecting, and Johnny did seem to be putting his past behind him.

Walking into the living room, he wondered what happened to those wonderful times and how people could change so drastically. *Why did people make life so difficult?*

"So, you deliberately disobeyed me." Seth's dad appeared right in his face.

"What are you talking about?"

"You know damn well what I'm talking about. I can see. I saw you talking to that Styvers boy."

"Wow, Dad, years ago you would of call him by his real name. And what's wrong with talking…? And you've got to be kidding! I was walking past his house. He was sitting on the porch."

"I told you I don't want you to talk with that kid anymore. He's bad news, Seth, and a bad influence."

"You don't know what you're talking about, Dad. So the guy made a few mistakes. That doesn't mean he hasn't learned from them."

"His father is an arrogant drunk. The apple doesn't fall far from the tree. He will get you into trouble, and when that happens, don't expect me to bail you out! I'm warning you, Seth, don't let me catch you talking to him again."

"You don't know jack," Seth blurted out, feeling moisture in the inner corner of his eyes.

"I know enough, and that's more than you."

"Yeah, right, Dad, I won't talk to him anymore," Seth said pushing past his father with defiance to the stairwell. "I would of thought you'd have some compassion for him since he has no mom."

"Oh, he has a mother all right."

Seth jerked around and demanded, "What do you

mean by that?"

"Don't be messing with other people's business."

"Why are you holding back on me what actually happened to Mrs. Styvers?"

"Conversation over! You stay away from him. You hear me!" His father turned, slamming the front door behind him.

14

BRIAN KOGAN SAT IN FRONT OF his computer mystified. After all that, he didn't even get her cell phone number—just a swan key chain that maybe wasn't even hers. *What the hell was up with Mr. Manteria popping a cork on him? The guy just freaked out in the hall in school.* Even Mr. Smith had a funny look on his face when he passed him in the hallway. As God was his witness, there was no way he was going to give up his only possible link, clue, to the girl of his dreams.

Larry Jones should have backed him on the party invite, after all the pain and suffering he continued to shell out for him. *Well, screw him...user.* But, then again, if he didn't go with Larry to the mall, none of this would have transpired. He would not have met Dadia. *Dadia who, though? Moreover, how could he find her?* But the biggest atrocity was Ashley Wentworth, the rich girl who invited everyone else to a party and blamed him for Dadia storming out of the food court. His blood wanted to burst out of his veins. Seth was sure to go. He wouldn't miss an opportunity to go to a party, and he spoke nothing to him about it. He wouldn't even tell Brian what happened after he left the food court.

Somehow, he had to get an invite. She would be there. No, it was useless; he was useless, like his life, one speeding bullet after another, each one puncturing his skin with a small pinprick to leave a large, gaping hole on the inside. Things would never change for him. He should expire, right here, right now, clutching the only friend he had—his lone little computer mouse, Rollie. No one would care, or for that matter, no one would even notice. Thoughts ran to her, and he started to type.

> Every time I sleep it's your face I see
> all the days that pass it's you I need
> through this wait I go through
> hoping I see you again
> Were you just part of my imagination?
> Or are you part of me
> now that I've seen you
> All the breaths I take, they don't compare
> for the feeling I get when I'm with you
> The air I breathe isn't as precious
> as you to me
> But you don't know that (will you ever?)
> But you don't feel that
> (can you give me a chance?)
> All I ever did get from you
> was the sense that you might care
> BUT WERE YOU JUST A DREAM?
> Or are you becoming part of me?
> Can I see you one more time?
> Can I just speak to you for one moment?
> The deprivation from something so
> important…
> it all leads to this one single act
> This solemn act of depression
> Working against time to break the cycle
> of pain
> For you…For me…ONE MORE TIME
> I'm risking my life, but for you
> it's worth it
> I'll spend every minute of every day
> To search for the perfection of you
> Me being with you would make it

the most perfect imperfection
But I know, for you I'll change
For you I'd do anything
These thoughts of LONELINESS
Won't break in my sleep
I'm always with you
So put me down for good,
cause this one is worth it.
Please be worth it.
I can't imagine eternity without you.
Please be waiting for me
Please don't leave me there alone
For you this act of depression
For me this final happiness
for us, to be together…

When the dreams feel real—Brian

He clicked on Rollie to post his words. *How could he be so blind? No one would go for someone like him.* It had been proven, more than once. How he fell into Tori Halley's trap! He thought she saw something in him, and now, how could he entertain the idea that Dadia might? She was no doubt just like Tori. Tori, nice in the beginning and then fooled him royally, a conniver. She couldn't see past her own mirror, and he fell for her and her lies. He'd hear girls talk; they wanted a guy who was nice, who would listen to them, who would never dream of taking advantage of them. In squeaky voices they'd ask, "Why can't I find a nice guy?" Brian was that nice guy. That was just who he was. But then he'd watch them hook up with the jerky con artist next to them. *Were they blind? Couldn't they see?* Then the other line would be "Oh, he's *too* nice to go out with." But the best one a girl could say after a guy put her up on a pedestal, gave in to her every beckoning whim, and would be what she'd announce to anyone who would listen: "Oh, we're just friends." *If he heard that line one more time, he was going to puke.* But Tori took it a step beyond and made a fool out of him, played him on a dare, a prank, with all her friends watching, and they snickered and jeered.

So, how could he even think this Dadia saw something in him? Yeah, she was nice, but that's how they all started out. She was maybe just playing "nice" just to use him, like everyone else. *At this point, did she even remember who he was?* He hoped his grandma would forgive him, for he wasted her precious gift on a girl. The bleep on his computer came with a reply to his post.

15

EXCITED, SHE PULLED THE WINDOW down dumbfounded that he was standing right there on the sidewalk.

"Dadia, would you like to go to the movies tonight?" the mesmerizing, green-eyed boy asked, looking up at her, as she sat in the window seat of the bus. "I think there's a romantic comedy playing at the cinema. Come with me," he begged with a commanding smile. His eyes sparkled with the luster of deep emeralds.

"How did you find me?" she replied with exuberance.

"It wasn't easy, but somehow, this swan guided me." He held in his hand her key chain. "I would go to the ends of the earth to find you. Come with me," he said, with an inviting stretch of his hand.

Just as she got up, the school bus started to move while the green-eyed boy walked, keeping in step with her window. She could see his mouth move, while she strained to hear his words. The bus churned into second gear, and she found him quickening his pace, but still looking into her eyes. She looked to the driver. He seemed hell bent to race the old, rusty tub straight out of the parking lot. Turning back, their eyes met once more, and he gave her a "don't-you-know-what-I'm-thinking" look. Now instead of the swan, he held a red rose arm's length in the air toward her. Taken aback, she smiled. The beautiful red of the rose appeared soft like the velvet of her mother's most beautiful Christmas dress. Dadia remembered how she would cling to it, saying, "Mummy, I could hug you forever!" Dadia could just reach out and touch it. It was spellbinding, with a glow warm as the green hue of his eyes.

Focusing her thoughts on the rose, her smile turned to dismay. The rose faded, and without warning the brilliant red turned to jet black and shattered like tempered glass. The boy still kept up, alongside of the bus. Did he care or notice? Closer and closer he appeared to be getting to the side of the bus.

Watching these events unfold, trepidation took over. Her face felt hot. She pressed her hands against the glass first, asking, and then yelling, "Stop. Stop running!" She could feel moisture build up on her palms. She pressed harder onto the glass. "What are you doing? Stop running so close!" Her eyes pleaded with him. He just kept smiling, running with the side of the bus. She looked in horror to see him disappear, then a hop from the back wheels of the bus, while it continued on its hell-bound path. "Oh, my God! Stop the bus! Stop the frickin' bus!" she cried. Tears swelled, and her heart pumped uncontrollably. In the mirror above his head, the bus driver howled. Wincing, she turned to see the green-eyed boy's limp body lying on the macadam. She let out a bloodcurdling scream.

"Dadia, Dadia! What's the matter?" Ashley grabbed her shoulder and shook.

"Oh, my God, Ashley!" Make the bus stop!" Dadia said, looking in horror.

"Why, Dod? What the…? You jerk face, ya fell asleep!" Ashley looked at her. "Wow, what the hell were ya dreaming? Ya scared the crap out of me!"

"Oh…it was nothing."

"Well, a lot of screaming for nothing. I think everyone on the bus is looking at us." Ashley laughed, shaking her head.

Relief came looking out the window. Ashley's stop

was in sight. She'd get off there and cut through the park. Stepping off the bus, Ashley turned and gave her a smile.

"Hey Dod, you OK? Did ya want to come over to my house?"

"No, no, that's all right. I'm just going to cut through the park."

I'll talk to ya later?"

"Yeah, later, Ash." She walked in the opposite direction, getting her heart under control. Coming up to the park, she hastened past the small swimming pond and the playground and hurried over the footbridge to the cul-de-sac. *Safe,* she thought. Opening the front door, she heard pots and pans hitting the stove and the smell of -- *yes, spaghetti and meatballs.*

"Hey, Mom, I'm home."

"Hi, honey, how was your day?" Katie Paola echoed from the kitchen.

"Good, other than the scene I made on the bus about ten minutes ago. I, like, fell asleep and had this real scary dream. I even screamed aloud! Oh, my God, Mom, I was so embarrassed."

"Oh my…" her mother said, glancing over from her place at the stove. "Would you like to share?"

Dadia walked over to the refrigerator and poured herself a glass of iced tea. "Mom, when you dream about someone and it's the best dream ever, and then it turns bad, what do you think it means? I mean, it's not like you even know this person, but they are in your dream."

"Well, it might mean you have some sort of feelings for that person, but you're not sure. Maybe a little confused or a little scared."

"Is that what you dreamed?" Dadia's mother said in a grave voice.

"Nah, it was nothing like that. I don't even know why I screamed out loud!" she laughed. "I was just interjecting. I'm going to do some homework."

Grabbing a piece of fruit from the counter, she made

her way up to her room. Thoughts meandered to the mall Friday night and that boy in her dream. *Yes, he was mesmerizing, but sometimes first impressions were wrong.* That's what got her in trouble the first time. That's why she acted the way she did. *Maybe he was different. No, forget it,* she thought. Unsettled, she searched her nightstand. *Damn it, where the hell is it? Was it an omen? Did he have it? The dream, what about the dream?*

16

DEFIANCE RAN THICK THROUGH SETH Kogan's veins as he double stepped the stairs to his room. My father is not going to tell me who I can and cannot be friends with. Who the hell is he? His father's chokehold was school, nothing more.

Reaching the top landing, he heard the bedroom doorknob turn, catching the latch. "Damn you, Brian," he said through his teeth. Silence discomposed his inner feelings as he stopped halfway to his own room and turned back.

A knock on the door was soft but firm. In a low, sarcastic lull, the voice on the other side of the door spoke. "Come in-n."

"Bri, we need to talk," Seth bellowed closing the door behind him. "Did you tell Dad that I was hanging out with Johnny?"

"No, why would I do that?"

"Well, he just reamed my ass out downstairs."

"I don't know what's up with dad. He thinks Johnny is bad news." Brian paused. "Why are you hanging with him anyway?" he pressed.

"Come on, Bri. You know Johnny and I have been like brothers since we were small. Just because his family is messed up doesn't make him a bad guy. How would you be if Agent Kogan, OK, mom, walked out one night never to return? I think you'd be a little off at times, no?" Seth proceeded to the window and looked out toward the Styvers's home. Brian took the opportunity and went back to playing his computer game. Maybe if he ignored Seth he would just go away. Instead, Seth turned and surveyed the room, his eyes memorizing every intricacy, taking photographic pictures in his brain. Systematically he surveyed each item and placement in Brian's domain and honed in on the key chain, sitting on the desk.

Brian felt his brother going into search-and-destroy mode and stuck his body in front of Seth's eyes while he spoke. "Well, Dad said he heard that Johnny had been talking to some Crags in Harrier. We all know the Crags are trouble, Seth."

"Oh, so now Dad's telling you crap he knows nothing about? Hearsay? And what do you know?" For your information, there's no proof. Johnny's a friendly guy. He talks to everyone. You should know that."

"No, you got it all wrong, Seth."

"Sure, Bri, and guess what? You were invited to a party through Johnny this Saturday night. Why don't you come and see for yourself how much of a fool Dad is for talking jack about things he knows nothing of."

"I was invited to a party? By Johnny?"

"Well, it seems, little brother, those two girls you and Larry were talking to at the Galleria are having a party, and for some odd reason, that girl Ashley invited you."

"No way. I don't believe it. Larry told me that Ashley was pissed at me and hated my guts."

"Why the hell would that be? You didn't even talk to her. Anyway, Johnny and I are going…are you in or are you going to be an oinker?"

"No, I'm in. I'm no snitch."

"Good, keep it quiet, even at school. If dad is upset about anything, it should be the fact that you're hanging with Larry," Seth said, wandering over to Brian's computer. "What's wrong with you, man?" He looked down at the swan key chain on the Brian's desk.

"That's funny coming from you," Brian replied.

"Aww…what's this?" He picked up the key chain. "Is this Mom's?" Seth could swear he had seen it somewhere before. "First mom's Precious Moments dolls, now her girly stuff? What's with you, Bri?"

"It's *not* mine and *no*," he adamantly replied.

"A bit feminine, don't you think?" Seth was intrigued.

"I said, it's not mine…that, that girl Dadia…she dropped it, I think…Friday at the Galleria."

"Sure, bro." He studied the key chain. "Word on the party?"

"Word."

"I got stuff to do," Seth said. He wasn't sure letting Brian go to this party was a smart move, though he was determined to prove his father wrong about Johnny.

"Hey, shut the door!" Brian squawked.

"Yeah, right," Seth yelled from down the hallway.

Brian was reeling. *No way! Was he invited to her party?* Maybe Dadia had something to do with it because as far as he could tell, Ashley was the conniver. She would never just invite him. *But who gave two craps about Ashley?* He was going. He was going to see Dadia there. This time, he would have more to say. Intelligent words other than *hi,* and he could return her key chain. *The universe is finally on my side,* he thought, falling back into his bed.

To dream…or not to dream…that was the question.

17

ARRIVING AT THE FAST N Easy Convenience Store was the last place on earth Johnny wanted to be, but he needed money. Yawning, he slowly walked through the front entrance to survey what the hell he got himself into, and he wondered what his mother, if she were still in his life, would think of him. Canvassing each aisle for his new boss, he noticed every item was perfectly spaced, shelved, and alphabetically sorted. Why didn't he notice this last week when he came in looking for a job? *Could someone be that anal?* He wondered how much work and abuse would be propelled upon him in this new job. There, bent down in the bread aisle, he found the guy whose picture was in the dictionary under the words "anal retentive."

"Mr. Halley, I'm here for work."

With eyes of a mutant fly, Mr. Halley looked up through his spectacles and then back down to his watch. "Hmm, yes, yes," he said, counting the inventory on the shelf.

Yo, was he deaf? Johnny's brain scanned for a reaction. "Um, Mr. Halley, I'm here to start work today, John Styvers? Ya hired me last week?" He was becoming perturbed at himself. *What planet was he on when he landed at the Fast N Easy, thinkin' this would be a good place to rack up some dough?*

The word *hello* swirled around his head. He eyed his new boss's vintage polyester pants. *Was this guy stuck on the carousel ride in 1974? Where was Johnny Styvers the day he said yes to this job?* He stood as a soldier at ease. He could play the game, refusing to utter another word; he looked at his own invisible watch.

"Yes, Mr. Styvers, I heard you the first time. Please try to remember, patience is a virtue," Mr. Halley said, smacking the inside of his cheeks while he chewed on a wad of gum.

Now the ol' man was quoting crap and chewing his cud. Johnny was definitely starting the wrong job. There was no way this guy had any lineage to Tori Halley.

"Mr. Halley, yo, call me Johnny."

"Now, Mr. Styvers, follow me to the back room, and we shall set you up."

Johnny followed. His eyes scanned the store to find the other poor slob who worked this cellblock. There he was, stacking the candy shelf—the sorry soul he had run out on the other night when he saw this guy in front of him melting. *Would he remember him?* His new cellmate wore a yellow polo shirt with the Fast N Easy insignia on it. Johnny forgot how much he hated the color yellow, but he needed the money to support his new baby—an old, piece-of-crap car, from the last decade.

As they reached the back office, Mr. Halley unlocked the door to a small room consisting of two chairs, a desk, and four filing cabinets. The walls showed outlines of memories of what once was. On Mr. Halley's desk, papers piled high. His phone was the original, standard, black Bell telephone from the beginning of time, which sat on the left hand side of the desk. *Odd,* Johnny thought.

Mr. Halley pointed to the chair. "Please sit." Johnny thought he smelt the sweetness of cotton candy. *Nah couldn't be.* It did make him want a cup of coffee. Every vacation down the shore his mom would get them both some cotton candy and a cup of joe -- black. There was just something about the two together. It was sweetness meeting brawn, his mother and him. Johnny clutched the key around his neck and fell into a trance – back to the night she gave him the key with a promise of buried treasure.

Mr. Halley proceeded to walk over to the second filing cabinet from the door and unlocked it. Inside were polo shirts in clear plastic wrap.

"What size are you, Mr. Styvers?" he asked, and then he pulled out a large shirt.

"Extra-large."

Mr. Halley turned and eyed him up and down. "Yes, yes, I understand you kids like wearing your clothes larger than normal. A clean image is what this store portrays. A large will do the trick. Make sure that you tuck it in and wear a belt. Those fancy, studded belts you kids wear are a no-no; a regular black belt will do. Sneakers or shoes are acceptable. I will accept jeans as part of the dress code, but they must cover your backside. We are not running a plumbing store here. If you would prefer khakis or Dockers, they will be more than acceptable. Blue, black, or tan in color. No visors or baseball hats at all. Every Friday is payday after four p.m. You can put this shirt on now. If you are not wearing a belt, just make sure when you come in next time that it is tucked in."

"Sure," Johnny said, looking glum.

"Yes, yes, I almost forgot. Every new employee is awarded tickets to any concert being held at the Foundation Center in Rolling Hills." He opened up the third filing cabinet with his key. The bottom drawer inadvertently shot out, frightening him. Inside was a stack of videotapes. Startled, Mr. Halley pushed the drawer in and pulled out the top drawer. "Hmm, yes, yes." Mr. Halley handed him six tickets. Johnny was amazed. *Maybe this guy wasn't so bad after all.* All the best bands played at the Foundation, and tomorrow night his favorite band, Negative Zero, was scheduled to play.

"Now, with that all done, Mr. Styvers, I will introduce you to Mike Johnson. He will clue you in on how to work the register, greet our customers, and show you your day-to-day responsibilities." Mr. Halley turned toward the door. "Mike, how long have you been standing there?"

Mike shrugged his burly shoulders.

"Well, Mike, this is Johnny Styvers. He is the new employee I told you about. Show him what he needs to know."

"Hey, Johnny," Mike stretched out his arm and ever so slightly snapped his wrist, shaking hands. Though manly, Mike's grip gave him the impression he was born with an empty tool chest. *Probably drank tea, pushing paper instead of dirt,* Johnny thought, wondering if he had some device under his shirt that pumped up his shoulders and pecks to be shaking hands like that.

"Hey, Mike."

"Come on, I'll show you the ropes." They both walked into the store while Mr. Halley closed the office door and locked it.

"So, Johnny, where do you live?"

"I live right here in Park View."

"Oh, really." Mike looked skeptical.

"Yo, where you from, Mike?"

"I live over in Harrier, off campus, nice little apartment. I'm studying at the university there. Law."

"High hopes, my friend," Johnny said with apprehension.

"Well, if you're going to reach, you might as well reach real high."

"Yeah, well, there were a few times I reached high, with both hands, but somehow it didn't have the effect I was looking for. I don't think the law and I see eye to eye."

"Ha, well law can be very interpretive." Mike looked at him and cleared his throat.

"Ya got something stuck in there?"

"You could say that." Mike laughed. He liked this new employee's sense of humor.

"Yo, Mike, what's the deal with fly eyes?"

"He has some strange quirks, but overall seems to be an OK guy. He's quiet, keeps to himself. Just don't bring up anything about Park View. Actually, I'm really surprised he hired you. He has never, in the two years I've worked here, hired anyone from Park View or anyone from Park View High School."

"What makes you say that?" Johnny asked as Mike's reply piqued his interest.

"Well, I've heard rumors. I don't want to repeat them, because I am all about facts. But once I asked him how it was funny no one from Park View worked here, and Mr. Halley started to rant and rave about some guy at the high school. He lost it in the store, in front of the customers!" Mike paused. "It was kind of like you the other night." He poked his eyes in fun at Johnny without letting Johnny say a word in defense. "So, if you know what's good for you, don't ever bring up anything that has to do with school or Park View, unless, of course, you're looking to get fired."

"Well, ya don't have to worry. I don't go to Park View High School. I frequent a small school over the border in Harrier. "An' what's with his obsession with this store an' his office? It's like, yo, complete Doctor Jekyll and Mister Hyde."

"Word of advice, don't ever mention his office or how it looks. He spends very little time in there, as it's spooked or something. Come on, we'd better get to work."

As the night progressed, Johnny felt Mr. Halley here and there, studying him. He had met odd in his lifetime, and he knew that Mr. Halley never lived or worked on the even side of the street.

18

ASHLEY WENTWORTH STEPPED INTO THE foyer. "Mom? Dad? Jarred? Anybody?" Her voice echoed through the spaciousness. Plopping her books down on the table, she headed toward the kitchen. Rounding the island, she grabbed a banana from the fruit bin and eyed the familiar note on the counter.

> Ashley dear,
>   Out shopping with Carla from the club. Be a honey – find something to eat. Daddy is working late. So be a dear...have something delivered. Don't bother waiting up...BE GOOD!
>   Love you, Mom

A fifty-dollar bill was attached to the note. Pressing her lips tight together, Ashley read the note again. The corner of her lips began to turn upward. She rubbed the fifty-dollar bill between her thumb and forefinger then dialed her phone.

"H-E-Y, Julie. It's Ashley."

"Hey, Ash, waz up?"

"I was wondering if ya wanted to come over to, um, study. We both have that test in history tomorrow, and I haven't got a clue. I just thought you and I could maybe bond or something. We haven't been close, but I would like to be better friends."

Julie wondered what was up with Ashley, but at the moment, she didn't care. This was Ashley Wentworth, and maybe she really did like her since she invited her and Stephanie to a party Saturday night. *What was with advance notice though?* Now it had a few days to be spread around. *Was she out of her mind?* But maybe Ashley was smarter than that. *No one seemed to know* where *the party was—only that there was going to be one.* Sparking Julie's curiosity and the fact Ashley did invite those guys from Park View, she contemplated Ashley's offer. Julie especially wanted to meet Seth, the one she overheard Ashley telling some girls about, when she sat behind her in history class.

"Um, yeah, I'll come over," she said with anticipation. "What time?"

"Well, my parents are out for the night. So why don't cha come over now, and we'll get some food?"

"I dunno; my mom is making dinner now, I think."

"Hey, tell her we need to study all night—and time is a wasting!"

"Yeah, she may buy that, considering my grades haven't exactly been good this year. So, I'll take care of my mom, and I'll see you in, like, a half hour? You're on Chestnut Street, right?"

"Yeah, it's the big one with the water fountain in the front, set back; you can't miss it." Grabbing the note, Ashley plopped it in the garbage can, skipped over to the staircase, and ascended to her room. Tossing her cell phone on her bed, she went right to the closet and proceeded to search with diligence. Before she could find her secret box, the cell phone beeped. With a sigh, she stopped searching. It was a text message from Dadia. *Hey Ash, was just wondering what was up. Call me when you get this.* She dropped the phone back onto her bed.

Back in her closet, she found the box. Opening it, she eyed hundreds of bills. It was the easiest cash she had ever made. Sticking the fifty in the box, she exchanged it for a twenty-dollar bill, closed it, and put the box back to the dark corner from whence it came. The doorbell rang.

"Jules, you got here quick."

"Yeah," Julie said slowly, looking around in wonder. "Wow, I love your home."

"Yeah, it's nice," Ashley replied. "Follow me. Oh, throw ya books on the table, next to mine. We can look at them, later," she said with a wink and a smile. "Hungry? I'm sure we can find something in this house to eat!"

As they scavenged in the refrigerator, Ashley asked, "hey, Julie, are you in any clubs?"

"No, not really."

Ashley pondered, "Well, I have a friend, Larry, whose dad is the Grand Numen of the Foundation Center over in Rolling Hills. It's a club that has so many different things you can do. I hang out there."

"So, how did you get involved in the Foundation Center all the way over in Rolling Hills?" Julie asked.

"Well, I have a lot of free time on my hands and love to go to the mall. I met Larry Jones there about a year ago. We just clicked, and he invited me to become a member. My parents don't know about it. They'd freak out!" She laughed. "Anyways, I have so much fun over at the Foundation, and Larry is always available when I'm just downright bored to death."

"Wow, is the club part of the Foundation Center where all the bands play?" Julie was in awe.

"Yeah, it's a really cool center. We do so many fun things, and ya can do stuff for them and in return get tickets to see the bands!"

"Hey, would you be interested in maybe coming to one of our club meetings? I'll show ya how to make some good money too. They have a program that if ya become a scout, for every person ya get to join the club, ya get a finder's fee. It's all very legal, and there is no work to be done."

Julie thought about it. She could use some money to get that expensive bag she saw in Neiman Marcus. Going in to a store like NM and just looking was no fun. "What kind of money are you talking about?"

"I'm talking like two hundred dollars a week! Tax free! You only have to recruit one person a year."

"No way, it sounds too good to be true."

"Believe me, it's all legit."

"Do you need the money?" Julie questioned.

"Nah, I do it for fun, and I like being in charge of things." She laughed, "I'll invite some of my Foundation friends to the party Saturday night, introduce you to them. They are the nicest bunch."

"Sure," Julie said. "Are you inviting those boys you talked about in school? The ones from Park View?"

"I did say I would invite them." She smiled. "Ya know what? Let us go out and get something to eat. I'll make it even more fun; we'll rent a limo!"

"No way," Julie said. That sounded so awesome.

Julie followed Ashley up to her room where she showed Julie her secret box with all the cash inside. "A few hundred will cover it tonight, don't cha agree?"

Julie was smiling ear to ear.

Ashley's cell rang. "Talk about ESP," she whispered, "It's Johnny Styvers." Julie eyed her with excitement.

"Hey. Was up? Oh—Dadia?—um, sure, but I'm with my friend Julie right now." She looked at Julie and smiled. "Who else is going? Seth? That be great—cool—I love them too—I know. Don't cha worry how we're gonna get there. I'll take care of it—Great. We'll meet you there in a little more than a half an hour." She hung up the cell phone.

"Oh, my God, Ashley! What is going on?" Julie asked with anticipation.

"We, my love, are going to the Foundation to see Negative Zero tonight! Johnny just invited us. He has six tickets for the show! But I have to call Dadia."

Julie frowned, "Does she need to come?"

"Yeah, I know. It would be more fun just you and me. But Johnny said Seth's brother, Brian, was coming, and I think he's sweet on her."

"Oh," Julie said. "Is he as cute as your description of his brother Seth?"

Ashley hesitated. She was ready to burst, but replied, "See for yourself when you meet him," and proceeded to call Dadia.

When Dadia arrived they were hopping into the limo. She looked at Ashley with surprise, seeing Julie there. As the limo pulled down the driveway, Ashley nonchalantly spoke. "Driver, take us to Park View, to the strip mall on Russell Avenue. We'd like to go to the Fast N Easy Convenience Store, please."

Julie looked at her questioningly.

"Johnny works there. He's friends with Seth."

Julie was in heaven. *Why weren't they friends long ago? What did Ashley ever see in Dadia?* Dadia was way too boring and quiet to be her friend. She looked over to see Dadia looking out the window, being her usual not fun self. Tonight was going to be a blast, even if Dadia was there. With Ashley in her corner, Julie would get first dibs on Seth.

19

READY FOR THE CONCERT OF a lifetime, Johnny walked down the aisle at the Foundation Theater in Rolling Hills. While sounds of unrecognizable voices scratched grooves through the air, he wondered how he got a ticket in the VIP section. He couldn't believe he was there, looking for his seat with Dadia. Ashley and the others were seated in the middle. Poor Brian was seated in a section by himself, and Johnny hoped the kid wasn't afraid of heights.

He liked the idea that Dadia's ticket was a seat next to him. Though at first glance, she carried a prudish, don't-screw-with-me persona. Johnny couldn't help but see an inner beauty. She had a stunning face with long brown hair, but her standoffish attitude could keep any guy away. To him, however, that would be a challenge. But she was different. Her inner being emitted something—something he connected with—and at the moment, something he just couldn't put his finger on. Maybe they had experienced life in the same way, which somehow bonded him mentally to her, as if he knew her all his life. Whatever it was, he felt comfortable just being with her. Ashley was a second thought, and Dadia seemed OK with the fact she wasn't with the rest of the group. She seemed comfortable just sitting next to him. *Was she thinking the same thoughts?* At this point, he didn't even know what his thoughts and feelings were. Shrugging it off, he decided to enjoy the moment. It was the first time in his life he felt peace and contentment since his mom, Hanna, disappeared. It felt good, but he had to mull it over. Intense voices hammered his brain reminding him, *pleasure entwined with immense pain left scars.* Slowing his step, he filed in behind her to keep his thoughts unseen behind his eyes.

Making their way down to the front rows, they checked their tickets. It was strange how they all came with the tickets Mr. Halley gave him until they were scanned at the door, and then they were assigned new ones, and shuffled forward to move along. Though they received the new tickets one right after another, they were seated in different sections. *Funny,* he thought. *They were broken apart from the rest.* He and Dadia received additional backstage passes on lanyards, and it seemed they must have won the golden tickets. His eyes scanned around to see how many others had passes. Not many. He was never lucky in any endeavor, and *winner* was omitted from his vocabulary. Maybe this was a sign of something good to come. Or, maybe, he just happened to get his ticket scanned right after Dadia. She could be the one with the luck.

Brian must have been pissed, Johnny thought. Ashley, Julie, and Seth were somewhere in the middle tier, while Brian seemed to have a seat in some obscure section, all by himself. *Poor little Bri. Maybe that was his lot in life,* he thought. *Maybe some things ya just never get past or grow out of. Those certain traits you're born with that just seem to harden you, and follow your soul to the grave.*

Once they realized they were all being separated, they made a quick pact. After the show started they would meet in the last row, middle upper tier. No one ever cared about the seats in the nose bleed section.

Johnny could have sworn he caught a glimpse of Larry Jones and Tori Halley at the show. If Larry came within a twenty-foot diameter of him, he would beat him down. He knew it was wrong, and he needed to control his anger. But it was Larry Jones, and Larry had no regard for the living or the dead. Larry would be getting what he deserved with the stunt he pulled at the Galleria talking trash about his mom.

Hmm, never, ever been a VIP, sputtered out of Johnny's brain. He looked down at the laminated pass around his neck. *So, this was what it was like to have clout.* The lights went low. The stage lit up. Pyrotechnic flames shot upward, and the band began to play.

"Johnny, I'm going to the ladies' room."

"Now? The show is just starting!"

Dadia scooted past him while Johnny focused again on the stage. Sighing, she started up the steps. Brian was on her mind. *Where could he be sitting?* Her swan key chain was pressing on her brain, but she had felt awkward to ask Brian about it in the limo in front of Julie. *Hmm,* she remembered, *he was in Section Sixty-Six, and it really was not fair he was by himself.* She walked through the arch to the hallway.

An attendant stepped in front of her, startling her. "Excuse me, madam. May I help you?" he said, looking down at her to see the pass around her neck.

"Um, I'm looking for Section Sixty-Six?"

"Section Sixty-Six. May I see your ticket?" The young man snatched the ticket out of her hand. "It seems you're in the right section," he told her, looking at her with a face of stone.

"Yes, I know, but my friend is in Section Sixty-Six, and I need to talk to him."

"Section Sixty-Six you say?"

"Yes, Section Sixty-Six. Just point me in the right direction. I'm sure I can find it."

The attendant looked at her with question. "I'm sorry, madam. There is no Section Sixty-Six. You must be mistaken. Do you need an escort back to your seat?" The attendant placed his hand on her arm.

Dadia looked at him with forced eyes. "I guess I was mistaken. Um, can you tell me how to get to the nearest bathroom?"

With a reluctant look, the attendant smacked his lips together. "Yes, madam. Pointing down the corridor, he said, "The ladies' room is the second door on the right.

As she walked she felt the eyes of the attendant still on her until the door of the ladies' room closed behind her. She sighed. *What was going on?* At the sink, she splashed water on her face. *No Section Sixty-Six? Where was Brian?* She could have sworn that down in the lobby an attendant pointed in the direction Brian was to go. She saw Brian asking; she saw the attendant point.

"May I help you, madam?" a voice came from the dark corner of the bathroom. Taken back, she turned. Out of the shadows, a woman twice her size and age emerged, holding a hand towel.

The woman looked at her with a smile, and eyed her backstage pass. Instead of handing her a towel, the woman spoke. "Welcome, my dear."

Welcome? "Excuse me, can you tell me how to get to Section Sixty-Six?"

The woman tapped Morse code with her pointer finger on her nose. "Section Sixty-Six?"

"Could you just tell me where the stairs are to the upper section?" Dadia stared at her.

"Oh, my dear, the upper section is no place for you. You are on a special list. You should rejoice in that. May I help you back to your seat?"

This was absurd. "No, I think I can find my way back. My friend must be worried about me. Thank you, and yes I am glad," she lied. The woman smiled.

Touching Johnny's shoulder, she sat down. He was still in a trance. He reminded her how Ashley's brother, Jarred, could focus on the TV and be oblivious to all that encompassed him. He'd be so focused on what he saw nothing around him would matter. The house could burn down, and the crispy critter in front of the burned-out box would be him. Ashley would say the meanest, most outrageous things to him, and he'd say, "Yeah, Ash, whatever you want," never taking his eyes off the TV set. She looked at the stage. She looked to Johnny.

"Johnny, Johnny." She grabbed his arm and tugged. No response. He just smiled and stared ahead, bobbing and singing lyrics she could not understand. Grabbing his head and gently forcing it toward her, he came to and looked at her.

"What?"

She screamed into his ear. "Jay, there is something really, really wrong here!"

"What ya talking about? This concert is outrageous." And then it hit him. No one had ever called him Jay, only his mom. He looked at her in bewilderment.

"No, really, listen to me. They're telling me there is no Section Sixty-Six. That's where Brian was headed to, Section Sixty-Six."

"Maybe you're mistaken, Dod." All of a sudden, it felt so natural to call her that. "We're gonna meet everyone up at the top. So what's the problem? Let's just enjoy this VIP status. Brian will find his way. Yo, he is a big boy, ya know." He smiled at her. "Then, at the end of the show, we can go meet the band," he told her, flashing his VIP badge.

"Johnny, they told me there is no way up to the top from here."

"Don't believe it. We all came from the lobby, so there has to be a way. We'll just go back to the lobby and go from there—but after this song." He looked at her with the pleading face of a child, trying to convince his mother to buy a toy.

"Dod, let's just enjoy at least this one song. VIPs, we got the passes. Let's take advantage of it. Brian can handle himself, believe me."

"VIP might just be the problem," she said, sinking back into her seat. *Impressed? No.* More pressing thoughts were pushing on her brain. Dadia then lit up with the best idea. *Text him*…Yes, that would put her mind to rest. "Jay, what is Brian's cell number?"

The music had swallowed his soul. Hand in pocket; Johnny pulled out Seth's cell number, never losing focus on the show and handed it to Dadia. Dadia opening up her cell phone to text him. She took a deep breath and felt heat dissipate from her neck. She stared down at the screen on her phone. *No service.*

* * *

This is ridiculous, Brian thought, *as ridiculous as not saying anything to Dadia about the key chain. Was it even hers?* She didn't ask, and he didn't find the nerve, especially in front of everyone in the limo. Now it seemed every working sentry gave him a nod and a finger pointing in a direction that seemed to be the opposite of all the other cattle in the Foundation hallways going to their seats at this concert. "Section sixty-six?"

"To the right, sir, move along. The concert has already begun."

"I know, I know," he replied.

The last sentry seemed to know where the section was. "Through this door, sir. Go down the corridor to the last door on the left."

Brian followed his directions impeccably. Pushing through the door, he felt a pressure pushing on him, only to find he was outside in the back by the Dumpsters. "What the?" he said, pissed. He heard a bang and a click behind him. He stood there, miffed. *"This could only happen to me."*

20

"LARRY!" BRIAN YELLED DOWN THE hallway. His gait quickened, almost breaking into a run. "Larry!" Again, he listened for a response.

Larry Jones continued looking in his locker, shuffling the books and papers inside. He caught himself in the mirror suction cupped inside the locker door. Pausing, he combed his hair with his fingers. "Just the worm I was going to track down. Got that report for me? I need it now."

"Yeah, I got it."

Larry pulled himself away from the mirror. "Well, let's have it."

"You'll get it," Brian said defiantly.

Larry looked at him with contempt. "What's that mean? I'd better get it, worm."

"You will," Brian said, looking at the floor. "And what's with telling me that girl Ashley hated my guts?" His body tensed, and he felt moisture ooze from his pores.

"Hey, that's what she told me, man." Larry went back to the mirror.

Wrong answer. Everyone had a limit. Brian's limit was three times taller than he, but somehow he was already at the top. He had two choices he could make: stay the course, or with a surge of brawn, blurt out, "Well, maybe she's playing *you,* because she invited *me* to the party Saturday night. Actually, a personal invite." Brian chose the latter, and he smirked.

Larry forced his locker closed and turned to Brian, speaking in a nonbelieving voice, "She called you?" He stared Brian down.

"She called Johnny." *Damn it,* he hated himself for breaking under pressure.

"Really…Johnny?" he said. Brian caught the questioning in his voice.

"Yeah, and I think she's got a thing for him. We all hung out last night." He prodded simultaneously while the late bell rang. As if Brian Kogan had a bodyguard hovering above him, he slapped Larry on the back. "Gotta go, Slick."

"Hey, where's my report, butthead?" Larry asked dumbfounded.

"Don't worry. I'll get it to you next period. I'm late." Looking back, Brian yelled, "Find me in room two-fifteen!" He disappeared down the crowded hallway.

Find him? Room two-fifteen? Find Brian? Did he just call me "Slick"? Damn that Johnny, Larry thought. *Trying to move in on my Ashley? Now Seth is best buddies with Johnny?* He would finish an old fight if Johnny got in the way.

In the empty hallway, Brian stopped in front of classroom two-fifteen and took in a deep breath. A good start to the morning did not constitute walking into Mr. Manteria's class late, but today Brian didn't care. Today nothing was going to bother him in that dreaded classroom, two-fifteen. Detention and all the crap he was going to get would be well worth it for that priceless look Larry just gave him back in the hallway. It was awesome. He shocked Larry, and he liked it. Smiling, he realized he had the upper hand, from now. Seth was so right about Larry, though he wondered why his brother would put Larry up to torturing him. *He did, didn't he?* No matter. A smirk rose upon Brian's face. He flung the door open into Mr. Manteria's classroom. Reality met his eyes, and he was ready for it.

Mr. M. was in the middle of a lecture about the dark visions of Damen Blaine. He watched Brian saunter in.

"Sorry, Mr. M.," Brian said, walking to his seat still smirking. *I'm going to get my butt nailed to a chair for this one,* he thought. *So what...*He was ready to take his punishment with a smile.

"Mr. Kogan, we were just discussing the art of Damen Blaine. Would you like to contribute your thoughts?"

Brian was flabbergasted. *What happened to yesterday— when he wanted to rip his head off in the hallway?* Mr. M. was never shy about embarrassing him in front of the class. Mr. Manteria hated him.

"Well, I understand her art, and she's abstract...some might want to say, hmm," Brian replied.

"A very astute thought, Brian." Mr. Manteria continued his lecture. Brian's disruption was trivial to the marvels of Blaine's work. Brian sat in astonishment. *No punishment? No berating? No big deal, nada? What—was today a get out of jail free day?*

The class bell rang. Larry was waiting at the door. His neck was pumped, eyeing Brian. Brian took a deep breath and put his game face on.

"Larry, my man!" His heart raced, acknowledging Larry without delay.

"Bri," he said with the breath of the dragon. "Where's my god damn paper?"

Brian pulled the report from his binder.

"You had it all along?" He seethed, making sure no eyes of authority were upon them. Larry punched square on the shoulder with the full force of his fist; Brian stumbled backward, hitting the locker with his spine. His brain screamed. Flat out, he refused to acknowledge the pain.

"Yeah, man, I forgot it was there," Brian said, looking up with a wide-eyed gaze.

"Don't you dare, do that again, worm."

"Oh, don't worry, Larry. I wouldn't dream of it." But in truth, he would never do another piece of homework for that toad. He didn't need Larry. He, right then and there, refused to continue to be anyone's slave. He didn't care how many friends Larry had. Larry was a selfish user, and Brian was done being his lackey.

Watching Larry walk away, he stretched his back and rubbed his shoulder. Malevolence glistened in his eyes, while a vindictive grin materialized. Larry would now have to pay the piper, even if it meant Larry was going to pummel him in a dark corner or be a punching bag in between class—so be it. He didn't care anymore. *Revenge?* No, he had too much honor in his name, but he would claim back what was rightfully his—his own respect.

21

FOURTH PERIOD HISTORY, THEN A reprieve, lunch. Larry Jones couldn't wait. Today he and his buddies planned on sitting with Tori Halley and her crew. He just had to get through this class, and the rest of the day would be a breeze. Yesterday he handed in his history report. Now he sat smiling, looking at Ms. Choleric's back while she wrote crap on the blackboard. All was good. Brian certainly wrote the best papers, which propelled him to be the star student in Ms. Choleric's eyes. This was a feat unreachable to the rest of the male population in her class. Ms. Choleric hated the opposite sex in general, but she liked him. She, on the other hand, made him think of an old trophy that the school kept around reminding the staff and students that old fossils and history served some sort of purpose.

"Class, turn to chapter ten in your textbooks and continue reading about World War II," Ms. Choleric screeched.

The sound of rustling papers and books ceased. Larry looked at the page and pretended to read. Ms. Choleric circumspectly shuffled behind each student, eyeing the page he or she was on. Washing saliva around in her mouth, she stood behind Rolf, making a *tsk, tsk* sound, pushing her tongue between her two front teeth.

"Rolf, *tsk*, catch up." She cleared her throat and moved on. "Class, history is like war. If you don't attack it, it will most definitely attack you."

Torture, Larry thought. *Two more kids, then she would be hovering over his back like that smelly girl who had a locker next to his.*

"Nice reading, Mary, *tsk.*" She smiled at her with approval. Mary smiled back.

How do you nicely read? Larry asked himself, tapping his pencil on the desk. Ms. Choleric looked at the clock and returned her personal hovercraft back to the blackboard. She sucked the inside of her upper teeth, *tsk,* and she wrote, *tsk,* and wrote, *tsk.*

Get that bad taste out of your mouth or get a pacifier or something, Larry thought, and rolled his eyes. *Would she ever stop?* Today the sound was worse than normal. *No wonder she never married.* He laughed to himself while he watched her write some more crap on the blackboard. She spoke in a monotone voice even when she got excited about history. When it came to Ms. Choleric, she had no pulse. She epitomized that machine that showed a flat line when you died—except for that annoying sound she pulsed from her tongue.

Ms. Choleric finished writing the assignment on the board and turned to face the class. Her eyes fired straight to Larry and his smile turned into a hard question mark. "Mr. Jones, *tsk,*" she said in her gruffest voice, "I was shocked and dismayed that you had the gall to write what you did in your report about Adolph Hitler." She paused, and then continued, "It is hard to believe you referred to some song or poetry, writing about Mussolini's and Hitler's weenies."

Class, *tsk!* Quiet!" she shouted. "You, Mr. Jones, are to report immediately to the principal's office and to think, my star pupil." She shook her head back and forth, like she had some sort of shaking disorder.

"Ms. Choleric, I don't know what you're talking about. I didn't write that."

"Mr. Jones, did you or did you not write a report on

Adolph Hitler and hand it in to me yesterday, *tsk*?"

"Yes, but I didn't write that."

"Then you handed in someone else's work and put your name on it, which implies there is an additional layer to this atrocity. Do you know the additional charges you could be facing, *tsk*?"

Charges? What did that schmuck Brian write? He is a dead, dead, dead, man, Larry said to himself.

"Your parents will be called, and we will get to the bottom of this. March yourself right down to Mr. Thorn's office and let this be a lesson to the rest of you sitting here."

Larry took the hall pass, and the eyes of the class fluttered about.

"Just wait until I find that, worm," Larry said, tromping down the corridor to the principal's office. He felt his chest expand with hot moist air, ready to exhale a fiery steam, before charging like a toreador in a bullfight. Turning the corner the boy's bathroom door flung open and out walked an unsuspecting victim.

"Just the worm I was looking for." Looking both ways, he threw his prey back through the bathroom door. "You, Kogan, just messed with the wrong guy." Grabbing Brian by the shirt, he flung him into the urinals. The sound of cloth tearing rang out through the empty stalls.

"What the hell are you talking about?" Brian replied in pain.

"What did you write in that report, worm?" His anger seethed. He again pushed Brian up against the urinal.

"Oh, crap," Brian said, putting on his best surprised look. "Larry, I must have given you the wrong report. I swear. I was bored one night, wrote this off-the-wall piece—you know, I got carried away," he said, holding back the break of smile in the midst of his pain. Brian experienced pain every day of his life.

"I own you for life, worm; you're going to wish you were never born, and your sissy friend Johnny, he couldn't save his mother and he won't be able to save you. it's time to start your days in hell," Larry seethed as he threw his arm up, fist drawn just as the door of the bathroom flung open.

"Hey, you two!" A custodian with a mop and bucket eyed them both. He pointed to Brian. "You! Come with me." Grabbing Brian by the nape of the neck, he escorted him out of the bathroom, leaving Larry in bewilderment. Turning the corner, he walked Brian down the hall in the opposite direction of the principal's office. Turning the next corridor the custodian released the grip on his neck, looked him squarely in the eye, and winked. "Get to class, troublemaker."

Brian couldn't believe it. He held together the rip in his shirt and circled back down the hallway. Thank God, he had an extra T-shirt somewhere in the bottom of his locker. Finding it, he put it to his nose. Looking both ways with a Houdini exchange of shirts, he was off to class. Today was the first day of a new beginning. He grinned. Maybe things were starting to look up. Someone was watching over his shoulder. Maybe it was his grandma, pushing him to stand tall. Walking down the hallway, the smell of chocolate chip cookies filled the air in front of the cooking classroom. *Sweet,* he thought, reminding him of days of old and Johnny's mom. From today on, he would never be caught running again—well, maybe just to get rid his stomach everyone called his "beer keg". It was time to step into the light, no matter how difficult it would be, and there would be no turning back. He knew Larry would be watching and waiting to make his move. Somehow, he now had the strength to light the darkness that lay before him.

22

"HEY LOVE, IT'S ABOUT TIME you answered your phone. Are ya avoiding me? The party's tonight."

He ignored her first question. "Really, Ash, and where is that?"

"My house," she replied.

"Not a good idea."

"Larry, honey, don't cha worry. Everything has been cleared, and my mom just left for a last minute rendezvous with my dad in California."

"What about your brother? He doesn't know about the club or the party."

"Who, Jarred? My mom, of course, put him in charge. Once he heard she was leaving, he yessed her to death. The second she left the driveway, he was off for a weekend in Harrier with his—at the moment—love of his life, Darleen. He won't be home till who knows when, so all's good, love."

"I don't know, Ash, your house? I'll have to OK it."

"It's been OK'd. Like I said, don't cha worry. I took care of everything."

"I see..." Larry paused. "So why did you invite that guy Johnny?" He spoke in disgust.

"Because that was the only way I could get Julie to come. She is the target candidate. She wanted to meet Seth, and of course he wouldn't come without Johnny."

"She wants to meet Seth Kogan?" He saw how

Ashley looked at Seth and Johnny at the mall. He took a deep breath. "What the hell are you doing? I know these guys. This is a bad idea. You should of passed this by me first."

"I know what I'm doing, Larry, so drop just it," she belted back.

"So now you think you're a better spotter than me?" He knew he had ruffled her feathers. This conversation was over. He'd just go to his father, the Grand Numen. The Grand Numen would understand the risks and side with him. "So, then why did you invite that worm, Brian, after the fact?"

"Ya mean big boy?" She laughed. "I had a soft moment, OK. I invited him for Dadia."

"Dadia? She's not club material. This is not one of your personal parties. You saw what she did at the mall. Dadia should not be here tonight."

"Shut up, Larry. I know what I'm doing, and for your information, she fits the profile too."

"I hope you *do* know what you're doing, because there's going to be trouble, Ashley. And *they* will be the trouble."

"The only one who's going to be trouble is you, Larry. Maybe that's why ya dad picked me as a spotter. I had it all planned until you showed up Friday night at the Galleria with big boy. Ya ruined my plans, but being the quick thinker I am, I had to change a few things."

"Well for your information, big boy as you call him got my ass in deep trouble at school today. He's a dead man. Lucky for me my parents have been at the Foundation all week, and the school only had our house phone number. They're leaving the matter till Monday. So, now that I've told you everything—you know nothing, get it? Understand?"

"Don't worry, love. My lips are sealed, but now, more than ever, stay away from here tonight. We don't need you to do or to say anything stupid."

"What's stupid is that you invited Johnny and Seth. The Grand Numen specifically states no recruiting anyone from Mountain Crest and no inviting Park View people."

"Like I said, don't worry. No one else is being recruited, just Julie. I cleared her through GP."

"Oh, so now you're making plans and talking to GP without me? Do GP and the Grand Numen know about Johnny and Seth?"

"This has nothing to do with them. I know how to weave a web, and you're not going to say a word, got it? Ya wouldn't want daddy to know what went down today at school...now do ya? Don't want to bring any community attention to your family, now do ya? The truth about what happened in school shouldn't come out by mistake, now should it?" she asked harshly. There was silence on the other end of the line.

"Larry, honey, I will take care of everything tonight. Don't worry, and when daddy finds out about your school mishap, I got ya back."

"I am worried, Ashley. And I should be there tonight!" Larry insisted.

"You should know more than anyone else to stay away. If ya come here tonight, who knows what could happen?" There was a long pause.

Larry's voice softened. "You could slip away for, say, an hour tonight?"

Her smile radiated through the phone. "Aw...that would be sweet. But GP will be watching, and we wouldn't want anything to get back to the Grand Numen, now would we? I need to work. Recruit, recruit, recruit. Just think of it. A night off for you!"

Wrong response. "Ash," he said. "So, what's the story with us?"

"Aw, Larry, you and I are special. We are the chosen ones. Remember? You know that. Tonight is just work. You're gonna be in enough trouble come Monday. Let me handle this for us, for the club."

"But…"

"Tomorrow, you and I, love. I'll take you to the races; ya know you'll have a good time." She paused. "Please, just make sure ya don't show up tonight."

"Sure, Ash, whatever you say." He terminated the connection. He was pissed. They weren't supposed to ever recruit from the town they lived in, and no one under eighteen was allowed. Ashley had been the only exception because he begged his dad. *What, the rules changed, and no one informed him? Went over his head? Took control? How dare she even think about talking to the upper deck or his father over him? She was to go through him!*

His cell phone rang. "Yes, Grand Numen…Yes, sir, everything is planned for tonight…Yes, they are away…How come I didn't know? Wait, what do you mean…I'm not to be there? Since when? But…But…So when did we start recruiting from Park View? And no one asked for an opinion on this? Yes, sir…Sorry, sir. I'm to go to the Foundation, immediately? Why? Yes, sir, I understand GP will be there, but this is ridiculous! I should be there tonight! Yes, sir…I see, sir…immediately, sir." *What the hell was his father thinking?*

* * *

Ashley Wentworth loved being in charge. Find one club member a year—that was the quota. Slice of pie and she would do it right in Mountain Crest—her town. It was genius. She was good; she was very good at what she did. She smiled and opened her cell phone.

"Dadia, the party is tonight—here at my house!"

"Oh, your parents are letting you have a big bash?"

"No, no, Ms. Dadia, last minute my mom went to meet daddy for a weekend rendezvous."

"Wow, and they are still letting you have a

party, anyway?"

"Sure, sure thing, Dod," Ashley said.

"Well, I'm so sorry, but I can't come."

"What do you mean? You have to come! It's at my house!"

"My mom is going out tonight, which means I have to stay at home."

"Dod, no way, you need to be here."

"Why?" Dadia asked. They never hung out Saturday nights. Ashley always had things going on with her family.

"Because it's a surprise."

"I'm sorry, Ashley. I just can't."

Ashley paused on the phone. "Guess who is coming. That boy from the mall—ya know, the one that might have that special key chain? How ya gonna find out if he has it unless ya come and ask him?" She paused. "Ya missed your chance at the concert, ya know."

"Ashley, can you ask him for me?" Dadia pleaded. "I can't disobey my mom."

"Whatever, Dod, you did promise me you'd come to my party, and that's the only reason I invited those boys. And besides, everyone will be here; even Julie and Stephanie said they are coming."

"I can't, Ashley. Wait, you invited Julie? Stephanie?"

"Even if you just left the house for a half hour, your mom would never know."

"I really can't, Ashley."

"What does it matter? Whatever, thanks for the backup, Dod." She snapped her cell phone closed.

Dadia never disobeyed her mother, Katie. There was always that fear Katie had. Sometimes Ashley felt Dadia's mother made it up in her mind; no one was watching them. No one was following them, ever.

23

THE WENTWORTH HOUSE WAS FILLED with young adults from the Foundation who were preparing for the party. Julie and Stephanie were the first of Ashley's friends to arrive.

"Come in, girls!" Ashley spoke through the intercom, buzzing open the front door. "Go to the great room. Julie, you remember where that is. I'll see if 'you know who' is here yet."

Stephanie looked at Julie. "You've been here before?" Julie just looked at her and nodded. "And who is 'you know who'?"

Julie just shrugged.

Walking toward the great room, an athletic boy with sun-kissed skin stood smiling at them. "Hi, ladies, we are so glad that you could come. My name is Rob; welcome, can I get you two beautiful women a drink?"

Wow, Julie thought, *Ashley's friends with the male models from that store at the mall.* For sure she had some really nice looking friends.

"So, who are you two?" he asked.

Julie spoke up first. "Julie and Stephanie."

He smiled big. "Julie," he said. "That's so amazing! We make a drink called 'The Julie.'"

"Really?" she asked. "What's in it?"

"Some exotic tropical fruit and a secret little something that makes a Julie irresistible. Would both of you care for one?"

"Of course." Julie smiled at him and then at Stephanie.

"Do they make a Stephanie drink, like the Julie too?" asked Stephanie.

"Uh, no," he said and walked off to get their drinks.

Stephanie wrinkled her upper lip. "He's strange."

"Maybe, but he's cute," Julie injected. "Where is Ashley? I don't see her."

"She's finding 'you know who'," Stephanie replied agitated. She, Julie's best friend, didn't know who 'you know who' was. For some reason, Julie forgot to mention this small tidbit of information to her best friend.

* * *

Seth blew the horn. *Come on, Styvers,* he said to himself, *the party's already started.* "Bri, get in the back."

"Hey, I already called shotgun."

"Overruled, bro. Age before heiferism."

"Ya know, Seth, you're a Johnson."

"Yes, son, all real men have one; now get in the back seat. You're lucky you're coming."

Johnny plodded down the steps while Brian opened the door to get into the back seat. "Hey, Brian," Johnny called, gesturing a high-five handshake, only to stop and retract it.

Brian coughed and spoke at the same time. "Jerk."

Johnny just laughed. "That's so lame, Bri."

Seth looked to Johnny in the passenger seat. "A white T-shirt?"

"Yo, we're goin' to a party, ain't we?"

The car ride to Mountain Crest was quiet, at least in the back seat where Brian was forced to be a ghost again. Taking in the scenery, he noticed a swimming pond by a park before they turned onto Ashley's street. Right before they approached her house, an old beat-up white station wagon careened around the corner almost hitting them.

"Asshole!" Seth shouted.

"What a jerk!" Brian replied from the back seat.

Johnny just stared forward looking for her house. "Nah, he's not an asshole; an asshole serves a purpose."

Ashley Wentworth's house rested on a manicured knoll and from the street looked like a moderately sized home. Covered by shrubbery, the one clue that this was no ordinary, middle-class home was the flowing fountain by the front door. Trudging up the cobblestone driveway, the secret was no longer hidden. It was a mansion. Approaching the large double doors, Seth pushed the intercom button. Johnny said, "Yo, Ash, we have arrived."

The door opened as if she had been waiting for them. "Welcome!" Ashley bubbled over with excitement.

"Nice little beach house ya got here." Johnny's charm smiled, pushing in front of Seth.

"Aww…thanks sweetness. Most of the time it's empty and hollow, but tonight it is full of life." From within, the boys could hear the sound of music, laughter, and organized chaos. "Come in, come in." She gave two big smiles as Johnny and Seth passed her. Brian walked by and she held her breath, giving him a stony glare. He knew what she was doing, and he gave her back what she deserved—nothing. It was bad enough taking crap from guys; he refused to take it from a girl.

While her hand pulled the front door closed, she hesitated, looking into the darkness that fell at the end of the lighted driveway. "Anyone else come up the driveway with ya?" She could swear she heard the sound of disquiet.

"Nope, just us," Johnny replied.

She continued to look out. "Pumpkin?" Pumpkin her cat was always scaring her, appearing out of nowhere. Twenty-five pounds of pure kitty. Or maybe it was the wind playing with the leaves in the darkness beyond. *Man, you have some imagination girl,* she thought, closing the door. "Guys, if ya see a mutant cat, that's my Pumpkin." She turned to them. "Come, let's get to some good par-tae-yang!"

Beyond the sliding glass doors of the great room, the backyard patios were all furnished with expensive furniture; a heated, in-ground pool, adorning a waterfall half covered for colder weather; and in the distance a cabana, large as a small house. People were swimming and drinking out of red or occasionally blue plastic cups.

The three boys surveyed the backyard in awe. This wasn't a home. It was a hotel—a very expensive one. Standing with their tongues hanging out, Ashley waved to a young man who looked to be about twenty-five. He cut short his conversation with a young woman of mousey brown hair, parted on the side, picked up three drinks off a waiter's tray, and took them over to Ashley.

"You guys look thirsty," he said. "I'm Robert."

Seth's radar went into overdrive. He studied Robert, handing each of them a drink. Distracted, Robert turned to look at something by the pool. Seth noticed a small, circular coloration under Robert's right ear. *Interesting,* he thought. *A mole? A tat?* He just wasn't sure.

"Cheers," Robert said. Everyone clicked their cups and drank. Seth watched diligently to see Robert looking to Ashley. Her facial features seemed to release him.

"Nice party," Johnny said, downing his drink.

"Nice to meet you guys. Enjoy," Robert replied and walked back to the girl with the mousey brown hair.

Ashley meandered with the three boys over to the pool area and directed them to a patio table with a sign that said "reserved" on it. Guys and girls were splashing and having fun in the heated indoor/outdoor pool. *They knew how to live it up in Mountain Crest,* Johnny thought. Taking in their surroundings, Seth went into photographic-memory mode, soaking in every detail from the color of the cups they each had to the texture of the draperies in the great room. Turning to Johnny, Johnny didn't look right to him. Johnny was different when he picked him up, and he only had that one drink Robert gave him a short time ago. He filed that thought in his back pocket.

"Ashley, was that your brother who gave us the drinks?" Seth asked.

"Oh, no," Ashley answered back. "Just a friend."

"Wow, how old is he? Like twenty-five?" Seth kept seeing guys and girls that seemed a lot older than they were.

"Really? I think he's actually around eighteen."

On one side of the backyard, a group of kids were listening to someone as if they were in a training seminar. Over on the east side of the patio, Rob had Julie and Stephanie engaged in conversation while they sipped on their drinks. Seth noticed Julie from the other night and wondered who the girl was that stood beside her.

"Is your friend, Dadia, coming tonight?" Johnny asked. "She was a lot of fun at the concert."

"Oh, um, yeah, I think so, but Johnny, ya got a see the new hot tub daddy and I just put in at the cabana. Come…" She grabbed his arm, looked at him with seduction in her eyes, dragging him off, leaving Seth and Brian to fend for themselves. "Excuse us, guys; I just have to show Johnny my hot-tub attire." She gave them a sinister smile.

"You got a bathroom?" Seth shouted as she walked away Johnny on her arm. Johnny looked back at them with a shrug.

"Yeah, through the great room, to the right!" she yelled back.

"Bri, hold down the fort," Seth stated, getting up from the table.

"Hey, I'll come with you."

"Bro, only girls go to the bathroom together." Seth looked at Brian. "And don't drink the rest of that, OK?"

"Why? I sure am, aren't you?"

"No way, man, I'm the designated driver, if you didn't recognize that fact. Didn't you notice Johnny seemed different, right after gulping that drink Robert gave us? Don't drink that; I don't know what's in it. I've seen him down a six-pack of beer without being fazed."

"Well, he did gulp it down!" Brian said.

"No, no, something's amiss," Seth replied.

"You're just saying that because you don't want me to drink!"

Seth looked him square. "You want to see that girl, don't you?"

"Of course. I have her key chain. I'm just going to take a few sips; it'll help loosen me up."

"Bri, I understand that, but if you're interested in someone, don't drink—especially don't drink what's in that cup," he spat out under his breath.

"Well, when that guy handed us the drinks, you did. You're driving, and you seem all right," Brian protested.

"No, bro, everyone thought I did, but I didn't. Get it? Just stay here and look for your girl." Something just wasn't right about this party, and he was going to get to the bottom of it. Walking through the great room, he overheard the names *Rob* and *Robert* one too many times in different parts of the house. Could it be a coincidence every guy he ran into at Ashley's party had one of those two names?

24

DADIA COULDN'T STAND IT ANY longer. *Why did she have to sit home on a Saturday night while everyone else was having a good time?* Her mother was just a paranoid schizophrenic. She never disobeyed her, but tonight, well, maybe just for an hour. She would sneak out under the cover of darkness, leave the radio on in the bedroom and TV in the living room, and steal away for a short amount of time. She wanted to see if Brian had her swan charm and maybe even look at his pretty eyes once more. She had no interest in him—no interest in boys at all. Anyway, if he were coming all the way from Park View to return her key chain, she should at least be there to get it from him and at least thank him.

Out the door, she scurried down the street to the cul-de-sac and over the footbridge that led into a public park. Quickening her pace, she passed the swimming pond, feeling her heart race, and continued on to the street. *Safe.* Slipping through the gate of the Wentworth estate, she walked up the driveway to the front door. She pushed the intercom button, remembering the security camera and how it perturbed her. She bit her lower lip. Refusing to look up, she closed her eyes, feeling the camera watching her. Ashley knew she hated that thing, but human nature took hold and forced her eyes to open and look at it.

He watched her on the screen and studied her. He just knew those eyes had to be the color of chestnuts. She was beautiful and haunting. She looked to the camera. He spoke through the intercom. "Yes, yes, beautiful, may I help you?"

She didn't recognize the voice and focused her eyes now on the door. "It's Dadia. I'm here for Ashley." She felt her body vibrate. *Come on,* she thought. *Buzz me in!*

"I'm sorry. There is no Dadia on the list. Please, step back and look into the camera."

She stepped back. With reluctance, she looked into the camera. With mixed emotions, she scrunched her face to ask with uneasiness, "Mr. Wentworth?" Silence. Something brushed up against the back of her calf. Jumping, she shook as if electricity surged up her spine. "Pumpkin! Oh, my God, you scared the crap outta me." Pumpkin purred, pushing his orange coat against her. She scratched behind his ear, momentarily forgetting the camera's eye upon her.

"You may find my dear Ashley in the second-floor study," the voice through the intercom said, buzzing open the door for her.

"Thank you!" Relieved, she walked up the stairs hearing the sounds of laughter and talk from the great room and beyond. *What the hell was Ashley doing up in the library?* Reaching the door, she noticed it was ajar. Pushing it open, she threw her voice into the dimness of the room, "Ashley?"

"Yes, yes, come in, come in. My Ashley will be with you in just a moment."

"Mr. Wentworth?" she asked again. She never met Ashley's father. He was always away on business. She walked to the center of the room, and the door slowly closed.

"Um yes, yes, beautiful," he said.

"It's so nice to finally meet you," she said with a warm smile, putting her hand out.

"And you too," he replied with a gentle shake of her hand, feeling her soft, supple skin.

"I'm sorry. I thought Ashley said you were out of town this weekend with Mrs. Wentworth. I must have gotten it mixed up." She knew the Wentworth's had money, but it was apparent Mr. Wentworth had no sense of style or what year it was. She was surprised Mrs. Wentworth didn't intervene. Then again, with the way Ashley talked, he worked the graveyard shift, and Mrs. Wentworth took care of the day shift.

"Oh, yes, yes, plans changed I had to return, attend to business here at home." He put his hand in his pocket and pulled out a square object. "Gum?"

"No, thank you."

"Would you like something to drink while you wait for my Ashley?" he asked.

"No, thank you," she said again. Dadia started to feel an uneasiness she hadn't felt in a long time.

He walked over to the table and presented her with a tray of finger foods. "Take one, please. My Ashley spent all evening making these for the party."

She wasn't hungry, but to be polite to Ashley's dad, she took one off the tray and took a bite.

"Ooo, Ooo." She tried to hide her dislike of the finger food. "Um, could I have something to drink with this?" Out of nowhere, a drink appeared. She gulped it down. "I'm sorry. It was a little salty for my taste, but it was good," she replied.

"Sit, sit. My Ashley has told me so much about you but forgot to mention how enchanting and beautiful you are." He led her over to the couch.

"Maybe I should go look for Ashley," she said.

"Don't worry; she'll be here momentarily."

She sat down; feeling that momentarily was going to feel like eternity. Sitting on the couch oblivious to what to say or do, she listened for the sounds on the other side of the library door. "Wow, the music from downstairs is getting loud," she said, raising her voice. Not knowing why, she got up, becoming entranced by the rhythmic sounds from the first floor. Making her way around the room, her body and mind swayed to the dark rhythms and beats. Nestled in the corner of the room hidden behind a statue, he pushed a remote button to a video camera. She was lovely. She was more his speed. The other one was not up to snuff. He watched every inch of her while he curled his fingers to stroke the palms of his hands.

"Ooo, I think I'd like to take a comfy nap," she said, plopping herself back down on the couch, putting her hands in a praying position as she laid her head upon them. "I'm so sorry, I feel so heavy. It's comfy here." She closed her eyes. "Where's Ashley?" she said in a faint voice.

He hovered above her. *Patience, patience. Only ten more minutes.* The cell phone in his pocket buzzed. It was the Grand Numen. "Yes, yes, sir, I see. I will take care of it immediately." He looked at her on the leather sofa, an angel. "I'll be right back, my dear." He hesitated to touch her. The thought of waiting, wanting, excited him even more. He took a deep breath and locked the library door behind him.

25

ASHLEY HELD TIGHTLY TO JOHNNY'S arm and led him to the cabana. Feeling the firmness of his skin, she maneuvered him to her private lair that had become a little project her daddy gave to her to fix up.

Locked and off limits to everyone, it was still under construction. Ashley had the only key, which was a ruby charm bracelet, set in platinum. She could unlock any room in the cabana, or, for that matter, the house. She only had to stand within five feet of the door and pushed the stone to the right and down. Her daddy had this unique gift made just for her, after the countless times she had misplaced her house keys. It was a piece of jewelry she would never take off. Each door of her home opened with a key or a keyless device like the one on her bracelet. She promised her daddy that she would take total charge of getting the cabana completed, and that was one of her rewards for an almost-complete job well done.

As her baby project, the cabana was hers to put anything she wanted into it. Right now, the one thing she wanted to put in it was Johnny Styvers. She felt his essence extruding an inner strength that appealed to her. *Did he go to the gym? Nah, not the type.* Holding on to Johnny's arm, she felt his essence of manliness, and she wanted to feel more. In stature, he towered over her like an umbrella held high, and she felt protected from any element Mother Nature could shower down upon her. Larry, on the other hand, had strength but possessed no umbrella.

"So, Ash, what's behind the cabana?" He looked beyond the hedgerow. A forest stood. "Does ya dad own all that and the mountain too?" he quipped.

"Well, ya could say that. We have over twenty acres of property beyond the hedge that ends somewhere a quarter of the ways up the mountainside. Daddy wants to put in a nine-hole golf course and driving range back there—ya know, just so he can practice driving, chipping, and putting, when he isn't traveling all around the world."

"Impressive." He looked to the vastness of the mountain behind the cabana. "Is that where the Mountain Crags live?"

She nodded. "Yeah, they don't bother anyone. They're a very quiet bunch."

"Yo, they're fine in my book. Actually, a few weeks ago, I bumped into one over in Harrier. Elgin Von somethin'. I was standin' in line at the deli, buying a pack of Reds, and he bumps right into the back of me. At first, I'm thinkin' he wanted to start somethin', lookin' all odd and such. Like outta a Davy Crocket movie. I wasn't sure what to make of the guy as if he came from a different part of the earth, ya know? Maybe it was his shirt, an odd-lookin' thing. So's I shot back at him. 'Man…what the hell ya doin'?' I say, getting in his face. Yo, with a face like mine, it just attracts all sorts. So I give him my crazy look. Instead of getting' all scared and such—the normal reaction to my crazed nature—he just smiles an' looks me smack in the eye. I watch him pull somethin' out of his pants pocket; yeah, I'm thinkin' it's gonna be a knife. I brace myself for trouble. But no, he pulls out these little wood animals he'd made and starts babbling about how his pop taught him how to carve figures outta materials ya find layin' round—like wood, soft-stone mica, animal bones, and antlers. He tells me his pop, Myron, as if he was some sort of hero or something, taught him how to use his hands to create. How his pop would scavenge the

Dumpsters in the industrial area over in Harrier looking for scraps. That one day he stumbles upon this thing called Lucite at the DuPont plant. He then blows me away by pulling out a carving in the stuff, a pyramid shape his dad carved with a chisel and polished to a smooth luster. Man, the guy's skills were crazy good. Inside of the clear plastic was a scene of these trees and a bear—neva seen anything like it."

Realizing he just said more than he had in the last five years, he wondered what the hell got into him. Ashley just stood there, taking it all in. He was giddy without a care in the world. For a second he wondered *why*, and then continued. "Yo, gotta have mucho respect for a guy that works with his hands. I knew he was true talking, seein' his hands, and all. Reminded me of my…back when…anyways we just kinda hit it off." He paused. "I like working with my hands, too." He looked at her, searching for something sweet, eyebrows pulled up by an invisible puppeteer with a can-I-have-it-please smile.

She laughed. "That's so funny, I know Elgin. He lives on the mountain, way up beyond the cabana. We use to play hide-and-seek in the woods when we were young. Funny he never spoke to me. I always thought he was a mute. He'd just nod and such."

"Maybe he couldn't get a word in edgewise," Johnny said, joking.

Ashley smirked. "Hmm, maybe it's my turn to make believe I can't speak."

He sized her up. "Yo, how'd ya know his name was Elgin?" He was digging to see if he would catch her in a tall tale. He felt somewhat woozy, though he only had that punch Rob had given him. He steadied himself.

She grinned as if she knew the secret of life. "He wrote it in the dirt with a stick one day, silly. Just cuz he didn't talk didn't make me think he was stupid." She shook her head. "Come now, follow me."

Ashley buzzed the door open with her bracelet and

motioned him to take the lead. Hesitating, she looked out beyond the hedge into the woods again. "Pumpkin?" She dismissed it.

"Sweet charm bracelet, Laura Croft," he said, looking around in awe like he never saw a bathhouse before. She beamed at her own handy work.

"So, ya like?" she asked.

He nodded.

"The hot tub is just what we need, don't cha think? The workers finished it yesterday." She gave him a sultry look. "Want to steam things up in the new tub?" She grabbed his hand.

"Nah. I don't swim."

She couldn't believe it. She was throwing herself at him. *He didn't want to get wet?* He kept looking around. *What was up with that?*

He walked into what looked to be a game room with the finishing pieces of furniture, waiting to be put in place. Over in the corner, he eyed an oversized couch in front of a wide-screen TV. "But I do like that cozy couch over there." He took her hand. She smiled. Then he led her to the couch.

Looking into his Mediterranean blue eyes, he became irresistible with every movement, motion, and facial expression. Even the sound of his voice became deeper, darker with a tint of hoarseness. She knew right then and there: she could be his slave.

"Do you like to race?" she asked.

"Race?" he asked. "It depends. If it refers to you, I think I'd like to take it nice and slow."

His eyes looked down and then, without hesitation, moved upward, amorously to gaze upon her.

Her question backfired, and her heart began to race. She swore he could hear it, pumping loud and hard. She was losing her edge, her control. Sitting beside him, he put his arm around her and looked into the depths of her soul. He moved in, closer, to kiss her, and then ever so slightly backed away.

"This is no good," he said.

In almost a whine, she squeaked, "Why?" Her mind screamed, *what is he doing?*

"It's when I look into your eyes…it's what I see."

Tie a rope around her neck. Add a weight. Throw her in the lake! She thought. "What?" she asked aloud. "What do you see?"

He hesitated and smiled. "I see….my reflection."

She moved back and looked at him with a sour face.

"Nah—just playing wit cha. It's your eyes, so fine, like a looking glass, seein' all the colors of the rainbow."

"You're such a tease," she whispered.

"I'm in love with rainbows," he added.

She melted a smidge more. With that his lip slowly, gently, brushed against hers. He hesitated. She felt his breath. Touching her gingerly, he kissed her soft and slow. She felt a tingle roll up her back to end at the nape of her neck, only to burst out like the grand finale of fireworks, wrapping around her shoulders like a warm blanket on a cold winter's day. She had never felt a sensation like that before. She didn't want it to stop, ever. *Again,* she thought, *again.* Like a fountain, it flowed, and she continued to lose herself in his presence.

The sound of a bee buzzing awakened her from her trance. She now realized it was her phone and jolted to answer it. "Hey," she said, pulling her composure together. *How long had they been in the cabana? Oh, my God, the party? Her job? Julie?* Everything was a blur. She had gone to heaven, and now hands were all over her body, pulling her back down to earth.

"Yes, GP…I know, yes. I'm sorry. I was busy, and I didn't hear the phone…What do you mean there's been a change…Yes, I'll be right there." Closing her phone, she looked at Johnny. "I gotta take care of a few things. I won't be long. Will ya wait here for me?" She leaned over and kissed him passionately.

"Sure," he said. "No problem." She straightened herself out and blew him a kiss closing the cabana door behind her.

Johnny sat there and held the key around his neck. The key that was the last thing his mother gave him so long ago. A sadness came over him with a new realization - - he had to say "goodbye" to what he yearned for, and so desperately needed. Maybe it was time, time to start living again, time to let go of a wish, a dream of a life he could never get back.

Eyeing the empty room. It was time to connect again with Seth. Slipping out the cabana, he caught the sound of rustling leaves and low voices past the hedgerow somewhere in the woods. Curious, he found an opening in the hedge and made his way down a small slope and came upon a small clearing. Keeping himself hidden, his eyes could see the back of two dark, hooded figures, chanting in front of a third, who was kneeling on the ground, bent over at the waist. The brightest light source came from candles placed meticulously on the ground encircling the three figures. He strained to see. The one standing to his left held in his hand a short whip, like the whip ancient Romans used on their slaves. The other held above his head a knife, wielding it in the air in the shape of a figure eight. He never witnessed anything quite like it.

26

BRIAN KOGAN REMAINED AT THE PATIO table, waiting for Seth's return feeling isolated and alone. A ghost in the midst of Ashley Wentworth's party, he watched guys and girls talking, teasing each other, and having a good time. *Why couldn't he be one of those guys? What was wrong with him? Why did girls always say they wanted a nice guy and then dump them for the horny toads? What was wrong with being a shoulder to cry on, and why was he the type always getting the "oh, we're just friends" line. What was it the toads had that he didn't?*

Jessica Harper was all that. She seemed to take an interest in him. He tried to help her with homework and somehow ended up doing it for her. She would call him during an intense Internet game, and he would drop everything to help her, only to sit and listen to her problems with other guys. She would tell him how she wanted a nice guy, who respected her, was her friend, and someone she could confide in. He figured he was that guy. He knew he was all that and more and waited. Remembering that morning, he decided to surprise her in the hallway at school. Walking up from behind, he overheard her say she could never like him like that, only as a friend because then it would ruin everything. That was a bullet, right between his eyes blowing the back of his brains out, dropping him flat on the floor. Ruin everything? She then proceeded to go out with the toad she complained about numerous times to him. The same one that dumped her after getting what he wanted, to get what he wanted again, just to dump her again. He finally realized girls wanted a guy to be an "honorable player, a gentleman wolf." Girls were an oxymoron or maybe just morons. He tried to be everything she wanted and then that wasn't what she wanted. He swore to himself that there was one thing he would never do was bow down to the toad level to get a girl. Never. His motto: honor before false glory.

What was he doing wrong? Why did girls hate him? So, he had a small, keg-size stomach instead of a six-pack. If you had a choice, wouldn't you want a keg at a party instead of a six-pack? He was smart, caring, and would go out of his way for a girl. He treated girls the way his mother told him to, with respect and dignity. She said girls were fragile flowers, treat them with care. He now realized how she came up with all that crap. She was born his mother! She was a transplant from another world. And he was the token specimen to be studied, so some female alien could see how much pain and agony one human male could endure.

Maybe back in her day, girls were sweet, but the girls of today were insidious, deceitful, and nasty. Why did they always go for the guy who treated them like crap or had money? Why couldn't he be born with a Rolex and a silver spoon in his mouth instead of a Twinkie and a Purple Heart?

A hand on his shoulder brought him back to the party. "Dadia?" he whispered to himself, then the hand turned into a vice grip.

"Hey, worm, fancy meeting you here." Larry stepped in front of him. His friend, Frank Halley, kept Brian pinned to his seat.

"Larry, you getting in trouble was the last thing on my mind. I swear, that writing piece, it was a mistake," Brian blurted out squinting in pain.

"Right, you've made your last mistake, Kogan." Larry

seethed as Frank pulled him out of the chair, sticking a pointy object into his kidney. Flinching forward, Brian felt the point through his shirt.

"Smile, and start walking, worm."

"Sure, Larry, anything you say," *Where was Seth when he needed him?*

* * *

"What did GP do?" Ashley asked herself out loud, hurrying from the Cabana to the main house. She was supposed to be in charge. *What the hell did he mean that there has been a change? When did he decide to switch who the target candidate was? How dare he! She set this up. This was her house, her party, her show. She was a Wentworth, and she was in charge.*

Opening the private side entrance with her charm bracelet, she ascended the staircase. Only she and her father used the secret passage that ended at Daddy's private library. There she could survey what was going on without anyone being the wiser. She slipped in, staying out of the security camera's view. She was certain someone would be monitoring all the cameras. On the shelf of the bookcase, she pushed the button. The security camera would replay the last two minutes in repetition for ten minutes. Rounding the desk, she caught a glimpse of a body sprawled on the couch.

"Dadia?" The switch. He wanted Dadia, not Julie, that son of a bitch. That's why there was that mix up at the Foundation concert, though she still wasn't sure where Johnny fit into the picture. *The bastard—lying to her. He wanted Dadia. Dadia was her friend. A club member? No way.* She didn't want Dadia involved. It was her game. It wouldn't be for Dadia.

"Dadia, are you OK?" Dadia opened her eyes and just smiled. *Damn you GP,* she thought.

"Ashley, I've been looking for you," she said in a

slow, animated state.

"I'm gonna get ya home, Dod; don't worry." She went over to her father's desk and pushed a few buttons that opened up a side draw with a video screen. Viewing all the rooms and hallways from the security cameras, she caught Seth walking toward the library. *Man, he was a snoop!* Any other time she'd be pissed but not tonight. She buzzed the library door open as he walked by. "Seth," she said in a hushed tone. "Seth!"

He popped his head into the room. "Hey, Ashley, just looking for the bathroom," he told her, eyeing the room.

"No time for spreading bull. Dadia's in a bad way. Can you take her back home?"

"What happened?" he asked, looking at the pathetic state she was in.

"She lives at two eight four Sutton Lane. Follow down the road into the park. Go past the pond, and find the footbridge that leads to a cul-de-sac. She's the third house on the left."

He asked again, "But what happened to her?"

"I dunno. I just found her here." Seth looked at her with suspicion. "So, what else were you looking for in my house? I doubt ya have a bathroom fetish." She eyed him back.

He silently stared her down. "I'll take care of her, but what kind of parties do you throw, anyway? And what's with the guys down the hall?" Seth helped Dadia walk, and Ashley didn't answer. "It's interesting that all your party cronies are called Rob or Robert or Robby."

She had no time for idle chit-chat. "Just keep her walking, and go out this way. Ya won't be seen. Then head through the garage, out the side door, and down to the street. I'll make sure the doors are unlocked. Now go, fast!" She left him in a hurry. She had business to attend to. *What the hell was GP doing? He would not get away with it, not with her friend and not in* her *house!*

27

JOHNNY HAD NEVER WITNESSED ANYTHING like it. His mind took in what his eyes perceived before him. He was appalled. Two figures, one with a whip, the other a knife, stood over their prey.

The figure with the whip in hand spoke. "It's now time to pay for your sins, worm. Bow before God and His keepers, for you shall wear your sins for all to see." The figure spoke in a distorted roar as if it came through a voice box.

Johnny was certain this one was the ringleader of the two. He tried to make out whom the person bent forward on his knees could be in the dim glow of light from the candles, blindfolded and gagged, his hands duct-taped. The whip cracked. It spiked the poor soul's back. Johnny watched its body flinch, while its lungs held tight. This infuriated the hooded figure, and he cracked the whip again on the victim's back.

Feeling a sickening anger swell faster than a cheetah in pursuit of its prey, Johnny realized *he knew* the victim. With a roar, the earth rumbled as he burst out of the shadows to startle the robed figure with a knife, twisting its arm and grabbing the knife. Faster than a tornado, Johnny swung the knife up against the robed figure's neck. The figure's hood fell back to reveal the evil that lay beneath it. He knew this guy from somewhere but couldn't pinpoint where. Pure hatred kept him pumped. He looked with shooting flames to the other hooded figure with the whip. "Take the blindfold off my brother's eyes, or I'll slit your lackey's throat!" he bellowed.

The hooded figure took its whip and cracked it. Johnny stood his ground and held tight to the knife, feeling liquid ooze down his fingers.

"Oh, my God, Larry! Do as he says!" Frank Halley spoke through his teeth.

"Larry?" Johnny fumed. "Take off my brother's blindfold, now!"

Larry's hand pulled back his hood, revealing his soul.

"Do as he says Larry!" Frank pleaded.

"Frank, you disgrace the robe on your back," he said to the boy Johnny held at knifepoint. Larry proceeded to take the blindfold off Brian's eyes. Then he stepped back, ready for war.

Frank became dead weight, and Johnny dropped him and ran to Brian on the ground.

"Yo, Bri, are ya OK, man?"

Brian looked to his savior as Johnny cut the tape from his hands. "I thought I was gonna die."

Larry stood his ground, watching Johnny release the pathetic worm. "You, Styvers, deserve a whipping for every miserable day I have looked in the mirror to see this scar." He pointed to the scar under his right eye. "I've imagined this moment since that day, and now I will have my revenge."

"Revenge? For what?" Johnny sneered.

"That summer—at Shepherd Lake? I believe right after your mother left your pathetic family. You remember, in the woods, by the boating area? You left me for dead, you cry baby. Your poor mamma disappeared. What's a momma's boy to do, now that she's gone?"

Johnny looked at him squarely. "My mother and I had mutual respect, like any man and his mother should. Ya got it ass backward, Larry. You hate ya mother, but ya jump when she speaks, even when she's weaving wickedness. You're the one born without a spine."

At that, Larry cracked his whip. "I'm gonna give you what your mother got a long time ago, Styvers."

"Bri, get out of here." Brian froze. "Yo, Brian…get the hell out of here, N-O-W." Johnny spoke not taking his eyes off of Larry's every move. "Come on, Jones, I'm gonna settle the score now."

Brian found his feet and started to run. He had to get Seth. Fearful of looking back, the only sound he heard was an enraged voice, piercing through the night air.

"You psychopath, don't you *ever* lay another tainted hand on my brother or speak my mother's name, you sadistic son of a bitch."

Brian was now running a marathon. He was on the football field, and the enemy was closing in fast. Zigzagging through the trees as if they were his opposing linemen he had to get through. His objective was to find Seth and fast. His heart, beating hard, pushed against his chest, ready to explode at any second. He couldn't stop. Like World of Warcraft, he was Modarth, running to warn his clan that evil had awakened down in the depths of the dark portal. He felt the dark, ominous cloud above, waiting for the right moment to suck out his living energy. *Serpentine, serpentine,* he thought. Make it back, warn, and gather the clan for battle. Tonight, a terrible tragedy would not befall his comrade in arms. He was his brother from an oath forged long ago behind a willow tree on a hot summer night when the moon held bright.

He followed the hedgerow until there was an opening. Running through it, he could see the garage to Ashley's house. As he approached, the side door opened. It was Seth.

"Seth, Seth!" He felt his breath, hot and heavy, pushing on his face.

"Oh, my God, Bri, what happened?"

"It's Johnny," he blurted out sucking the darkness into his lungs. "Follow the hedgerow back behind the cabana, in the woods; he's fighting Larry Jones."

"Oh, crap," Seth said with trepidation. Brian then realized what his brother was holding.

"What happened to Dadia?" The pain in his chest pounded and couldn't stop.

"Take her man. Help her. I think she was drugged, bad. Make her walk or something. If she falls asleep, get an ambulance!" Seth gave her to him. To Brian's surprise, she felt like a feather.

"Don't worry, Seth. I will. Run, Larry has a whip and Johnny a knife!"

Seth ran toward the hedgerow. In the woods, the sound of a gun permeated the air, stopping him in his tracks, only to push him to run toward the sound, faster than his feet could go. Reaching the cabana, a figure came from out of the woods.

"Yo, let's get out of here."

"Shit, what the hell happened, John? Are you all right?"

"I'll tell you in the car. Come on. Let's take to the woods down to the street."

"Was that a gunshot?" Seth prodded.

"I dunno, man, but let's get outa here fast. Ya still got that jug of water in your trunk?" Johnny asked. "I need to wash my hands."

28

ASHLEY WENTWORTH SLID OUT THE back door of the cabana and called Rob. "Rob, the party's over."

"Where is GP?" he asked.

"He is on his way back to the Foundation."

"Oh?" Rob questioned.

"Yes, it didn't go as planned. GP has a weakness."

"You didn't know, did you?" Rob interjected. "Hey, was that fireworks from the mountain?"

"No," she said, perturbed. "I have a few other problems to resolve."

"I see," Rob said. He nodded to himself and passed the word to the other Foundation club members. Julie and Stephanie looked around. Black plastic bags were out, and it seemed that everyone at the party was cleaning up. Stephanie's eyes scanned with question.

Rob moved them along. "Party's over, girls."

"Where's Ashley?" Julie stammered, "I want to say good-bye before leaving. I haven't seen her all night."

"Don't worry about Ashley. Worry about getting out of here before the cops come. Do you girls need a ride?"

Stephanie tugged on Julie's sleeve and replied, "Thanks, Rob that would be nice." She looked at Julie. Her mom would flip if she saw her condition. No way would she call her to pick them up. Rob seemed like a nice guy. He practically spent the whole night with them. But Julie was out of character, and how she got that way from drinking fruit punch was beyond Stephanie's reasoning. She wondered if Julie brought something with her to the party. *There had been talk in school, but she never believed a word of it. But now Julie was hanging out with Ashley on the sly?*

"My car is right in the front. Come on, I'll take you home." Rob proceeded to push them along.

* * *

"My son, he is not worthy. He has no backbone."

"Hey, I told him so."

"And you must learn the first rule of conduct. Keep your anger under control."

"I know; you're right. But now, what are we to do? Do you think this situation will get out?"

"This was no small altercation. We must think hard for a solution. Come, we will work this problem out together. Tell me everything that just happened. You will be the one on top when all is said and done."

"I'm sorry. I will do better next time. The sight of him, here...well, I just wanted to kill something."

"I understand. This whole situation has infuriated."

"Come, let's talk. We will create a plan." He knew he could handle the girl and clean up any loose ends, but this time, the boy went over the top. And it angered him. Driving away from the house, his hands turned to stone gripping the steering wheel. This would be held over his head for as long as he lived. And that would not do.

* * *

Her cell phone connected to her father's emergency number. "Daddy, it's me, your little Pookie. Something happened, and I need you right now...Jarred? He's in Harrier. Please, Daddy. I'm in big trouble."

29

BRIAN WALKED IN DARKNESS TOWARD the main road with Dadia slumped in his arms. He was torn. He should be back helping his brothers. He never dreamed Larry would go off the deep end, the lunatic. It was just a stupid report. To him, the report was just comical. Nothing was ever funny to Brian, but that report? Now that was funny. He wished he had seen the face of Ms. Choleric when she read it and Larry's reaction when she sent him off to the principal's office. Thank God his guardian angel sent Johnny into the woods tonight; otherwise, he knew he would be—six feet under.

Dadia was a feather a few minutes ago, but she was gaining weight with every step. He looked at her. She stared back with eyes of candied apples. Remembering a park with a pond just before Ashley's house, he decided to take her there. Staying near the tree line out of sight, his pace slowed. His back stung and now his breath began to labor. Determined he would not falter, he would get her there any way he could, away from whoever did this to her. There he would watch over her and try to keep her walking.

Seeing the pond in the distance, the night moon sparkled upon the water. *Did she feel his heart thumping?* He was exhausted, and for a moment, sat her down on a park bench. Her head lay on his shoulder. He tried not to touch the back of the bench with his back as it stung from the lashing he received earlier. His felt his adrenaline subsiding while his pain increased. But his only concern was her. She was breathing, all was good. Drenched in perspiration, he sniffed the air around him in hopes her sense of smell was muted. Whatever it took, he would stay there all night and guard her. A faint moan touched the air.

"Here," he said, "let's try to walk some more." His shirt stuck to his back and stung like a harsh slap after a midsummer's day of overexposure. In control, never again would he show pain. Car lights started to pass by the entrance of the park, and he got her up and walked her off the path, out of sight. "I think your friend's party is over," he said to her. "Come on, let's try to keep walking."

"Brian? How did you—where am I?"

"Do you know how this happened?" he asked.

"Last I remember I was going to Ashley's party. Oh God, what time is it?"

Brian opened up his cell phone. Three missed calls. "It's ten forty-five p.m."

He powered off his phone. Placing it back into his pocket, he felt the key chain.

"I'm in deep trouble. I've got to get home," she said.

"I'll walk you there. Where do you live?"

She hesitated and then started walking fast with her hands on her stomach. "Don't follow me!" she winced.

"Why? I just want to make sure and give you—" She ran, stopping behind a bush, with her back to him. He heard the sound of water swooshing.

She pleaded with him again. "Don't come near me."

Brian stood, respecting her request. Chunking was a part of life, but even he would not want anyone to witness himself in the throes of it, especially if he was with the opposite sex. "I'll be over here," he said, "on the bench if you need me."

Waiting, his back throbbed. He was doing it again, being the good guy, sealing the fact of never getting the girl. He knew his waiting, helping, would be futile for any type of future that would include her in his life. After a while, she came out from the bushes.

"I'm so sorry," she said.

"Hey, no problem," he replied. "I'll walk you home."

She led him to an arched footbridge that spanned over a small, meandering brook into a cul-de-sac development of modest Cape Cod homes.

"I'm going to be in so much trouble if my mom came home early tonight."

"Which one is your house?"

"It's that one, on the left." She pointed. "Oh, good, her car isn't there." They walked around to the back of the house. Brian stepped in front to open the screen door for her.

"Oh, my God, were you running from Freddie Kruger tonight?" The shirt on his back was wet with numerous slash marks. "What ungodly creature did this to you?" she asked in fright.

"Your girlfriend throws a strange party," he said. "You don't remember anything, do you?"

She looked to him, and then unlocked the door. "No," she slowly said, still feeling the effects of the night, but somewhere within, she regained her strength. Dadia dropped her keys on the kitchen counter next to the door. "Come inside, please, let me take care of that for you."

He followed her like a lost puppy. "Nah, that's all right. I'm fine, but I have something…"

"Take you shirt off. I have an extra-large one I sleep in; you can have it." She walked into the next room. "You can't go home like that."

Brian sat down and clasped his hands in his lap, rubbing the upper part of his palms in a circular motion.

"Here it is," she said, bringing in the oversized shirt with Negative Zero on it. "Johnny gave it to me. Did you get one too, from that strange concert last week?"

He made no reply. He looked to the ceiling and just sighed.

She bit her lower lip. "Come on. I'll help you with that shirt." She took his wrists to help him stand up. He pushed her hands away, and he pursed his lips.

"I'm sorry. I was only trying to help." She still felt woozy inside but kept her composure. She knew whatever he went through tonight was bad.

Taking off his torn shirt, he turned his back to her. *His physique would seal his fate. His death certificate would state: "Died without ever getting the girl."*

Her eyes bugged at what she saw. "Wait, sit backward on the chair," she said.

Over at the sink, she gathered some towels, soaking one in water and ringing it out. She went over and with a soft hand tended to his wounds.

"You a nurse or something?" he asked.

"No—but when I was little, I was something of a tomboy who got hurt—a lot!" She laughed. "Ooo, and now my head hurts, badly! I'm gonna kill Ashley when I see her." He found a small smile within her weariness.

"I bet you're a lefty," he said.

"Yeah, I am," she said, with surprise. "How do you know that?"

"At the food court in the mall, when you walked away to the end of the corridor, you made a left turn at the T. You turned left. It would be natural to follow the turn to the right."

"Really," she chuckled. "And I thought you were going to say my watch gave it away."

"Your watch?"

"Let me ask you," she grinned, "what wrist do you wear your watch on?"

"My left, of course."

"See. There ya go."

Brian turned, stood up, and took both her hands in his. "Wait, you're not wearing a watch!" He caught her.

"Yes, but if I were, it would be strapped to my right wrist." She smiled at him then turned her face away, walking back to the sink. Wet towel in hand, she turned on the water and bit her lip.

She got a good look at him, he thought. He gingerly put on the T-shirt she had given him.

Headlights flashed through the front window. "Oh no, my mom—she's here! I'm so sorry. How are you going to get home?" she asked.

"Don't worry. I have a ride." He so understood. He grabbed his slashed battle armor of cotton. He had won the fight but lost the war. Dadia scurried to hide the evidence.

Opening the back door, he hesitated, pulling out of his pocket the only connection he had to her. He placed it on the counter next to her keys. Closing the door behind him, he slipped out into the darkness, where night crawlers crawled and creatures hid within their own madness.

30

"SOBRIETY IS THE DEVIL'S ADVOCATE—and tonight I'm on a mission to kill it."

"You don't mean that, Johnny."

"You bet I do, Kogan."

"Come on. You've already had way too much fun, and I'm tired of being the designated driver. Let's go to the Beanery and get some hoe—I mean Joe," Seth said, trying to lighten up the conversation. "I think you need to talk to me, buddy. Maybe you should start with that key around your neck."

Johnny grabbed the key in one hand and in the other as if it were his puppy, a bottle of Jack Daniels. He bent his knees and slumped down in the passenger seat. "Shut up, Seth."

"When you got that key, it was just about the time you started with this anger unmanageable management business," Seth continued.

"You know my mom gave the key to me...so, yeah, you go get a Joe," Johnny said in jest. "I'll meet ya in the cemetery, and I'll introduce you to my friend, Stella. Remember Stella? Yo, ya know, she had wondered why ya don't come visit her anymore." He laid his head back on the headrest, closing his eyes. "Next stop is the cemetery, I need to talk to Stella, explain some things I need to let go of.

There was a long silence only old friends could share.

Johnny spoke first. "Yo, better yet, take me back, and I'll finish off that Larry Jones."

"Ha, I think you already did that, my friend. That's why we're in the car! I don't know if you've noticed, but you're in no condition to finish off anything, especially the rest of that bottle." Seth looked over to him. "OK, it's time for the drunk-o-meter test; say the alphabet—"

"A-B-C-D-E-F-G." Johnny paused. "then proceeded with M-L-P-P. There, satisfied?"

"Ha. Yeah, right, John."

Johnny looked up through the sunroof. The stars seemed to sparkle and dance in front of the heavens, letting things in and keeping things out. Tonight they danced that same dance of darkness. They were still keeping secrets from him, but he wasn't sure why. *Why wouldn't they tell him where his mother went? Why did she give him that key—treasure she said—and what did it open?*

"I'd say Larry's at the emergency room by now making some lame excuse to his mom why he has all those gashes in his face. Or, he's squealing like a pig!" Seth injected with a priggish grin. "And your old man should be getting a phone call, right about now I'd say. Wait, no, changed my mind. I doubt your old man's getting a call...and lucky for you, knowing how strict Larry's parents are. I bet Larry's making up one hell of a story. His parents would cause more damage than you would, if they ever found out he was in a fight and lost. They are one weird family." He paused. "Actually, you never said what really happened before I got to you tonight."

"My Dad? He doesn't give two damns," Johnny slowly replied.

Seth looked at him from out the corner of his eye. Johnny was making a fist and then stretching his hand. They had been friends since as far as he could remember—at least diapers. *Johnny's old man, how could he not love this guy sitting next to him?* Seth still didn't know the depth of what Larry did in the woods to Brian, but Johnny put his life on the line for his brother Brian, without hesitation. Seth now understood what his mother saw in Johnny. Yeah, he could piss you off royally. But he had honor, and most of all he had heart. *Damn*, he hated when his mother was right.

"Let's get you at least a little bit sobered up, man, so you can tell me what happened before I got there and how I saved you." Seth laughed.

"You, saved me? Ha, you couldn't save a sinking bathtub in a boat!"

"So, then tell me—from the beginning, John," Seth said with raised eyebrows.

Johnny was still on his last sentence. "Saved me? Like crap, Kogan, I can take care of myself. Yo, I know what cha doing."

"And what the hell is that, Styvers?" Seth retorted.

"There's nothin' to talk about, Seth, so drop it." He put his fingers to his lips. "I don't think I can feel my lips, and why are my hands numb?" He looked at Seth. His eyes bulged then fell to emptiness.

"All right, Styvers, I know what you're doing. I think I know what the fight was about, John. Remember? I'm sober. If it wasn't for me, the next time we saw Larry Jones it would be a 'here's to good old Larry' drink between a bulletproof glass with telephones in our ears—you on the inside sharing a cell with a man named *Yurhorror*!"

"Aw, man, I could a stopped, but I didn't want to. And then the shotgun went off. Yo, that sorta got my attention. Everything else is a blur."

"That was a gunshot? Oh man, what kind of trouble are we in for now?"

Johnny sat forward and laid his head on the dashboard feeling the hum of the engine tingle through his head, vibrating his inner ear. He hadn't felt that sensation since days gone by—sitting in the back seat of the car with his head leaning just right on the door waiting in anticipation to reach the Styvers's vacation destination.

"She's never coming back, man."

"Who?" Seth asked.

"You know, my mom," he declared and clutched the key around his neck. "An' no matter what happens, life just goes on and on."

Seth wasn't sure what to say.

"Yo, do ya think what they said was true?"

"I remember the summer you slept on glass, and woke up someone else. Your mom—no way, never, man." He wondered what he was saying no way to, but whatever it was, it was a no way for sure.

Johnny was silent. "Pull it over, Seth. I think I'm gonna…yeah, I am." Seth turned down Eder Avenue. It was a quiet street alongside the cemetery.

On the shoulder of the road, Seth leaned against the trunk of the car, flashers blinking. Across the way, the cemetery fence eerily glowed in the darkness. It was the type of fence a person could impale himself on, if he didn't have the knack for scaling it. Running the length of the road all the way to the main drag, it looked ominous. When he was little, he always wondered why the cemetery needed a fence. The only people inside were dead people, and they weren't going anywhere fast. *Was it to keep the spirits in or evil out?* After all these years, he still wondered.

It seemed the first night they jumped the cemetery fence he didn't know there was a trick to maneuver over it. They had gotten into the cemetery all right, but then after visiting this headstone named "Stella" they got spooked. While his adrenaline rushed through his body to jump back over the fence, his shirt held tight to the wrought iron, his balance faltering, and he broke his arm. He rubbed his forearm remembering. That was a hard one to explain to his dad. Thank God, he didn't fall atop of it— impalement for sure. And of course, Murphy's Law would cause the worst possible area of the body to be hit. He learned the trick of jumping cemetery fences after the fact. He also got a good razzing by Johnny for being so stupid.

Like anything else in life, there was always some hidden trick or secret.

Now since connecting back up with Johnny, he realized that his friend never outgrew visiting the headstone of the woman called Stella. For some reason, he was still drawn to her. Then again, Johnny was a glutton for punishment, but Seth always found reasons to overlook his buddy's oddities. At this moment in time, it eluded him.

Tonight the smell of rancid stomach acid was becoming a burden. Johnny had gone about ten feet from the car into the woods, but it still permeated the air. At least it was the perfect spot to stop. No one every traveled this route unless they lived up the road at the new housing development, and this time of night most everyone was home, tucked away in their cozy beds, dreaming the night away. That was a good thing, just in case Larry did squeal, and they were looking for them. Johnny was in no shape for anything, and the last thing Seth needed was the cops to catch them together. His dad would be passed up for salesman of the month, and he'd be cleaning toilets with a toothbrush for the rest of his life.

The wind kicked up rustling the branches of the trees, while the sound of a dog barking in the distance made Seth anxious. Grabbing the bottle from the car, he threw it into the woods. "Come on, John! Hurry it up!" As he spoke, car lights came around the bend, blinding his sight.

"Damn it," he said, seeing the rack on top of the car. It pulled next to him, and the officer rolled down the window.

"Car trouble, son?"

"Yes, officer, my um dad is on his way."

"Do you need a tow?"

"No, no, sir. Like I said, my dad is coming. You know dads; they like to take care of things like this."

"How long have you been here?"

"Bout um ten minutes? Not sure of the time, sir."

"Have you seen anyone else on this stretch of Eder Avenue tonight?"

"Why no, sir."

"You got a cell phone?"

"Yes, sir. That's what I called my dad with," he said in respect, pulling the phone out of his pocket.

The officer scratched his nose with his forefinger and thumb. "You out by yourself this late at night?"

"Yes, sir, I just drove my friend home."

"I see," the officer said, looking at him. He put the spotlight in the car. "Do you live up yonder in the development?"

"No, sir, I live over on Ewing."

"So, what brings you onto this stretch of Eder Ave?" the officer pressed.

Seth thought quickly. "I was on the main drag, sir, and my car started sputtering. So I wanted to get off and turned down the first available street. And look, I had to pick a street next to a cemetery." He gave him a look of remembering all those horror movies with cemeteries.

The officer seemed to be satisfied.

"All right, son, but if an old white station wagon passes by here, you call 911."

"Hmm, sure officer. Anything I should know?"

"Well, we got a boy in the hospital. Allegedly beat up by a group of Crags—three I believe. They fled the scene in a white station wagon. Old, beat up." Looking at Seth, he smacked his lips. "You don't happen to know a guy named Johnny Styvers?"

Seth's body stiffened. There was no way he could pull anything over on this cop. He already told him where he lived.

"He lives two houses down from mine. Anything I should be concerned about officer?"

"Just want to talk to him. Did you see him tonight?"

Seth wasn't sure what to say and prayed Johnny was still passed out in the tall grass.

"Yeah, I did. Do you think he had something to do with the boy who's in the hospital?"

"No, no, just want to question him about the Crags. Well, have a good night, son."

"Thank you, sir. I will keep a look out for that wagon—white, right?"

"Yes, well, I'm sure they're back up in the mountains. Can't touch them up there, out of our jurisdiction," he said with disgust.

"They live up on the mountain in Mountain Crest, don't they?" Seth questioned.

"Yes, they do, son, but they might try to double back, take a different route."

"Well, don't worry, sir. My dad should be here any minute, and if I see anything, I'll be sure to call."

The officer pulled away toward the development up the road. Seth watched the headlights disappear and reappear in between the houses, then circle back. Slowing down the patrol car stopped upon reaching Seth's car. The officer looked at him.

"You smell that, son?"

"Yeah, it's awful! Think it's coming from over there in the old cemetery?"

"Hmm, well, have a good night, son."

"Sure thing. Thank you, sir." He stood there until the patrol car turned the bend out of sight.

Seth was reeling. This night was better than ever. It had to be Larry, the story weaver. Oh, my God, Larry had to get the prize for the best made-up story ever! The Crags! It was a legend: a group of people—vagabonds, mutants, everyone would say—that lived up in the mountain ridge of Mountain Crest in their own little society that dated back to eons ago. One dirt road led up the mountain to a makeshift fence that stated, "NO TRESPASSING." It was said that their clan began somewhere in the 1800s and that they were a mixture of all races and witchcraft. Some crazed British captain fled from the British Army, delusional about being of royal blood, and started his own civilization laced with voodoo. No one messed with them. Police included. They had their own society and laws and for the most part kept to themselves. The legend said that those who caught a glimpse of them told tales of grey skin, eyes black, and hair whiter than snow. A few that had blue eyes and dark wavy hair would venture over the mountain into Harrier. Here they blended into a bustling suburban city like Harrier. It was said that they could stare at a person and take part of his or her soul without ever speaking a word.

Seth could never decide if the stories were real or just another Loch Ness Monster. But every kid in Park View, at one time or another, told a spooky story about them wielding rifles and no-trespass signs, with other stories of brave souls venturing up there to get a glimpse of them— never to return. *Interesting, why would the cops want to talk to Johnny about the Mountain Crags?*

"Johnny, it's clear." Seth pushed down on his shoulder. "You're never going to guess what just happened. Come on, man; you should be sober by now." Johnny just grunted in the tall grass, hidden from view.

"Sobriety is not the devil, my friend. It's the Angel of God that just saved our asses." Seth smiled. "Other than that, the cops are going to go to your house, because they want to talk to you about the Crags! Your old man is going to hit the roof!" His cell phone rang. "Damn it. It's Agent Kogan." He opened his phone. "Hey, what's up?"

"Seth, is Brian with you?" she asked in a soft worried tone.

"Why, Mom, what's going on?"

"A detective from Harrier was just here."

Damn, Seth said to himself. He forgot all about Brian. He had left him with that girl, Dadia. If he told his mom he wasn't with him, she'd be pissed. If he said yes, she'd want to talk to him. *What the hell did Brian do to get a detective to the house?* "Oh, my God, Mom. Is everything all right?"

"Seth, is Brian with you or not? I've been trying to get a hold of him for the last hour. His phone keeps going to his voice mail." Seth could feel the steam, emitting through the cell phone.

"Um, yeah, we're at the gas station, and he's in the bathroom."

"When he gets out, have him call me right away. Seth, is Johnny with you, too?"

They were done for, so he'd better just fess up. It would be worse to double lie to Agent Kogan. "Yes, Johnny's with me, Mom. I'm sorry. It wasn't his fault."

"Seth, I don't know what you're talking about, but after the detective showed up, a patrolman comes to the door. It seems Mr. Styvers told him to ring my bell that I might—and I don't know why—know where Johnny was. The fact is…they found her, they found Hanna Styvers!"

"Oh, my God, Mom! Johnny's mom? They found her?"

"Yes, the police are looking for the person who dropped her off at the hospital. He was seen leaving the emergency room in a white station wagon."

Johnny grabbed the phone from Seth's hand. "Mrs. Kogan! This is Johnny. My mom, where is she? Is she all right?"

"Johnny, all that they would tell me is that she is at County Regional."

"Thanks, Mrs. K., I'm going there now. Seth, come on, get this rice burner revved up and get me to County Regional!"

31

MIKE JOHNSON'S SHIFT AT THE Fast N Easy Convenience Store was just about over. He gathered the last of the day's garbage and flung open the door to the back alley. Clearing his throat, he felt a noticeable change in the night's atmosphere, and his shoes did their ritual crazy glue to the floor. Thoughts of the dragon himself stood hovering over his shoulder, watching him, and he felt its breath singeing the nape of his neck. Intermittently, the dragon breathed, waiting for him to make the first move. He dreaded this part of the work. The back alley to the strip mall taunted him, as did the dreams of when he was young.

In ten minutes, the Fast N Easy would be a distant memory. In ten minutes, he would be meeting up with Johnny Styvers, the convenience store's newest employee, for a night of fun. They planned to get together a few days ago. Johnny said he could teach him how to make any girl feel attracted to him. When it came to girls, Mike needed all the help he could get. From what Mike could ascertain, Johnny was not inept in that department. He could tell by the first girl who walked into the store. Johnny only had to say a few words, and she was just about falling all over him. Now if that were a skill, he wanted to learn it, and fast. Johnny had given him Seth's cell phone number earlier in the day, and he was to give a call when he was out of work. This girl, Ashley, had a big house party tonight, and Johnny was going to get him in. Tonight, he needed to think about something other than work and school. He needed to find some fun with some new people. He was to call after his shift was over for directions to the party, and finally he would find out the secret that most guys prayed to possess. How animal magnetism worked to attract the opposite sex. You weren't born with it. It was a life skill. That's what Johnny said, and he was ready for his life to change.

The moist, heavy air continued to hold him back from proceeding down the alley to the garbage container, and now the faint odor of skunk rolled its way up his nose. He let out a big sigh and cleared his throat. Down the alley, the sounds of another poor soul must have been emptying his or her garbage as the metal container popped once, twice. *It must have been something heavy,* he thought.

The icy-sweet coolness from the air conditioners pushed past the door and tried to keep him a bay. He was surprised Mr. Halley was willing to turn them on, considering summer was becoming a faint memory. Like a beautiful girl, they whispered sweet nothings to tease him to go back inside, but duty called.

Exhaustion set in, and his mind wandered. *Why did he take those intense college courses this summer?* He had no break, went right into the fall semester, and his demeanor was showing its wear. The university sprawled between the towns of Park View and Harrier in the county seat of Sussex, and PV University was a no-slouch school. All courses, including summer, were of the highest caliber. October felt like it was already ending, and he was feeling the college/work burnout syndrome. *What possessed him to take on so much?* He didn't know. The one thing he did know was the fact that he so needed this night of mindless fun.

Leaning against the doorway, he pondered his choices of the past few months. Deep down his gut told him it was the right thing to do. He stood remembering his father's words: hard work now would pay off later. Well, tonight he wished his hard work was paying off now, not later. He needed to be at the Harrier courthouse, where all the action was, where life was happening—and ultimately justice. He wanted to be a big part of that. The dream of being a judge kept his nose to the grindstone, but tonight he wished for a reprieve.

Enough about his future, right now he had to deal with the dragon and to take out the trash. Every night was the same: stand at the door, shoes glued to the floor, take in a deep breath, let it out, quickly get to the Dumpster, and return to the back door. The alleyway and woods behind the Fast N Easy poked evil fun at Mike, reminding him the night his parents left him to suffer at the hands of his Uncle Eddie. He was only eight. *Why would they do that?* Uncle Eddie lived in an apartment over a strip mall with an alleyway just like the Fast N Easy. In the care of Uncle Eddie, day became night, and the dragon awoke.

"Mike!" A voice came from the front of the store. "Are we ready to lock up?"

"On top of it, Mr. Halley," Mike replied.

His boss, Mr. Halley, seemed different tonight. He left work five minutes after he arrived, saying he had some business to take care of. Well, that was six hours ago, and he just got back, yelling from the front of the store to lock up. *What the hell was that all about?* Mike pondered, poking his head around the corner, hearing a jingling sound. Mr. Halley stood in front of his office, fumbling with his keys. Mike watched him open the office door dropping what looked like a videotape. Picking it up, Mr. Halley disappeared into his office and locked the door.

Mr. Halley had never left the store, never left Mike in charge. He was a fly at a picnic. Now that he had returned, he was working in his office. He was never in his office. Mike wondered what was going on. Mr. Halley should have been out in the store, straightening cans on the shelves and being his anal-retentive self.

Garbage in hand, Mike, left the back door making his way into the abyss. With each step, the bags came alive to fight the fact they were being dragged behind him. Droplets of liquid appeared above his brow and upper lip. Thoughts bubbled back of Uncle Eddie, pushing him out into the dark, down the alleyway. Down a narrow alley, the darkness encroached, throwing out the perception of abandonment with each step he took. *Get the job done, now,* seeped through his brain. A small overhead light on a lone telephone pole was the only shimmer of sight. Keeping his mind on the task at hand would keep the eerie darkness at bay. "Damn." He sighed under his breath passing the back door of the cleaners, the Bagel Barn, then to the back of Sal's Liquor Store, where the large container rested.

The container, a large metal box filled up by all the stores in the strip mall, sat to the back of the woods, separated by a narrow alley, and just missed the glow of the telephone pole light. Every Sunday morning the Piepa Container Company would empty the garbage from the container.

Proceeding to hold his breath with every garbage bag he threw, he felt sweat starting to flow downward from his temples. The smell of skunk lingered. *Damn, I'm going to be permeated with the smell of skunk,* he thought. The night was just spiraling downward. His feelings started to race. I can't go to a party smelling like skunk. *By the time I take a shower, change, and am ready to go out, everyone will be going home,* he thought. *Damn it.* He rolled this over in his mind. The last bag of the night, he thrust into the air. No sound, only a thud when it landed behind the container. "Son of a…"

Each bag had the Quick N Easy name on it, so he had to retrieve it. It would be easier than hearing an hours' worth of crap from Mr. Halley. He then heard something rustling in the woods behind the container, and the hair on the back of his neck stood up like a feline anticipating trouble. The ghost of Uncle Eddie?

With trepidation, he walked to the back of the

container. As if it came alive, it grabbed his foot. He started to slip, falling forward, and he stretched out his arms to feel the sensation of weightlessness. It was a futile attempt. Face first, he hit the ground landing on something large—hard, but soft. He strained to focus on what lay below. Distorted looks, visions, and images of a darker side of life popped into his mind, and the smell of skunk seeped into his lungs more, with each heaving breath. Eyes now fixated on the realization of what was beneath him, his hands felt a lifeless torso. He tried to push himself off of it, but the mass consumed his senses. The dragon had come to life, standing below and above him.

"Oh, my God! Oh, my frickin' God!" he screamed, scrambling to his feet. Shooting his hands to his mouth, the dragon's wet breath sprang upon his face. Jerking away, his eyes popped out in horror. A body. He had never seen or experienced anything like this in his twenty years on earth. Turning, his stomach bubbled, and his throat began to contract.

32

JOHNNY'S MOM STIRRED FROM THE sounds of chatter echoing in the distance. Senses rising, she felt she were floating with the light of the day dawning. *Was she home? Still on earth?* Hanna Styvers tried to move only to realize every inch of her body ached. Yes, she was still on earth, trying to focus on the presence of someone steps away from where she lay. A voice spoke in a familiar, but somewhat deeper, tone to another beyond the walls, beyond her ability to hear. *That voice...could it be?* She couldn't recall where she was but recognized the scent of antiseptic and flowers.

"Mom!" a voice rang out, "I thought I lost you." Johnny tasted the salty liquid that ran to the corners of his mouth.

"Johnny?" She said faintly, pain immeasurable, though a small smile emerged.

"Mom, I've missed you so much."

"I'm so sorry...my memory," she said in a soft shaken voice.

His joy overtook him, and he wrapped his warm arms around hers. The feeling was back. "I never gave up hope, Mom."

"Myron told me I was hit in the head," she whispered. "I screwed up."

"Myron?" he asked. Where had his mother been all these years?

"My angel." She smiled at him.

"Mom." He lovingly smiled back. *She was always talking about angels.*

"Jay, you must know the truth," she said in a small, weak voice. She tried to focus, to gaze once more upon her son, how he looked so different, but the same. "Look at you, you're all grown up," she said. A veil of peacefulness filled her face, only to change with question from her eyes. "Johnny, how long have I been away?"

"I'm so sorry, Mom. I know it was my fault—everything, that day, the fight, that night. Yo, I'm gonna make it up to ya, Mom; I promise. And whoever did this…" His eyes turned dark, and his facial features became razor sharp. He tightened his hand around hers as he spoke with each word, sensing he needed to quell the surge within him. "There'll be no mercy—I promise you."

"No, no, Jay, you don't understand…it wasn't…no, not you…no," she said, going in and out of consciousness.

"Mom, I'm gonna make everything good again. You'll see. Rest. We have a lifetime to catch up." She was silent, but he saw the pain in her face. "I'll get the nurse to give you something." He pushed the call button.

"Do you still have it?" she asked.

"Have it?"

"The key."

His face illuminated. "Yo, see, it's been around my neck ever since ya gave it to me." Proud, he showed her the key attached with rawhide. To him, it signified his strength to endure all—past, present, future.

She smiled a sign of approval. "Get the box…the swan, the one on the key chain," she said.

"The box?" he asked.

"The buried treasure."

"What do you mean, Mom?"

With a burst of unexplained energy, she spoke in fear. "Don't let anyone else find it!" She gave him a hardened look that scared him, though he had felt this intensity before—within his own skin. Her adrenalin dissipated and her pain returned. She continued in a shallow voice. He cocked his ear closer to her mouth to hear.

"Remember that secret place we would go? The spot where we hid things?"

"Yeah, I remember."

"The wishing rock—don't let them get it," she spurted out. "Johnny, where's your dad?"

"Dad, um, yeah, he's coming."

"He needs to know everything." There was urgency in her voice.

"Rest, Mom." How long he yearned to say that again! He hadn't said her name for so many years. He refused. He spoke of her to no one. "Don't worry. Right now, you just need to get well. I love you so much." He paused. "So much has happened."

"They did this—took me from you and your father." The nurse appeared out of nowhere and looked at Johnny. She seemed to be holding back some important piece of information. The nurse then gave his mom an injection, only to disappear down the hall.

"I love you, Jay, with all my heart."

"I love you too, Mom."

"I'm so cold," she replied, closing her eyes. Hanna Styvers slipped into a deep sleep. He got her an extra blanket and wrapped it around her. Sitting back in the chair next to her, Johnny became oblivious to his surroundings. He focused on every part of her face, from the small indent under her right eye she gotten from scratching her chicken pox as a child to her dark eyelashes and the smooth wavy texture of her hair right down to her long delicate hands. He watched her in quiet, and he breathed deeply to catch the scent of flowers from the other side of the curtain. The woman next to her had four or five bouquets, wishing her well. His mind sparked. *Roses, yes, roses, that was her favorite flower. White ones, pink ones, red ones.* He would go downstairs, find a gift shop, pick out the most beautiful roses, and take them to her. She would smile. He would smile. She would heal, and life would be right again.

"Mr. Styvers?" the doctor asked, standing in the doorway. "I'm Dr. Blank." Johnny followed him. "Is your father here?"

"Well, sort of," Johnny replied. "He's on his way, but I can relay whatever you have to say about my mom to him. What happened to her, and how did she get here?"

Dr. Blank looked at his clipboard as they walked to the visitors' lounge. "It says here that a young man in his twenties—pale complexion, ice-blue eyes, brown, wavy hair—carried her into the emergency room and told the nurse her name. They asked if she had insurance, and he said yes. He had left it in his car and would be right back. While they were attending to your mother, they realized that the young man seemed to disappear, so they called the authorities. Upon a thorough investigation in the emergency room, one eyewitness who was coming in at the same time said a young man of his description got into a white station wagon and drove off."

Johnny was silent. One thing he learned from being on the street—never give out any information until you know all the facts.

Dr. Blank continued, "Well, whoever dropped her off knew she was in a bad way. Nurse Kimball was on duty at the time, and she states here that the young man was apparently upset and crying. He then kissed her on the forehead. There was no reason to suspect anything was amiss."

Johnny didn't care who it was. She was here at the hospital, and Dr. Blank was going to make her well. "So, Dr. Blank, how is she?" he asked, wanting to hear only good news.

"Well, from what we can surmise, your mom has an old scar from a knife wound, and we ran an MRI and X rays on her with a few additional tests. We are waiting for the rest of the results.

"What? She was stabbed, beaten?" Johnny's heart raced with the heat of molten lava.

"It appears at the same time she was stabbed she also suffered other blows, one to the head in the temporal lobe, affecting the hippocampus. That's the primary auditory area of the brain that controls recognition and memory. It is critical to the memory process. The hippocampus is located between the surface and the center of the brain. A blunt force struck the outer shell that sent a shockwave from one side of her head to the other. The hippocampus was damaged or affected."

"So what does that mean for my mom?" he asked.

"In layman's terms, it's called amnesia. Your mother's memory was spattered like when you drop mercury on the floor. It breaks out into separate pieces, but with gravity and pitch, each piece finds its way back to the whole. Now, there are two types of amnesia: anterograde amnesia and retrograde amnesia. Anterograde is the inability to learn new things. That was not affected by the blow. Your mother suffered retrograde amnesia, which is the loss of memory of events that occurred before the injury. From this trauma, memory lapse can last from months to years. What triggers regenerative memory back? Only God knows, but we're working on it."

"Does my mom have all of her memory back?"

"That is unknown at the moment, but it is promising that she will. Until the police find this mystery person, only your mom can tell us what happened."

"Yo she's gonna be all good, right doc?" Johnny's face lit up.

"Well, there's another complication. The MRI and X rays also show she suffered other internal injuries years ago. We're guessing it was at the same time she had the blow to the cortex of the brain. These injuries were not physically seen or attended to, probably because she was traumatized. Over time these injuries healed, only to leave other problems."

"Problems? Like what?"

"One of the injuries was to her kidney. From our findings, she was also hit with a blunt force to that area. Normally the kidneys are well protected by the muscles in our back and our skeletal frame. Your mom had a penetrating trauma or extreme blunt force that damaged them. There may have been no evidence of external injury other than slight bruising on the back or abdomen in the area the kidney is located." Dr. Blank stopped. "You've received bruises, right? We don't think much of them. Your mother has renal acute kidney failure a result of direct damage to the kidney undetected from long ago."

"But ya can you fix it now, right Dr. Blank?"

"The renal condition shows many blood clots in the kidney vessels. We are doing all we can for her, but right now the biggest thing you and your father can do is pray." Dr. Blank tapped his hand on Johnny's upper arm. "We all will be praying for her."

Walking back into her room, he knew he would never need a picture of her again. He gazed upon her, burning her total essence into his memory. Nothing on earth could ever let him forget every nuance of who she was. So much lost time, too many questions unanswered. Sitting, his leg bounced in a quick rhythmic motion, and he grabbed her hand again. Night and day meshed into his weary muscles, making his head feel like a bowling ball as he laid it down next to her.

* * *

"Room four-twenty-two, please, Hanna Styvers." Seth stood with Brian in front of the reception desk looking down at the woman behind the computer.

"Room four-twenty-two, please, Hanna Styvers?"

The woman put on a pair of black-rimmed glasses, squished up her bright red lips. Seth flinched.

"One room pass left," she said through her nose. "There is a restriction on that room and someone must be up there now. One, just one of you can go up." She squinted, taking her glasses off.

Seth looked to Brian."OK. Thank you." Seth rolled his eyes. "Bri, you take the elevator up. I'll sneak by the rent-a-cop and meet you up there."

"Sounds good." Seth was better at sneaking around than he. Brian was just too truthful.

Seth walked around the lobby. He eyed Brian make it past the security guard to the elevators. *Hmm*, he'd take the stairs. Noticing a woman in the corner of the lobby fiddling in her pocketbook, he approached the guard.

"Excuse me, sir. The woman—the one sitting over there—asked if I would get you. She seems to be having some problem and wants the security guard. That's the one—that woman over there." Seth pointed. The guard nodded and walked over to the woman. Seth hesitated then made his move. He opened and closed the stairway door and double stepped up the first flight. Rounding the landing, he bumped into a woman out of nowhere, descending the steps. His speed knocked her off balance, and she fell onto the step. The woman, in her mid-twenties with mousey brown hair parted on the side, was wearing one of those colored tops with matching baggy pants that hospital employees wore. "Oh, my God, I'm so sorry," he said. "Please, let me help you up."

She looked at him with reluctance. He realized she could ask him for his pass or question why he was in the stairwell. He smiled at her, shrugged, and double stepped two more flights up to meet Brian on the third floor. Brian was waiting nervously at the stairwell door.

"Seth," Brian whispered. "There's a guy in uniform standing in front of her room. What are we going to do?"

Seth looked. The man stood wide and brawny looking as if he placed each brick into the Berlin Wall all by himself.

"No wall is impenetrable," Seth replied. "Come on." He took the lead like a bulldozer ready to mow down anything in his way. The man eyed them approaching Mrs. Styvers's room.

"Seth and Brian Kogan?"

Dumbfounded, they both spoke, "Uh, yeah."

"Your art teacher, Nekos Manteria, told me where I might find you, I need to speak with Brian." In his pocket, he pulled out a photograph of a swan key chain.

* * *

Awakened by the warmth of a hand on his shoulder, he looked up to see Seth and Brian standing behind him.

"Hey, man, we're here for you," Seth said.

"Thanks, guys. She came back. This time she's here to stay."

Still holding her hand, he just experienced the deepest sleep in five years. He was determined to nurse her back to health. His mom was strong. She would overcome this. He looked to her only to see her face—the face of an angel—slowly draining in front of him as he felt her hand go lifeless. Seth and Brian both looked to his mother. Their lips went thin, and tears welled up in their eyes.

33

AT THE FUNERAL PARLOR, A man in a suit smiled as the corners of his mouth turned downward. Without a word, he motioned Johnny and his father down a hallway adorned with old green paint and a lone portrait of a man in a suit, no doubt the owner. An office door with no name on it opened into a small, drab room that held no pictures, no trinkets, and no soul. Three empty chairs surrounded a lone phone and unclaimed pen set that perched atop a barren desk. The suit motioned them to be seated, while he walked over to the front of the desk to start the questioning process. It was a time for many questions. It was a time no one wanted to speak.

"Would there be an obituary announced in the papers? Which papers? Would a picture of your loved one accompany the obituary?" The man fiddled around in a drawer and pulled out a standard contract. "What would you like to say about the deceased in the paper? Would you like to say donations to a favorite charity in lieu of flowers?" Then he went on to ask, "How many days will you have your loved one laid out? Open casket? Closed casket? Do you have a plot? Alternatively, would you prefer cremation?" He pulled out a catalogue. "Please choose a remembrance card. Religious? Nonreligious? Please pick out a saying for the back of the card for your beloved." Decisions had to be made. Through all the questioning, the suit's lips continue to point to hell. No time to think, just do. Read this; sign here and here and here, as if there were some major urgency for the deceased to catch a plane to heaven. "Don't worry. We will take care of you, of everything. We are here for you and your loved one." Then the suit asked the question that stood out in Johnny's mind the most. "Do you have insurance?"

Insurance for what? They're betting you're gonna live, and you're betting you're gonna die? Life was so messed up, he thought. Johnny couldn't get the images of the last few days out of his head. The funeral home's basement was a sea of caskets, each with a name and a price list, all dependent upon the options one picked out. *What were they buying? A car?*

"Which would your loved one like to have eternal rest in?" the suit said. "Would you prefer the Royal II? It comes in twenty- or eighteen-gauge steel or copper or stainless steel outside to prevent rusting. Or maybe you would be interested in the Royal IIS? It sports an eternal-rest, adjustable-bedding feature plus a pillow and a throw. Some have a half couch, while other caskets, a full couch."

A couch? They had to be talking about something else. Just thinking about it returned him to that queasy pressure surrounding him the past few days. He was in a submarine twenty phantoms under rushing up to breathe. *Metal ones? Wood ones? Vacuum-sealed ones? Vacuum sealed? So bugs couldn't get inside? Caskets had warranties in case of decay? Five years, ten years, fifteen years? What was the point? It still would decay and who the hell was going to check to see if it were true?* It was all too much for him to comprehend. He loved his mother more than life. It was her spirit, her soul, which mattered. That was the questions he wanted answered.

People he didn't know looked at him as if they had a concern for how he felt, but he knew they were just doing their jobs. The second he and his dad left the funeral parlor, their caring would cease. Of course, his dad seemed to think they were genuine. No asking of opinions or discussion—it was his dad's word, final: metal casket, vacuum sealed. His father worried about the bugs in the ground. His father said his mom didn't like bugs. However, Johnny knew she would have preferred wood. It grew from the earth and returned to the earth. Johnny thought his father, being a carpenter, would have understood that.

* * *

Looking out from the limousine, the water droplets on the window made the world appear surreal. *Of course, it rained. It always rained when it's time to bury a loved one,* Johnny thought. As the small procession rolled into the cemetery, Justin and Billy flashed before him. Justin and Billy had arrived there one year prior. It rained that day too. They died in a head-on car crash the night Justin was to pick him up. The three of them had planned a night out, starting with a party invite from Tori. Tori Halley's mom had no clue, or if she did, she didn't care. There was always a gathering in the basement, and Tori's mom never popped her head in to see what was going on. She believed she had an alcohol-free house, never realizing Tori would bring it in through the basement window. That same night Johnny and his father almost came to fisticuffs in the front yard, right when Justin and Billy pulled down the street. Seeing a show of violence being played out on the Styvers's front lawn, they kept going. Johnny didn't blame Justin. Everyone was afraid of his dad. He was big as Paul Bunyan. So instead of meeting up with them, he spent the night at Stella's grave over on Eder Avenue. *That's where mom should be resting, not at this cemetery,* he thought. *It was a shame mom never got a chance to meet Justin and Billy. She would have liked them.* She never threw down a gavel of judgment by sight or hearsay. She always came to her own conclusions about people by looking into their eyes. She always found something different—that one thing no one else could see. She always said you had to look with your own heart, which was the only way you could see deep into the soul. In the center, you would find the truth. She could always see God's hand in everyone—the good others refused to see or acknowledge, and then she would help them to recognize and share it. He never realized how amazing she was until now. *What could anyone expect? He loved her, but hey, he was only twelve.*

Seth told him the guy he saw with melting eyes at the Fast N Easy died. He was also being buried today. The poor guy had worked with Seth's dad. Johnny knew of his impending demise that night at the Fast N Easy Convenience Store. Seeing melting eyes all these years, knowing they would die within days or weeks. He felt an anxiety attack coming on that now, at this moment, he had to quell. At times, he felt he had the power to make people die. It just freaked him out. *Was he doomed to be a grim reaper?*

As the cars proceeded to the gravesite, Johnny looked through the rain-drenched window. He focused downward as the cold air hit the warm ground, forming a blanket of rolling fog. The cemetery seemed peaceful enough, nestled on a knoll that overlooked and bordered a golf course. *Yes,* he thought, *At night the spirits, if they felt privy to, would play. Why else would anyone put a cemetery next to a golf course? Didn't his father know that his mother hated golf?*

All of his memories about her came flooding back—everything she ever said. She believed that everyone had a plan and called it a blueprint, which set each and every one of us apart from the other. She spoke of the uniqueness that each soul possessed from the fingerprints on your hands to the unique shape of your teeth. When he got a little older, she was to tell him all she knew. He needed her now. He wanted to know right now all the knowledge his mom had possessed, and right now, he wanted back all the years that were taken away from him. A pain rose from his chest into his eyes, causing stars to appear. He saw the very same stars the day he sat in the dentist's chair, seeing a hairy fist poke a larger-than-life needle into his mouth, wiggling it around and around until shiny, bright stars appeared out of nowhere.

He was tired of floundering through life. *Could he make people die by looking at them? So what was Justin and Billy's purpose in life?* She would have had the answers. He wondered, *If you had a lapse of judgment and took your best friend's life with your own, could you still make it to heaven?* He wished he were able to talk with his mom. *God gave us answers, she told him, all you had to do was ask and then wait. The tricky part was being able to hear.* Maybe he needed to learn how to listen.

God certainly had known all the bad things he had done in life, and he realized that saying had to be true: only the good died young. The bad ones never died. They lived here in hell forever. He decided, at that very moment, he didn't care what anyone said, Justin and Billy made it to heaven, and of course, his mom went straight there, too.

He hadn't thought about his mom's philosophy of life for a long, long time, and now nothing at all made sense. Now he would never learn the mysteries she spoke about. *The box,* he thought. *Maybe it held what she promised to tell, what she had promised to share.* He had to find out what happened to her. *Why was she so scared for him?* He had to find that box she told him about so many years ago—the one that held the family treasure.

Looking over to his dad, he realized no words or eye contact had been made since the night mom was found. By the time the old man got to the hospital, she had already passed. He wondered who would say, "I got to take a shower boy and straighten the house some. I'll be right there." *His father hadn't laid a finger to clean the house in years. And then all of a sudden, mom is found. No one can say if she is going to live or die, and he has other priorities?* It took the man four hours to get to the hospital, and then it was too late. Some things, Johnny realized, he would never understand.

So here they were, at the cemetery to say their final good-byes for the last time. He had found her and lost her all in one day. Life was useless. Life sucked. *How could he ever believe there was a God? How could God let this happen? How could He be all loving and righteous and allow this to be?*

The priest must have presided over a million funerals, for as far as Johnny was concerned, the man had no feeling. *Where did his dad find this guy?* He went through the funeral motions like he spent his life knowing his mother. *How could he listen to anything the man said?* His intensity rose within. This guy had no right. He knew nothing about his mother. He never even met her. Here he stood, talking about his mom like they were childhood friends, telling everybody about who she was. He had no right. He had no idea.

The smell of roses filled his cavities, and for the first time since entering the cemetery, he took his eyes off the ground. He saw Mrs. Stevens and Mrs. Mendelssohn standing there. *How dare they?* They spread rumors about his mom when she disappeared. They weren't there for her. They were here to get the town juice.

Seth and Brian stood to the side. Seeing them, he lightened up and caught a glimpse of Dadia, too, in the background. He looked their way and sent an acknowledgement of thanks. Somehow, it seemed to help ease the fidgeting pain running through his body. Standing under the tent at the gravesite, he looked to his father, who stood a few feet down from him. For a moment, he thought he caught a glimpse of a tear. *Wow, the man did have feelings, somewhere deep down in his pit, or was it just the rain?*

While the priest continued, Johnny's stiffness subsided, and he took in more of his surroundings of the cemetery and its rolling hills. The rain came down, and he felt the fresh, quiet peacefulness about it. Down below from his mother's final resting place, the road hugged a horseshoe-shaped mausoleum like arms around a loved one. He looked to the mausoleum that held many wreaths and sprays of flowers that hung on individual squares. Johnny's ears heard the rustle of stone and pavement popping. His eyes moved to the road, catching the outline of a white station wagon, rounding the mausoleum as if the eyes in the car were upon him. When the car passed by the mausoleum, Johnny noticed a tall, slim woman standing alone in the rain, watching. Her figure replicated his mother's stature. Droplets of rain glistened on her short, wavy hair, and the misty fog sauntered around her feet. He squinted. It was odd that she held no umbrella and wore sunglasses. The fog that crept around the slopes of the cemetery became unsettling, and the woman below seemed to be floating in it. He looked harder. The woman took the dark glasses off and wiped them. He put his fist to his mouth. Electricity surged, and the rain shorted out his body. "Mom?" He spoke under his breath. Wiping his eyes in disbelief, he looked again to sharpen his view. Panic set in, and his heart raced. She had gone, just disappeared, and the station wagon was gone too. *Was she, was this, real, or was he hallucinating?* No one else seemed to notice what he had just witnessed.

"Mom!" he shouted. The priest stopped short. With no regard for interrupting the prayer and all that had gathered, he ran down the knoll. She was there, around the corner. He felt it! He knew it! Down the graded slope, he ran to the corner of the building. Reaching the spot in which she stood, he stopped. *Had he just seen a ghost?* There was no one in sight. "Mom," he beckoned, pleading. "Come back!" Emptiness ensued and the rain poured from his eyes. All of his energy dissipated as his knees buckled him to the ground. Bent over, he threw his hands to his face, and he rocked, back and forth.

Seth, Brian, and Dadia caught up to him in distress.

"Johnny! Are you all right?" Dadia blurted out.

"I saw her. I swear!"

"Saw who?" Seth interjected.

"My mother! She's here!"

No one knew what to say. Looking to each other, Seth was the first to speak up. "Yeah, we know, John."

"Yo, I *saw her*. She took her sunglasses off. I saw her face. It was *my* mother. She was right *here*, this place."

Uneasiness showed on Dadia's face. She knelt next to him and put her hand on his shoulder. "Jay," she said.

"No, Dod, it was her; it was my mother."

"Come on, Johnny, before your dad throws one of those fits," Seth said, prodding his friend. "Everyone's waiting for us".

Helping Johnny up, Seth put his arm around him as he supported his friend back to the gravesite. Only then did Seth understand the depth of pain his friend was besieged with all these years. Mr. Styvers stood silent, and just stared at his son.

34

JOHNNY'S DAD STOOD ON THE front porch of 284 Ewing Avenue and tried to grasp the fact his wife, Hanna, now lay in peace. He hoped he could rest amid the questions that still abounded. *Would he ever know? Would the truth ever be shown or was her secrets too dark, too deep. Had she been unfaithful?*

Joe Styvers knew for a fact that "he," that foul man, would pay for all the sins he cast out in God's almighty name. He had ruined his life and Johnny's life. He just knew somehow that man was the cause of his wife's disappearance and now death. *What you give, you get back. No one could dispute the Old Testament. It stated it three times—in Exodus, Leviticus, and in Deuteronomy 19:21: Lex talionis—and so it shall be.*

Joe sauntered back to a time when the day felt warm, and a cold night was inviting. A time when his neighborhood was alive, with neighbors, friends, and children who played in the street. However, the few guests today were like vultures, other than Sue. Sue Kogan stopped by with some brownies. Her actions spoke louder than her words. Then there was her husband, Henry. Henry Kogan thought he was superior to those without a college degree. That made him think he was all knowing to those who worked with their hands. *Best he didn't show up,* Joe thought, for he would have only made it to the bottom step of the front porch.

Johnny was outside in the back with the Kogan boys. They had more sense and compassion in their pinky toes than their father did in his body. Meandering through the house to the kitchen, Joe looked out the window to see the boys sitting on the back deck, while he contemplated the future for him and his son.

* * *

"Johnny, I wasn't sure when to bring this up," Seth said. He looked to Brian. "Bri, show him the key chain. I swear it's the same one, the one in the picture the detective showed us at the hospital. And I swear I remember seeing the same swan here at your house, here when we were kids."

"I don't remember anything like that, but why didn't ya say something earlier?" Johnny questioned.

"I didn't think it was the right time to talk about his investigation. He wasn't giving us any information but wanted us to reveal all we knew. How dare him, with your mom in such a bad way."

Brian looked at Seth.

"What?"

"I don't have it. I gave it back to Dadia."

Seth rolled his eyes.

"Yo, it's Dadia's?" Johnny asked.

"Well, I think it was," Brian said.

"Think it was?" Seth chimed in.

"Well, I don't know for sure; the waitress found it in the booth at the café after we left. It could have been hers."

"So you gave it to Dadia. Did she say it was hers, or it wasn't?" Seth prodded.

"Well, I didn't personally give it to her. I kind of left it on her kitchen counter."

"Why the hell did you do that?" Seth asked in raised voice. Brian went silent.

Johnny cut in. "Yo, there's one way to find out. She invited us to her house later. Wasn't gonna go, but if ya think it has something to do with my mom, I'm game."

"Who knows?" Seth stated, looking to Brian. "I know little bro here would like to go." He grinned. Brian shot him back a look. Johnny laughed for the first time in days. Seth smiled .

Johnny got serious again. "My mom talked about a box this key opened. Johnny held in his hand the key he swore to protect. "She said the box was hidden, down by the willow tree."

"Well, let's go find it bro. Brothers of the Domain." Seth put a comforting slap to his back.

The boys walked down to the willow tree, to their old secret spot hidden from view. It was a place where they could take off their war paint and be who they really were in a universe that was their playground so many summer nights ago.

From the tall brush, Brian peered up to the back of the Styvers's home. "Oh, my God, Johnny," Brian whispered. "There's a cop with your dad." His eyes squinted as if they could hear too.

Joe Styvers shouted from the back porch. "Johnny must a left with the Kogan boys, officer. I know he didn't do anything, and we'll get this matter straightened out. I just know he didn't do it." His father's boisterous voice spoke loudly.

Johnny continued his quest, bent on finding the box. "She said it was here, under the wishing rock." He turned the stone over and started to dig. Nothing.

"Are you sure this is where she said?" Brian asked almost in a whisper.

"John, we have to get outta here." Seth realized the time was now to get the three of them far away from Park View as possible. "Come on, we'll circle around, get my car, and go over to Dadia's." Seth pressed him. "I don't like the idea the cops are here talking to your dad. I don't like the idea of what your father is implying. Which, by the way, I have no idea what that is, but it doesn't sound good!"

Seth pulled Johnny away, and in silence they made their way through the tall grass. Johnny retied the key around his neck. *The box…where was it?* He was befuddled.

* * *

"When he gets home, Fred, I'll bring my boy down to the station," Joe assured the officer.

"All right, Joe, we've known each other for a long time. Make sure you do that," Fred stated. "And again, I'm so sorry for your loss. She was a good woman."

"Thanks, Fred, I know. Don't worry; we'll clear up this misunderstanding," Joe replied.

After the last mourner left, Joe Styvers sat down in his easy chair, surveying his shabby, empty living room and started to shake. He wished he were back in time, when the universe smiled upon him—to the bench where they had spent hours talking, cuddling, and looking up to the heavens. He wanted to be back in the day of living dreams where life was alive and new, but now life had faded and weathered, just like the window boxes on his house. Jack Daniels kept nudging him to keep his company again. Jack would insist on going down to the willow tree with him. He was starting to get sick of Jack. Maybe Jack wasn't his friend after all.

"Forgive me, Hanna; forgive me for everything I thought all these years. Was this the justice you sought? "

35

DADIA CAME IN THE BACK door to the kitchen and gently put her bag on the counter. "Mom? Where are you?" Katie Paola lived in the kitchen; it was odd she was not there. "It was so sad at the funeral today."

"Don't forget to wipe your feet," her mother replied from the living room.

"You're in the living room?" Her mother was on the couch, curtains drawn.

"Yes." She looked down and away.

Dadia sat next to her. "What's wrong?" she asked.

"I had a dream the night Mrs. Styvers passed away."

"Are you OK?"

"Yes, but the dream, it still haunts me." Dadia took her mother's hands to feel them trembling. "Have you gotten a hold of Ashley yet? Her mom asked. I've tried Jacqueline a few times but no answer. It doesn't look like she's returning my calls."

"I don't know, Mom. After that Saturday night party she had, she left me a text message she was going away for a while with her dad. Her dad is kind of strange…But what happened in your dream? Tell me."

"Well, this isn't easy to say." Her mother paused. "I dreamt I was at a wake with strangers, but everyone knew me. They treated me as if I was family and kept hugging me and calling me Hanna. I found myself surrounded by the smell of roses, and then something poked me in the back. I turned to see. In the distance, an open casket surrounded with pink and white roses. My first thought was to pay my respects, only to find myself right there, right in front of the kneeler. I knelt down, afraid to see who it was. Saying a prayer, I kept my eyes closed until I mustered up some courage to peek first at the hands. They were feminine, belonging to a woman, and in her hands, instead of a rosary, was a key chain—my key chain of the swan, like the one I gave to you. At first, I thought, oh, my God, maybe it was you in the casket, but it was me." A tear flowed from her eye as she bit her lip.

"Mom, don't worry." Dadia put her arm around her. "It was just a dream."

"I know, Dod, but I was looking at my own reflection. Ever since Mrs. Styvers passed, I feel a heaviness inside of me."

"What do you think it means?" Dadia interjected.

With a deep breath, her mother crossed her beautiful, long hands over her shoulders. "There's more," she said, head sullen. "When I found out I was I lying in the casket, I fainted and fell to the floor. In the blackness, I could hear everyone, but I was in a cocoon, sightless, motionless. I heard footsteps rush toward me, and this voice shouts, 'Mom!' The voice was that of a young man. Then another man grabs the young man, and the young man shouts the name Darius, in an angry voice." She paused for a long time. Dadia sat in silence with her.

"Mom?" Dadia said, "Johnny was so distraught today he thought he saw his mother at the cemetery. He swore it to us all!" Her mom sank her shoulders into the couch.

"The poor thing, it must have been frightful for him."

"I hope you don't mind, but I felt bad so I invited him and his two friends over to our house. Is that OK? He had invited everyone back to his house, but I just wanted to come home. I don't think he wants to be alone. Sorry, I didn't ask first."

"Well, I guess, yes, that would be fine."

* * *

The smell of homemade chocolate chip cookies permeated the house. Baking always helped Katie Paola relax and think. In a little while, Dadia's friends would be in her small home. She had to have something to offer them. Thank God, the kitchen was the largest room in the house.

She smiled at the thought Dadia had made some new friends. This time she was determined to put down roots and stay put in this nice town. She felt comfortable here— a comfort she hadn't felt in years. Ashley Wentworth was Dadia's only friend since moving to Mountain Crest, and she was interested in meeting these new boys. *Maybe Dadia was getting over the trauma*, she thought. *It was some time ago.*

She didn't know Johnny, but her heart ached for him. To lose a parent was devastating, especially under those circumstances. *And what about the dream she had?* This Johnny was maybe the key. She had many questions, but they would have to wait. Meeting him today would be a good start.

Brian was the first to come in. "Hey, please take your shoes off," Dadia said. "My mom likes to keep the floors clean." She smiled. He smiled back. "Go right ahead into the kitchen and introduce yourself, OK?"

Brian's nose awoke. "Umm…do I smell cookies?" Dadia stayed at the door letting Seth, and then Johnny inside.

"Hey, Johnny," she said, looking at him with a wish to take away his suffering.

"Yo, thanks for the invite." The corners of his lips ever so slightly curved up.

Brian stepped into the kitchen as Dadia's mom turned to greet him. He froze in his steps. Seth was next only to be halted into silence next to him. Johnny followed with his head held low, while Dadia came up behind him. Johnny was the first to speak.

"Thanks for the…" His voice cracked, as his eyes gazed upward. Someone was playing a cruel joke. Mrs. Paola looked at him with pursed lips and wide-open eyes, noticing the key around his neck.

"I, uh, I'm sorry. I gotta go." Johnny turned, bumping into Dadia, almost knocking her down as his feet flew to the front door. He grabbed his shoes and bolted out the door. The sky opened up, as swirling wind and rain sponged down onto the street.

Dadia looked to Seth and Brian. Neither of them moved. They stood there speechless, eyes fixated on her mother.

"Dadia, is he all right?" Mrs. Paola ran to the door. "Maybe it wasn't a good idea to invite him over so soon?"

"Mrs. Paola, you don't understand," Seth chimed in. You don't just look like her; you could be her!"

"Be who?" Mrs. Paola said with a worried look.

"No questions about it. We should know. We grew up with Johnny and his mom. You could be Mrs. Styvers! I'd say her identical twin." Brian nodded his head in agreement.

"Oh dear," she said. "Where do you suppose he ran off to?"

"We should go after him," Seth said. "I have an idea where he's headed."

"Yes, definitely," Mrs. Paola said. "Please, please bring him back, all of you please, and we can figure this all out. I just baked some cookies."

"I bet chocolate chip, with a Hershey's kiss in the middle," Brian said in jest, putting on his shoes.

"And baked with love!" she replied, raising an eyebrow. "How'd you know?"

Seth and Brian looked at each other. Then Seth spoke. "See Mrs. Paola, this is real spooky. Even down to the cookies, you *are* Mrs. Styvers."

Dadia piped in, "We'll find him and bring him back, Mom."

"I'm glad you're coming with us, Dadia," Brian said. She returned him a blank stare.

I'm such a jerk, he said to himself, getting into the back seat of Seth's Acura letting Dadia sit in the front. His alter-ego ghost pushed him into silent darkness once more.

* * *

Katie Paola stood in the kitchen, tapping her foot, waiting for the tea water to boil. Every idea led to another question. Opening the cabinet door, she reached to the back of the shelf and pulled out a box. At the table, she contemplated opening it up. Out of her pocket surfaced a key identical to the one she noticed around Johnny's neck. She hadn't opened the box in years, and time had helped her forget some of the items and questions that still lay inside. *Where did the money come from? What did the swans mean? And the pictures?* Everything was still a mystery—a mystery she wanted to forget.

With a slight shake of her head, she put the key back into her pocket and placed the box back on the shelf, pensive to what it all meant. She hoped the smell of the cookies baked an hour ago would soothe the pain of her daughter's friends. *Yes, some cookies and a hot cup of black tea would do the job,* she thought.

The kettle whistled in harmony to the rhythmic banging on the kitchen-door window, making the glass angel bounce in repetition against the pane. The bell never worked, but her angel did make a nice homemade door knocker. Cautiously, she peeked through the window.

36

DADIA'S MOM OPENED THE DOOR, while he stood motionless, hair dripping, shirt stuck to his body like Saran Wrap. A mournful fear shot from his meek blue eyes. He looked to her in silence.

"Mrs. Paola, sorry for runnin' out like that, but…" Johnny wiped the rain off his cheeks.

Quietly, she took his hand and led him into the kitchen. Her eyes started to itch with a deep sensation, like a joyous reunion for a long-lost son. Her emotions ran, holding back the Hoover Dam behind her eyes. "There is so much I need to know," she said to him.

"Only the darkness of my room has scared me more than this," he replied.

"Please, come. Sit," she said, bringing him to the kitchen table. She then scurried out of the room.

Taking a deep breath, he could hear her opening then shutting drawers in the distance. A moment later, she returned.

"Here." She gave him half a smile and handed him a T-shirt and a towel. "I now understand that I look like your mother, and I am as perplexed as you. Maybe that is why I've been having these dreams." She poured a cup of tea and set it in front of him.

Above the sink, she pulled out the box for the second time and laid it before him, watching every nuance of his facial expressions. His face told the story of deep thoughts and betrayal.

Johnny said, "My mom once said there was a box this key opened." He took the key from around his neck and held it tight in his hand. "A buried treasure, she told me. There was no box. The secret hiding spot was empty." He continued in disgust. "It was all a hoax. My mother must have been delirious, thinking she put something important there, and all these years, I carried around this key, for what?"

She looked hard at him. "Who's to say you were the first one to the secret place?" she questioned.

With a slight cock of his head to the side, he squinted.

"Now, I look like your mother, and I seem to have a key like you. A coincidence?" He just looked at her. She continued. "This box came to me after my mom died. I was away at college, and a woman who called herself Ms. Rosemary—just Ms. Rosemary—came to my dorm. She handed me this box, a key, and my mother's urn. She said my mom died in an accident on vacation. My mother never took vacations, not by herself." She looked to the floor. "I was so young. I didn't know what to do." Her eyes moved back to him. "Can I see your key?" He gave it to her, and she placed it into the slot, turned it to the right, and then to the left, as the tumblers clicked.

"You can buy that box and key at any hardware store," he said.

"No, this box and key are custom made. That I am sure of."

He thought for a moment. Inquisitive, he asked, "Your mom, how could that be? Wouldn't other family members miss your mom?"

"I had no other family. It was just the two of us. I was so young…" The room lightened, and the sun wrapped around the remaining clouds in the sky while the rain continued its dance. She got up and looked out the kitchen window in a trance. "I went back to where we lived. Everything was gone—burned to the ground," she said, pausing in silence.

He could tell she held back what lay below the top of the water. It must have been dark and deep. She turned to look at him.

"I'm so sorry. Here I am talking about me, and I should be consoling you."

"Yo, that's fine." He rather meant it. He was feeling better just being able to talk to someone who seemed to have the same problems as he did. "I feel like she's here somehow. I just look at you and…" He had to change the subject. He had to shake that feeling. "May I ask your mother's name?" He felt extremely proper and out of place.

"Her name was Stella."

"Stella? No, man, can't be," he said in astonishment.

"Why do you say that?"

"I don't know why I'm sharing this with ya, but," he said, looking for her reaction, "there's a grave at Park View Cemetery that I visit a lot. Yo, been going there for years, ever since my mom disappeared…to think an' such. Mrs. P., don't ya go thinkin' I'm strange or anything, but I talk to the woman buried there. Her name—Stella." He had never told anyone this. Seth knew about Stella, but they hadn't been tight the last five years. Letting that thought out into the air, he felt a thin veil lift from his eyes.

"Please, call me Katie," she said. The pounding of nails on the roof from the hard rain subsided. A ray of colored light illuminated the glass angel on the door.

Johnny was done with this whole mess and was itching to just go, get out of there. He had enough. Looking at her, he became so conflicted. Enough was enough. His leg began to rhythmically bounce.

She took out a yellowed piece of notepaper from the box and then turned the box toward him. Inside were many photos. He looked at them, while she spoke, "This note was in the box." She read it to him: "Look for your comfort from your mother's urn. I believe that this was a note from Ms. Rosemary, the woman who came to my dorm room telling me my mom had died. There was no note or writing from my mother…only these pictures, money, and two key chains."

He took out the top picture of a woman with a child. "Is this your mother, Stella, and you?" She nodded in agreement. *Was it a coincidence?*

"Johnny, would you mind going to that cemetery with me? I want to meet your Stella." She touched his arm in reassurance.

"Sure," he said with apprehension. He had been around the block more times than he wanted for his age. For him, things never worked out as planned or for the better. Right now, he wanted to just bolt—get the hell away from her, his father, his life. He wanted to punch something. She looked and acted exactly the way he remembered his mother, and she reminded him of someone else—the girl from his journaling site whose name was…Stella, for whom he had grown to care about. Right now, he wanted to believe in something, in someone, but it was all too good to be true.

Katie left a note on the counter for Dadia. It had rained so hard earlier she tiptoed around the worms that surfaced onto the driveway, while the smell of earthworms permeated the air.

Driving down Route 10 to Park View, Johnny looked to the sky, searching for the rainbow. *There, there it was, right in front of them—maybe a sign and an omen.* He figured they would both be full of questions on the ride to the cemetery, but she kept her eyes straight ahead, only asking directions for where to turn. He looked to the rainbow and wondered if she felt the same calmness that somehow now enveloped him.

Taking a deep breath, they approached Stella's headstone, feeling the anxiety in the air before a static burst was about to snap. It was all too coincidental: she, looking just like his mother and he, visiting a gravestone of a person named Stella, the same name as her mother, and he, writing online with a girl named Stella.

He knew his Grandma and Grandpa Styvers, but it never occurred to him that he never knew his mom's mother or father. No one ever spoke of them, and the idea of two sets of grandparents never entertained his thoughts.

"Yo, Mrs. Paola, are ya sure ya don't have any brothers or sisters?" he asked.

"No, it was only my mother and I," she replied, arriving at the headstone. "Stella "Leda" Thestus, 1950–1986," she said aloud. "Funny, she died the same year as my mom."

"She was a loner, like me," he said.

"Well, someone spent a lot of money on this headstone," she said. "And look, under her name, a swan." She pulled out her key chain.

"Hey, that's the same key chain the detective at the hospital showed us."

"Detective?" she asked, her mind immersed in the gravestone. A swan carved in the headstone faced the same direction, and each feather was the same shape and form as her key chain.

"Notice her name. It is encased in a rectangle with each corner an engraving of what looks like a bird of some sort, maybe a swallow?" She rolled the last name *Thestus* in her mind.

"After my mom disappeared, I spent a lot of time in the cemetery with Stella. She and I, we're sometimes drinking buddies," Johnny said with a grin. "I never took any notice to the birds on her headstone."

"Actually, these swans look hand engraved by someone, maybe at a later date?" she questioned. "Do you know what happened to your mom, Johnny? How or why she disappeared?"

"Not a clue, I just remember my mom and dad fightin'. I always figured it had somethin' to do with me cuz since that night, my dad has refused to talk about it."

"Johnny, I don't believe that any woman would tell her child a wild treasure tale and repeat it to them five years later if it wasn't true. Maybe someone got there before you."

That thought freaked him out again and infuriated him at the same time. *Who else knew their secret hiding spot, other than Seth and Brian?*

Out of her pocket, she pulled a picture of a building under construction and handed it to him. "This also was in my box. Does it look familiar?"

"Yo, most definitely," he said. "It looks like a part of the Foundation over in Rolling Hills."

She raised her eyebrows. "The Foundation? I talk to a guy online that got free tickets to a concert there. Funny, his name is… Johnny, too."

With a precarious look, he asked with a dark voice, "Your screen name—it's not Stella, is it?"

"Johnny Styvers?" Johnny turned around. Two police officers came out of nowhere.

"Who's askin'?" he replied.

The officer pushed his arms behind his back. "I have a warrant for your arrest." Johnny tried to pull away but stopped when he caught Katie's eyes tense with fear.

"What are the charges, may I ask?" Mrs. Paola cut in.

"Homicide, madam."

"Murder? Right, of who?" Johnny shouted.

"Larry Jones." The officer sneered at him.

As the police car drove away, Katie swore she would find the underlying cause of this. No more would she look over her shoulder in fear. *Why didn't her mother tell her more, and why was this boy's dead mother an identical look alike to her?* There were too many coincidences. Hearing the sound of gravel popping, she turned to see a car approach. It was Seth with Dadia and Brian.

"Mom, what are you doing here?"

"Johnny came back to the house. He spoke of Stella's grave. Your grandmother's name was Stella, so we came here."

"So where is he now?" Seth asked.

"They took him away." Mrs. Paola stated.

"Who took him away?" Brian questioned.

"The police. They arrested him for murder."

"Murder?" The three of them chimed in.

"Of whom?"

"A Larry Jones. Do you know him?"

Seth and Brian looked to each other.

"What do we do now?" Brian questioned.

"We find out the truth. There's no way Johnny killed Larry. Johnny has a hot temper, but to kill? No way," Seth insisted.

"Well, I think maybe a good place to start is here, with Stella Thestus's grave," Mrs. Paola said. The boys and Dadia looked at her. "Come; let me show you what Johnny and I found."

37

THE FRONT DOOR FLUNG OPEN with an angry thrust. "Dad!" Seth yelled. Brian followed behind him, step for step.

"Hey, don't slam the doors!" his father yelled back.

Seth knew where he was and headed right to the family room to find his father sitting in the lounge chair, reading *PC Magazine*. He looked to him with contempt. "Tell me what happened to Mrs. Styvers," he demanded. "We have to know—now!"

Looking up over the top of his glasses, Mr. Kogan lowered his magazine. "And who the hell are we? You got a mouse in your pocket?"

Brian stepped out from the shadows. "Dad, we need you to tell us the truth about what you know in regards to the disappearance of Mrs. Styvers five years ago."

"Well, well, well. Now you boys both feel you're old enough to start spreading old gossip of the neighborhood. What good do you think will come from that?"

"Dad," Seth said, regaining his composure, "we're not going to go around the neighborhood kissing everyone's butt in Macy's window to get this information. We are going to get it one way or another. We would prefer to get it from you or mom."

"And why must we have this information?" His father put his hand to his cheeks in question.

"We need to help Johnny," Brian spilled it out.

"Let me guess; he's in trouble."

They both spoke at the same time. "Yeah, kind of."

"We need to help him, Dad. Please, just tell us what you know." Brian asked. "We need to do some detective work."

"Well, if you're looking to do detective work, go ask your mother. She knows more than she would ever tell, and then some." Mr. Kogan flicked his arms and stuck his nose back into his magazine. "Enough talk about the Styvers family for one day," he said under his breath.

Mrs. Kogan heard the whole conversation. The boys made their way to the kitchen, and she was ready for them.

"Mom," Seth said, sitting down at the kitchen table with Brian.

"I know; I heard you talking with your dad. There are two different versions of what happened to Mrs. Styvers. One, it was gossip around town—you both know how I hate gossip." She looked at them both with a stern face. "They said she was having an affair with Jack Jones, the Grand Numen of the Foundation in Rolling Hills."

"An affair? You mean cheating on Johnny's dad? Mr. Styvers?" Brian asked.

"Yes, but that was gossip, and of course it came from Mrs. Stevens."

"No, she was at his mom's funeral, " Seth said.

"Anyways, I also got wind Mrs. Styvers found out some interesting information back then that could have put Jack Jones in jail. When she disappeared, whatever information she did have—if any—never surfaced. This led people to believe she was having an affair, leaving town in embarrassment. Then, she shows up now, five years later. Who'd a thought…amnesia, I believe they said."

"Yeah," they both confirmed. Then Seth said, "When we were in the hospital with Johnny, a detective came in with a photo of a swan key chain, asking us a bunch of questions."

"Come to think of it, Seth, he actually looked

familiar." Brian stated.

"Who?"

"That detective— I've met him somewhere." He looked puzzled. Brian was no sleuth and nothing like his brother.

"A swan key chain you say." Seth's mom went into thought mode. "Was it a beautiful, brilliant white swan? In clear Lucite?"

"Yes. Why?"

"I vaguely remember something about a swan. Let me take some time and think some more about this. It was a very long time ago."

They both looked at each other. Seth motioned to Brian to be silent about the swan key chain that Dadia or her mother possessed.

"Yes, I believe she had a key chain with a swan on it. I noticed it one day at the ballpark, when you, Seth, and Johnny were playing ball. It well might have been a few days before she disappeared. She said it was a key to finding her lineage. I wasn't quite sure what she meant by that."

"Well, thanks, Mom. Brian and I need to check some things out."

She smiled. "By the way, what kind of trouble is Johnny in?"

They both stood silent.

"Bad, huh?"

"Yeah, bad, but I know he didn't do it," Seth said.

"Do what?"

"Murder Larry Jones."

"Oh, my God," she whispered. "The boy in the paper—the one found behind the Dumpster late Saturday night?"

"Afraid so, Mom," Seth replied.

"He's not the son of Jack Jones, is he?"

"Yep, bingo," Brian added.

38

INTERROGATION OF FRANK HALLEY

Detective: "So tell me, Seth, what exactly happened Saturday night?"

Seth Kogan: "The three of us were invited to Ashley's. She gave me directions. Brian, my brother, came running to the garage as I was coming out."

Detective: "Brian was running to the garage? From the street?"

Seth Kogan: "No from the cabana. He was sweating, hard, fear in his eyes."

Detective: "Go on. What happened next?"

Seth Kogan: "Well, he told me that Larry and Johnny were in a fight. Larry had a whip. He showed me what Larry did to him, whipped the crap out of his back."

Detective: "Larry Jones and Johnny Styvers were in a fight?"

Seth Kogan: "Yes. Brian said Johnny had a knife."

Detective: "Did Johnny have this knife earlier in the evening?"

Seth Kogan: "No, sir."

Detective: "Can you be certain of this?"

Seth Kogan: "No, but Johnny never carries a knife."

Detective: "How long have you been hanging around Johnny Styvers?" Seth looked at him. He knew where the detective was going with his questioning.

Seth Kogan: "About a month or so."

Detective: "Continue…"

Seth Kogan: "I cut through the hedgerow and ran to find Johnny up by the cabana."

Detective: "The cabana?"

Seth Kogan: "Yeah. I was halfway there and I heard a shot."

Detective: "A shot."

Seth Kogan: "I think a shot or an enormous tree fell in the woods. I run further into the woods, toward the sound. Johnny is running my way. He says, 'Let's get the hell out of here.'"

Detective:	"Did he have the knife in his hand?"
Seth Kogan:	"No. He told me Larry took off at the sound of the shot. So he did too. That's all I know. We got in my car and split."
Detective:	"And where was Brian?"
Seth Kogan:	"He was taking Dadia home."
Detective:	"Did Johnny have any blood on his clothing or hands?"
Seth Kogan:	"No, sir, the next thing I know Johnny's drunker than a skunk, and we're over by Eder Ave Cemetery, where he's puking his brains out."
Detective:	"Now Brian is where?"
Seth Kogan:	"Taking Dadia home."
Detective:	"Dadia who?"
Seth Kogan:	"I don't know, Ashley's friend—Dadia Paola, I think. I then get a call from my mom saying Johnny's mom was found, so I dropped Johnny off at the hospital, go pick up Brian, and then go directly back to the hospital. Brian got the last pass, and I snuck up the stairwell to the hospital room. To prove it, I bumped into a nurse on her

	way down. Actually I tripped her by accident in the stairwell."
Detective:	"And what did she look like?"
Seth Kogan:	"Well, she had on one of those nurse uniforms with a name badge. I think it said Thelma."
Detective:	"Then what happened?"
Seth Kogan:	"I ran up the stairwell, met Brian on the way to Mrs. Styvers's room. That's where the detective stopped us and questioned us."

39

INTERROGATION OF BRIAN KOGAN

Detective:	"So, Brian, tell me what happened Saturday night."
Brian Kogan:	"Seth, Johnny, and I went to a party at the Wentworth's."
Detective:	"Were her parent's home?"
Brian Kogan:	"I didn't see them."
Detective:	"OK. What happened at this so called party?"
Brian Kogan:	"There were a lot of people there. I was sitting out by the pool, and Larry and his henchman, Frank, sneak up behind me and stick a knife in my side, tell me to follow them. I did. You know, when you're up against the wall with a knife in your side, what else are you going to do? Well, Larry takes me into the woods."

Detective: "Frank Halley and Larry Jones?"

Brian Kogan: "Yes."

Detective: "Did anyone see you?"

Brian Kogan: "Probably, but he made me smile like we were best buddies."

Detective: "OK, then what happened?"

Brian Kogan: "He takes me into the woods and blindfolds me, tapes my hands up. I think I'm a goner. Now, I don't want to die. It seems like an eternity of walking, blindfolded— Larry laughing and making all those remarks."

Detective: "Remarks, like what?"

Brian Kogan: "You know, calling me a worm, loser, his lackey. And he says how he's going to take all his frustrations out on me. He was a jerk, and I'm glad he got what was coming to him."

The detective gave him a look. Brian realized what he said and immediately continued.

Brian Kogan: "We get to this spot, and he pushes me to the ground. I can hear him rustling through the leaves as if he had things there already."

Detective:	"Things there?"
Brian Kogan:	"Yeah, like you come home for dinner and the table is already set, but it wasn't set when you left in the morning, it just appeared somehow. Anyway, I hear the sound of a lighter flicking. Oh my God, now I'm thinking he's going to burn me at the stake. Like the witches at Salem. All of a sudden, Larry starts chanting some weird stuff. Then whack on my back. The pain was excruciating."
Detective:	"Did you scream out?"
Brian Kogan:	"No way, I was not going to let him have the satisfaction. He hit me two, three times. I didn't know when or where I would be hit next. I tensed up like a rock in anticipation. I'm waiting for the next blow, and I hear Frank saying he's first going to cut out my tongue so I can't tell anyone, then cut off my fingers so I can't write anyone, then cut out my eyes so I can't see who did this to me. Now I'm praying to the

almighty God to send out the National Guard: Where are the helicopters? The spotlights? Where the hell is the SWAT team? While I'm praying as hard as I can, I hear a war scream coming from afar—like someone running and yelling, like they're going to do major damage, kamikaze style."

Detective: "What do you mean kamikaze style?"

Brian Kogan: "Like, they don't care if they live or die as long as their mission is a success. I'm like oh, damn, I'm going to get bombarded from all sides. I crouch low in a ball waiting for the bear to smack me. I'm tensing up waiting for the worst, then the scream stops. I can hear a scuffle in the leaves, a voice shouts out the sweetest words I ever heard."

Detective: "And what was that?"

Brian Kogan: "'Untie my brother, or I'll slit your lackey's throat.' It was Johnny. I almost, right then and there, collapsed in relief. Right then and there, I

197

	thanked the powers that be. He is my guardian angel you know. I love him, man."
Detective:	"What happened next?"
Brian Kogan:	"Johnny cut my hands free. I take my blindfold off. Johnny tells me to run, so I run. I find Seth. He was with Dadia. He told me to take care of Dadia, so she could get home safely. Then he ran to help Johnny."
Detective:	"Where in the woods did this take place?"
Brian Kogan:	"I don't know; other than I came out somewhere by Ashley's garage. I guess somewhere in the woods by the cabana."
Detective:	"If you were blindfolded, how did you know which way to run?"
Brian Kogan:	"I heard sounds and saw lights. Where else would you run? Into a dark forest?"
Detective:	"Then you took Dadia Paola home?"
Brian Kogan:	"Yeah."
Detective:	"And what did you do for two hours before Seth came to pick you up?"
Brian Kogan:	"Like I said, I took Dadia

	home; she helped me with my wounds. You've seen them; they're real."
Detective:	"Did you hear a gun shot that night?"
Brian Kogan:	"Um, I don't think so."

40

INTERROGATION OF JOHNNY STYVERS

Detective:	"Johnny Styvers, you have quite a nice little file going on here for various minor infractions, including two misdemeanors under your belt. I see you've moved up to a felony status with this one."
Johnny Styvers:	"Yo, I don't know what you're talking about. I didn't kill Larry Jones."
Detective:	"Really, well the forensics lab says the evidence points to you. A knife with your fingerprints on it was found behind the Dumpster at the scene of the crime."
Johnny Styvers:	"Like I said, I didn't kill him. Dumpster? What Dumpster?"
Detective:	"The Dumpster behind the

	strip mall on Russell Ave. So then, can you tell us how your fingerprints got on the knife?"
Johnny Styvers:	"Yo. The only thing I can tell you is that he and I had a clash Saturday night in the woods. His buddy, Frank, was the one wielding a knife. I thought he was gonna kill my best friend. I got in the middle of it and took the knife away."
Detective:	"Larry's buddy, Frank Halley, in the woods behind the strip mall?"
Johnny Styvers:	"What's with the strip mall, man? In the woods next to Ashley's house—I don't remember her last name. She was having a party. She lives in Mountain Crest. I heard something in the woods. Went to check it out and found Larry and his buddy trying to torture my best friend. I stepped in to save him."
Detective:	"Save who?"
Johnny Styvers:	"My friend, of course, Brian, Brian Kogan."
Detective:	"Larry Jones's friend,

	Frank Halley, was there?"
Johnny Styvers:	"His name was Frank. I'd seen him hang with Larry here and there. I dunno his last name. Why don't you go ask him what happened?"
Detective:	"We did. He was badly beaten. He gave his statement to the police at the hospital. He stated two Crags and you beat him up, tried to slit his throat, and then you took Larry away by knifepoint."
Johnny Styvers:	"Who is this guy?! That's such a load of crap. He's lying!"
Detective:	"I see here that you have been seen in Harrier, meeting up with a Mountain Crag named Elgin Von Craig."
Johnny Styvers:	"Yo, now is it illegal to talk to people?"

Johnny was disgusted. *How dare they!*

Detective:	"Your friend, Brian, can he back up your story?"
Johnny Styvers:	"Of course he can."
Detective:	"Frank Halley has identified Elgin Von Craig to be at the

scene that night. He claims he passed out after being beaten by Elgin and one other Crag and saw you holding a knife to Larry as you walked him out of the woods."

Johnny Styvers: "Right, and then I drove Larry all the way to Park View just to kill him and dump his body behind the strip mall that I just happen to work in. Come on, man; I'm being framed. Listen, Larry Jones was no angel. He was torturing Brian. Taped his hands, blindfolded him. He was whippin' him with one of those short whips. So I stepped in."

Detective: "And what did Brian do?"

Johnny Styvers: "What do you think happened? I got the knife away from Frank and cut Brian free. I told him to run, so he ran. His back looked like it was ripped with a circular saw, man; the guy was in shock. Larry and I didn't even get a chance to start fighting. There was a gunshot. It startled both of

	us. Larry ran like a sissy ass, so I decided I'd better get out of there."
Detective:	"Larry Jones ran."
Johnny Styvers:	"Yeah, he ran, and that's all I can tell ya. That's all I know."
Detective:	"And what about the knife?"
Johnny Styvers:	"The knife? I chucked it, and like I said, I took off too."
Detective:	"And what about Frank?"
Johnny Styvers:	"Frank? He was lying on the ground, breathing, so I left him. Why should I care? He just finished torturing my brother, one of my best friends."
Detective:	"Well Johnny, you'd better get a good attorney that can find some hard evidence in your favor. They're looking to prosecute you as an adult, considering you will be eighteen in a few weeks. And the way I see it, you're looking at twenty to life."

Johnny knew right then and there, he had forgotten the law of the land. He should have remained silent.

41

"SETH, WE DON'T HAVE TO go to the library. Follow me." Brian led him to his room. On his computer, he knew he could find out anything.

"Here, let's look up gravestones and their meanings." He clicked to the Snoodle site. "Look," he said, "special emblems on tombstones have special meanings in Christian faith." He scrolled down the list. "Skeleton, snake, and here it is—swallow. It means 'motherhood.'"

"That's interesting," Seth replied, "considering she is the only one on the gravestone, no husband. Well, she still could have had a child."

"So, let's check out the swan." Brian scrolled down the page. "There is nothing for a swan."

Seth thought for a moment. "Let's see, her name was Stella 'Leda' Thestus. Leda—why is her middle name in quotes?"

"Maybe that was her nickname?"

"Strange nickname for Stella, don't you think?"

"Yeah, but she's old. Maybe back then it was something that was common?"

"Wait, put Leda into Snoodle." Brian clicked search: Leda, a suburb of Perth. Western Australia. Leda, a moon of Jupiter. Thirty-eight Leda is an asteroid.

"Here!" Seth quipped, "Click on this one: Leda, Queen of Sparta from Greek mythology." Snoodle brought up "Leda and the Swan."

"Oh, my God. This has got to be it!"

Seth read out loud, "King Tyndareus of Sparta had a wife, Leda. Zeus of Greek mythology became smitten with her. To seduce her, he turned himself into a swan. This seduction resulted in two immortal daughters of Zeus. Leda also had twin sons from Tyndareus, who were mortal children."

"Could it be that Mrs. Paola, Dadia's mom and Mrs. Styvers, Johnny's mom, are twins? I mean—they both look identical!" Brian contemplated.

"Well, a DNA test would prove that," Seth replied. "Let's see, Mrs. Paola has a swan key chain, exactly like the swan on Stella Thestus's grave. What we don't know is, did Mrs. Styvers have the same key chain? The problem becomes the box Johnny was to dig up. It wasn't there."

"Wow, if we can locate that information then Stella could actually be their mother—and wait, that would mean, Dadia and Johnny are—related?"

"This is too farfetched." Seth shook his head.

"No, Seth, I don't think so. Look—" Brian read more, "Leda and the Swan was also a poem by William Butler Yeats. Larry told me to do his next project on William Butler Yeats. He said that his grandfather was obsessed with Yeats and his poems." Brian stopped reading aloud and became immersed in the screen.

"What, Bri? Come on, what else does it say?" Seth was becoming impatient.

"Oh, my God, Seth, Yeats was associated with 'The Golden Dawn'!"

"What the hell is The Golden Dawn?"

"It was or is an occult group and in that group was Alistair Crowley! You know, the song by Ozzy Osbourne? Mr. Crowley!"

"Bri, focus, let's keep with saving Johnny's ass."

"Well, I've overheard talk from dad that there is speculation that the Foundation, over in Rolling Hills, the one that Larry's father is the Grand Numen to, has occult gossip surrounding it." Brian was fly-fishing.

"You heard that from dad?" Seth shook his head.

"OK, then, I'll query Larry Jones and Grand Numen Jack Jones on Snoodle. No, wait; let's look up the Foundation of Rolling Hills. I think that is a safe place to start."

Searching site after site, they finally came to some interesting information. "Look, the founder of the Foundation—Darius Jones, Larry's grandfather."

"Now this is getting ridiculous—Darius? Like Tyndareus?" Brian laughed.

Nevertheless, Seth was impressed. "Bri, you are the wiz man. When do you have time to figure all this crap out?" Seth looked at him in awe.

Brian rolled his eyes. "What good is all this information? We have no proof; it's only coincidences."

"But we have something to go on. Who knows where it will lead us?" Seth replied.

"Come on, let's go to the police station and see if we can talk to Johnny."

"Should we get Dadia? She is involved, somewhat." Brian was throwing out his fishing rod.

"Sure, bro, we can pick her up on the way. Maybe her mom can enlighten us on this interesting bout of coincidences we've just uncovered." Seth took a long, hard look at his brother. "You really like her, don't yo. Bri, the way you act, she's never going to be attracted to you."

"I know, so, why bother? That's just the way my life is," Brian stated.

"No, no, you just need the skills. It's like learning to walk or ride a bike. Once you get your balance, you can take off."

"Sure, it's easy for you, Seth. The girls just love you for some reason and Johnny too." He looked down at his round, keg stomach. "I have nothing to offer."

"See that's where you put yourself dead in the water," Seth replied. "Here, I'll teach you how to swim, and it all starts with the letter C."

"The letter C? What the hell does that have to do with swimming?" Brian looked skeptical.

"Yeah, C for *confidence*. And that is the foundation to building a skyscraper. Look, the first example: at Dadia's house, you were soo sweet. You ask, 'Dadia? Are you going to come with us?' in a squeaky, meek, Mr. Clean voice? See, there, no confidence. You're too kind, too sweet; I wanted to vomit. I bet she would of if she could. Big turn off, bro."

"Yeah, but that's me. I am a nice person. What are you trying to tell me to be mean?"

"No, see you don't get it. First, be yourself. I've never heard you talk like that to *anyone*!" he laughed. "And second, be audacious."

"Audacious? Like arrogant?"

"No, be spirited, fearless. Girls can smell fear, you know, just like dogs. Maybe that's why they call them Bi-at-ches!" He laughed. "And don't forget, you have to add in some fun. No girl likes a straight, boring guy. By the way, being nice and kissing girl's butts are two entirely different things."

"Oh, yeah, easy for you to say."

"No, bro, it's in all of us guys. We are all born jokesters; we just have to clean it up a bit in front of the ladies. Trust me; they like it. We just forget to use our God-given gifts when we put girls on a pedestal. A real girl wants an equal—someone she can go head to head with, and someone who is more of a mystery than she sees in herself."

"I think I understand, but—"

"Think of it this way: You like to read books, right? Would you rather read a book with the ending known to you right off the bat, or would you rather like the mystery of slowly turn each page to find out what happens? Because if you know the ending, why read the book?"

"Slowly finding it out. It's more fun," Brian injected.

"See! Girls are the same way as guys! They want to figure you out. They don't want you to be an open book—only after you hook them." He smiled. "They subconsciously want to figure you out on their own and then decide if they want to go further. We all like mysteries and want to figure out what happens. That's how we decide if we want to get involved."

"OK, I guess I understand that, but how do you get a girl to open up your book and read it?"

"There comes in the letter A—attraction. You can help that along by how you portray your letter with help from little H."

"My letter C, little H? Wait, now you're sounding jerkier than me."

"It's what some guys just know, and don't share, or just too stupid to realize what they're doing. Maybe it's competition. Yeah, that's it. But the C I'm talking about is *confidence* with a little humor. It's like playing a game of some sorts, and don't throw worry into the mix, worry ruins everything."

"But I don't like to play those kind of games."

"Oh, my God, Brian. That's all you do! Wake up; smell the Twinkies! And the last person a girl wants to spend time with is someone who lacks his own personality, his own being."

"So what do all those capital and little letters spell?" Brian was still confused.

"Nothing, you jerk, I was just trying to make a point!" Seth stopped talking and just stared at Brian.

"What!?" Brian got quiet.

"Bri, you never told me what happened in the woods, between you and Larry. Wait, you were going to do a report on Yeats—for Larry?"

"Come on, Seth. You know you set him up to torture me."

"What the hell are you talking about? Torture you? Why would I do that? Larry's an ass. I can torture you myself," he said with a half-baked laugh. "No, really, what happened?" He put his hand on Brian's back. Brian flinched.

"I'm still sore." He grimaced.

"Aw man, I'm sorry. If I knew, Larry was doing that to you I would have killed him myself. You're my brother, man. No one messes with you," he said, "except me."

Brian opened up. "Larry was pushing me around since the first day of school. He told me that it was all your idea. You paid him, and gave him secrets about me, and told him to make me do his homework."

"You were doing all his homework? Man, I had no idea. Wait, so that was your handy work? You wrote that off-the-wall report on Hitler? The one that sent Larry to the principal's office?"

"Yeah, that was my hand." Brian smirked as he nodded his head yes.

"Oh, my God, Brian, you're the man! That report leaked out all over the school. It's going down into the annals of Park View High School history!" He slapped him on the back. "Oh—sorry! Come on let's go get Dadia to help us solve this crime. Johnny's innocent. Larry had a lot of enemies, but what we have to find out is how many enemies Johnny had who would want to frame him."

"Call Dadia; I'll prompt you what to say. Her number should still be in my phone." As they sped off in Seth's Acura, Brian felt his hands quiver as he took in the breadth of the sky.

Seth looked over to him. "Hey, Bri, don't hide stuff like that from me ever again, OK?"

"Sure, Seth." He felt a spark of a long-lost connection, and it felt really good.

Stepping into the Paola household, Seth and Brian were speechless once more to see who was talking to Mrs. Paola.

42

MR. MANTERIA, WHAT ARE YOU doing here?!" the boys asked in unison.

How did Brian's art teacher know Mrs. Paola? Seth wondered.

"Good, we're all here. Nice to see you again, boys. I believe you two might be able to help shed some light on an old, unsolved police case. Mrs. Styvers and I, well, we were good friends way back in the day."

Seth looked to Brian with two eyebrows raised. Thoughts of a tryst ran through his head.

"Mr. Manteria, you work for the police too?" Brian asked.

"Yes the jig is up, as they would say in the movies. Because I also have a teaching degree in art, I was planted first in the middle school, then in the high school, as an art teacher to observe the Jones boy. I've been working on a case against his father for more years than I want to admit. The disappearance of Mrs. Styvers put a stop to the investigation five years ago because lack of evidence. Or should I say, the evidence went missing. So, I decided to stay at the school because, well, the kids just love me." He smiled. Brian tried not to cough.

"The case is recently reopened with the sighting of the swan key chain. It was part of the evidence Mrs. Styvers had acquired and had shown me." He looked to Brian. Brian looked to Dadia. Dadia looked away.

"Wait!" Brian blurted out, "The janitor—the one who saved me from Larry in the boys' room? He was a detective at the hospital, right?" Mr. Manteria nodded his head up and down with eyes closed.

Seth looked at his brother agitated. "Do you know what happened to Mrs. Styvers?" Seth asked, not taking his eyes off of Brian.

"The night Mrs. Styvers disappeared I spoke to her on the phone. We were to meet later that evening, but she never showed up."

"Why was she going to meet you?" Seth asked.

"Good question. Johnny's mom had in her possession information that could put Larry Jones's father, the Grand Numen Jack Jones, in jail and out of business— proof that the Grand Numen murdered Stella Thestus, who was her biological mother. She had told me on the phone right before she disappeared she placed this information in a safe spot. No one knew where that was, not even her husband, Joe."

"The box!" the boys replied.

"Yes, but I'm afraid that from what I have learned, whatever was in the box may now be in the wrong hands," Mr. Manteria continued. "Now you can see, Mrs. Paola looks exactly like Mrs. Styvers. We believe that she is Mrs. Styvers long-lost twin sister and that Larry's father had his hands in the homicide of Stella Thestus, their biological mother. Mrs. Paola has a locket of her mother's hair, and we are getting approval to dig up Stella Thestus's gravesite. We will be analyzing all DNA to see if my theory warrants truth."

"But why does Stella Thestus have a different last name?" Brian questioned.

"We believe that it was her name when she was a member of the Foundation. Kind of like a cult, they are given a new name when they are inducted into the group. Stella's killer also took the liberty to bury her and keep it all quiet. Her only other family was her daughter, Mrs. Paola here, and she was away at college. They figured what would an eighteen-year-old know about anything and who would believe her?"

Mrs. Paola blinked her eyes sporadically. Dadia handed her a tissue.

"But why would Larry's father kill their mother, Stella?" Seth questioned.

"Well, boys, it's complicated, but to paint this picture in oil, about six years ago, Mrs. Styvers started searching for her biological mother. While on her quest, she stumbled upon information linking Larry's dad with the death of Stella Thestus. Stella had given birth to two girls, twins. Mrs. Styvers learned that Darius Jones, Larry's grandfather, and Stella Thestus were—in fact—her biological father and mother.

"Larry's dad, Grand Numen Jack Jones, runs the Foundation, a large organization over in Rolling Hills. Grand Numen Jones knew he would inherit the business from his father, Darius. Darius had an affair with Stella, and she got pregnant with twins. Grand Numen Jack Jones did not want to share the business with two half-sisters and Stella. This also did not sit well with Jack's mother, Ester, Darius's wife. Got that? Now, Mrs. Styvers was in the process of proving after eighteen years that the Grand Numen Jack Jones found and killed her mom, Stella. She also learned her biological mom had key chains of swans made up for her and her twin. She hoped these key chains would reunite them one day. They are one-of-a-kind art, you know, purchased through a storefront in Harrier."

"So you're saying that Mrs. Styvers and Mrs. Paola are—sisters? Their mother was Stella Thestus from the cemetery, and their father—Darius Jones, who is also Larry's grandfather?" Seth immediately surmised. Mr. Manteria was impressed with Seth's sense of quick deductions as this web was confusing enough for an adult.

"Yes, but Larry's dad is only their half-brother. His mother Ester, Darius's wife, put her son Jack up to killing

Stella Thestus. Larry and Johnny are partial cousins, and Mrs. Paola is Johnny's aunt, making Dadia his blood cousin!" Mr. Manteria concluded.

"Oh, my God, Dadia," Seth replied. "You're related to Johnny." Brian quietly sighed in relief.

Mr. M. cut in. "Though we think Darius, somehow in his twisted mind, loved Stella, Jack knew this out-of-marriage union, especially if the birth of two daughters ever surfaced, would ruin the Foundation, his father's reputation, and ultimately his by association. Jack might have to split the Foundation with a woman and two half-sisters. Jack's mother would not adhere to that. All his father and he worked to build would be destroyed by this scandal. Before Stella ran, she was ready to divulge everything she knew about the Foundation to the police. She was a woman scorned with two babies to take care of." He paused. "The Foundation is big business you know, boys."

"Wow." Brian looked in awe.

"Jack was going to get rid of Stella, but she caught on to the plan. With the help of her trusted friend, Ms. Rosemary Little, Stella planned her escape. Jack found out the plan, and things spiraled out of control. In opposite directions, Stella and Ms. Rosemary fled to safety—one with Katie, the other with Hanna. Stella knew she'd be caught if she kept both children, that it would be too dangerous. Ms. Rosemary took Hanna, and Stella took Katie. We believe that Ms. Rosemary Little somehow found Mrs. Styvers and was in contact with her before she disappeared. We also believe that it was the same Ms. Rosemary who contacted Katie, Mrs. Paola, when she was in college."

Mrs. Paola sat, looking to the floor. Dadia moved closer to her mother and placed her arm around her shoulder.

"We are assuming that Ms. Rosemary got scared and left Hanna off at an orphanage in New Mexico. We have traced Ms. Rosemary to an antique-and-art store in Harrier during the time she was friends with Stella. She sold items of art from the Mountain Crags described as American art—for no one would buy from the Crags. The area people feared and hated them, as they could not look past their different outer appearances to see who they really were inside. However, Ms. Rosemary came from a different cloth and felt akin to them. The beautiful box and urn, in Mrs. Paola's possession is Mountain Crag artwork. We believe Ms. Rosemary found Hanna (Mrs. Styvers), and gave her the second identical box—the same as her sister, Katie (Mrs. Paola), but this box held damaging evidence against the Foundation. Sounds like a motive for murder to me."

"Is Ms. Rosemary Little still at that shop in Harrier?" Seth asked.

"Unfortunately, after she left she never returned. The shop changed hands, and no one has any information on her whereabouts."

"Why didn't Stella just go to the police instead of running?" Seth questioned.

"Scared I guess, for her children. I suppose she figured it was better to run, considering there was speculation that the Foundation was missing a hell of a lot of money. For a year or so, construction on the compound ceased. We have no proof but believe that Stella took the money. It was the only way she could stay hidden. Cash leaves no footprint as a credit card or check."

"Does anyone know what happened to Ms. Rosemary Little?" Brian asked.

"No one knows for sure. Hanna grew up in the Midwest. She met Joe Styvers and fell madly in love. Joe was working construction where Hanna grew up but then had a job opportunity to come back to the east coast. They married and settled in Park View. Talk about coincidences or maybe the powers of the universe at work." Mr. Manteria paused in deep thought.

"Anyway, Hanna, I mean Mrs. Styvers, received an anonymous letter one day about finding a box that started her search for her biological mother and father. When the trail led to a possible murder, she came to me. Imagine, her ending up back in the place where she began, two towns away from Rolling Hills and the Foundation."

"Wow, it sounds like something from a movie," Seth added. "Bri, show Mr. M. what we printed out. Look what we dug up." Brian handed it to him.

Brian looked to Dadia. Confidence oozed from his eyes. He reassured himself that he was a person that she would want to get to know. She looked at him with a question in her posture and a small raise of her eyebrow. Oh, my God, it was working, and he didn't even say a word. Yes, he could tell she was wondering something, and it had to do with him. He kept his cool, and then ignored her just as Seth said to do.

"Mr. M., does Johnny or his dad know any of this?" Seth asked.

"No, but they will."

"But what about Larry? Who killed him and how does this all tie in together?"

"Well, all the evidence so far points to Johnny with his fingerprints on the murder weapon. When we are done here, I'm going to ask that both of you come down again to the station. I have a few more questions for you." Brian glanced nonchalantly to Dadia. Did she tell her mother what happened that night? He needed to get his story right where she was concerned.

"Sure, Mr. M., we'll follow you down," Seth said.

"Well boys, on the way there let's go to the place where Johnny thought the box was buried. We have a lot of work cut out for us to prove his innocence and find out the truth once and for all."

Mrs. Paola looked to her daughter, Dadia. Her hands began to quiver. "Wait," she said. "That would explain my mother's strange death. If she is buried in the cemetery over on Eder Avenue, then—" She went to the mantel and pulled down her mother's urn attempting to open it up.

"Mom! What are you doing?" Dadia exclaimed.

Taking the seal off the top, she looked into the urn of her mother's ashes; horror came to her eyes.

"Mom, what is it?"

"Everyone, please, just leave, now." Putting the top back on the urn, she walked out of the room and down the hallway. The sound of a door closing, and metal clicking in the distance rang out through the house.

43

"DEATH, THE FINAL TERMINATION."

"I don't think you have it right, Johnny." Brian tried to quell his negativity.

"Come on Brian, what side of the table you think your sitting on? This is it. Someone has it out for me, and I don't exactly have a 'he's-a-nice-boy' rep."

"You're innocent until proven guilty, Johnny."

"Ha, they seem to have proof I'm guilty, even when things don't quite match up. But they'll find a way; they'll make it so. I'm sinkin' in cement here, Bri."

"Johnny, don't you dare sit there without a fight." Brian paused. "You're my hero. I don't believe your blueprint has you lying down and just giving in. Right now lot of people and I are going to prove you innocent." Brian caught him off guard.

"Blueprint? Where'd you come up with that?" Johnny questioned. He hadn't heard that word in years. He didn't believe in any of that crap anymore. *Why would God let his mother disappear from the most important years of his life then reappear only to die in front of him? What was his purpose in life?*

"Listen—I've read about a lot of different views, and I've come to the conclusion before we are born, we choose to come to earth with a plan, a blueprint, to get enlightened. We come to this negative world to experience and perfect our spirits—you know, who we are. Why do you hear so many people say this is a living hell?"

OK, Brian had him there, but he wasn't convinced.

Brian continued, "We are born to learn, and sometimes we can be deterred from what we need to learn. First off, alcohol and drug abuse deter us from completing our quest. If that happens, when we die we need to come back again to learn what we missed—with the same type of parents and obstacles. Once we decide to learn a new enlightenment, we must keep going through the same hardships until we reach the desired perfection we originally wanted to acquire."

Johnny sat there looking strangely at him. *When did Brian become the philosophical one?*

"Hey, I have a lot of time on my hands, and I started reading about other people's beliefs. Many people believe we are all under one God, but just as we are each physically unique, we each think uniquely about what we believe and don't believe in, you know, in regards to rituals and God. Some people don't want you to question when it comes to faith, but only in questions do we get real answers," Brian said calmly. "Your mom, she's in heaven waiting for you," he said softly.

"So why don't I just end it now and get out of this hell hole?" Johnny half taunted.

"You shouldn't. Suicide is never a solution, but you can make all the other choices in your life. Within your plan for life here, you give yourself adversity, because only in adversities can the soul progress to enlightenment. See? You know, live and learn? But when we don't learn, we repeat and repeat till we do. Hey, I should know; I've done a lot of repeating it seems." Brian chuckled and then got solemn before continuing.

Johnny was intrigued. *Was this Brian Kogan sitting across from him? The quiet little brother of Seth they always tried to ditch and mock any chance they got?* He looked at him from across the table. *A person he put his life on the line for, but never got to know on a deeper level? Who was the real Brian Kogan?* Immediately Johnny knew he had made the right choice to protect him, and whatever the outcome would be, he would do it again if he had to.

"Johnny, your mother loved you so much. I always knew just in the way she looked at you, spoke to you, and did for you. Believe me; she doesn't want you to be sad. I'm sure you've heard of the tunnel when you die and the white light? The light guides you through, and I just know when your time comes, your mom will be there waiting. To her, it will be only a blip in time, though for us here on earth, many years seem like an eternity. You'll be reunited, and she'll help you to readjust back to the other side."

"I dunno, Bri, even though I'm not sure there is a God…"

Heaven is just a different frequency from here on earth. What's cool is everyone on the other side is about thirty years old because thirty is the perfect age."

"Really—thirty, huh?"

Today Brian was feeling good about who he was. "I also keep an open mind to everything I read, and then I make my own decisions on what I think is right and good. You got to question, man, and make your own deductions, you know?"

"So is everyone physically beautiful on the other side?" Johnny searched.

"We all have flaws, but I think the most beautiful have acquired great knowledge and insights. That's probably why we put so much emphasis on beauty here on earth. The only difference is beauty here on earth certainly doesn't mean they are full of information and insights; actually I think it means the opposite." He smirked. "Look at Tori for example."

Johnny laughed. "Yeah, but—" He gave him a crooked grin.

"All right, all kidding aside—your mom—I'm sure she is drop-dead gorgeous on the other side."

"Maybe ya right on that one, bro. So then why are there so many religions? Ya know, each says they're the chosen people."

"Well, I think we should respect every religion's customs that speak of love, truth, and goodness. Just like all people are different and do things differently, so is each person's ideal of God and even God's image. There is a common thread in life that binds all of humanity together. The universe knows there is never only one right way to do something or to believe in something.

"If you know so much, tell me why I see people's eyes melt and then they die, and why didn't I see that with my mom?"

"Seth told me about Mr. Jacobs," Brian replied, "and with your mom, maybe it's because you can't see those you have a personal connection to. It always seems to work that way. You never get to see everything."

Johnny's silence threw an awkward surge into Brian's chest. Finally, he spoke. "Bri, I'm not gonna make it in here; they're gonna try me as an adult."

"Johnny, ask God for help."

"Why would He listen to me? Yo, I've said I don't believe in him anymore."

"All you have to do is ask. He stands in the shadows until you call Him. He'll never let you go through more than you can handle, just ask, k?"

"Sure, bro, I'll ask, considerin' how much time I have on my hands."

"Hey, just be patient and listen."

The door to the room opened. "Times up." The officer motioned to Brian.

"You mean there's a time limit? Damn it, Seth and Dadia are waiting outside to see you! And, oh, my God, Johnny, Dadia, she's—"

"Sorry, son, time's up. They'll have to come back tomorrow." He hastened Johnny out of the room.

"Hey, I'll always be here for you, bro," were the last words Brian hoped Johnny heard.

44

IN THE BARREN ROOM, HE sat. The cold of the bench felt like a block of ice through his clothing, but he had endured worse than that. While he studied the bumps in the wall, he realized there was nothing he could ever possess except his own thoughts, and he had many. *Where was his so-called dad?* If he ever had a son, he would be there for him, at least by now.

Where was he? Maybe his father decided to let him rot in a cell for a while to teach him some lesson or maybe he was celebrating with Mr. Daniels again. That seemed to be his father's answer to all his problems. But in the last five years, nothing had gotten better, and everything just got worse. It was only a mask. He now realized his father's problems weren't solved with alcohol. *Why did he think he could solve his own problems with the same fruit?*

What was up with Brian? He just spewed his guts out to him in the visitors' room. Maybe he needed to listen to Brian and stop living in the past.

Forget the "because-that's-just-the-way-it-is" world and live in the "why-is-it-so?" world. *Why didn't he question more?* Anyone who did anything great questioned. If he had done some investigative work, he might have found his mom. Instead, he, like his dad, lived in his own pity. If there was a God, He gave the world pity to give away to others, for self-inflicted pity could only lead to one thing: self-destruction.

45

"BRI, YOU SAID YOU JUST wanted a few minutes alone, to thank him. What the hell did you talk to Johnny about, and what you mean we can't get in to see him now?!"

"I know. I'm sorry. We just got—I mean, I just got—carried away, and I didn't know there was a time limit. And hey, he saved my life."

Seth shook his head, sighed, and looked at Dadia. "Little brothers, huh."

Walking in the lobby of the police station, Brian couldn't read Dadia's thoughts. Were they of sympathy or disgust? *Damn you Seth,* he thought. *What the hell happened to our earlier bro-to-bro conversation?* It was just like his brother.

"Mr. Styvers!" Seth's eye caught Johnny's dad walking in with two police officers. "Mr. Styvers!" he shouted. "Mr. Styvers!" he shouted again.

"I'm sorry, kids; you can't talk to Mr. Styvers." One of the officers stayed behind as they walked Johnny's father through the security door.

"But why?" Seth questioned.

"He is in the process of making a confession."

Now the three of them were confused. "I don't get it. All three of us," Brian firmly stated, as he looked to Dadia for her unselfish conviction to tell the truth, "gave our statements of what happened Saturday night. None of us saw Mr. Styvers, none of us."

"We need to find Mr. Manteria," Dadia said.

"Wait," Seth said. He walked over to the police officer behind the main desk, and they spoke. The officer picked up the phone, speaking to someone on the other line, and then relayed something back to Seth.

"What did he say?" Brian asked.

"The detective said they're keeping Johnny here until they can confirm his father's story. Then they will determine if he is to be tried as an adult or a juvenile. So he'll either go to the juvenile detention center in Harrier or Rockledge
Correctional Facility."

"Is that normal procedure?" Dadia asked. "I was surprised they were going to let us all talk to Johnny. Maybe they made a mistake, after realizing they let Brian in to see him."

"I don't know, but this gives us more time to figure out this mess. Come on, Mr. Manteria is on his way back to your house Dadia. Let's go see how your mom is."

"You don't believe Mr. Styvers killed Larry, do you?" Brian asked Seth.

"I don't know, Bri. I've been in the same room with Mr. Styvers recently. He's a real mess, man."

46

"I'M SORRY, SON; THEY DIDN'T believe an ol' drunkard could kill a strong, young boy like Larry Jones. My story wasn't bulletproof. I guess quick thinkin' isn't as easy as building a house."

He called him son, not boy. Johnny wasn't sure what to make of it.

"That's OK, but why did ya try to take the rap for something I didn't do? Ya don't think I killed Larry, do ya?"

"No, no, I'm sorry." His father closed his eyes. "I haven't been much of a dad since your mom disappeared. I drowned myself in pity."

"Well, it was a little more than just that, Dad, but it's all right. But ya really do need to get some help."

"I know. I've talked to an ol' friend here at the station. He's gonna help me get things straightened out."

Johnny looked pensive. "Someone is framing me, and I don't know why."

"You be strong now, ya hear? I still have a few—well, one—friend in this world. I promise ya, we'll get to the bottom of this."

"Thanks, Dad." He kept calling him *Dad,* and he didn't know why.

"Your mom was right, ya know, as always. I should a listened to her. It was my fault. I let my stubborn pride get in the way. She was an orphan and found she had family somewhere and was determined to find them. I wanted her to myself. Someone gave her up, and I didn't want to share her with strangers." His dad's eyes glazed up. "If I helped and stood beside her, maybe none of this would have happened."

"You mean it wasn't because of me, the night she stormed out of the house and disappeared?"

"You? Why would you think that?"

"Well, you guys were fighting, and I heard my name. Afterward, you wouldn't even talk to me about mom. What else would I think?"

His father gave him a solemn look. "Ya had nothing to do with it. Your mother loved you more than life itself." Johnny squirmed in his chair as his fingers pushed against the cement bumps on the wall. His dad continued, "John, you have an aunt and a cousin. They were in the dark, too. I'm just so sorry ya mother didn't live long enough to find out the truth."

"No way, I have an aunt? A cousin?" he asked in wonderment.

"Their name is Paola—Katie and her daughter, Dadia. What? Do ya know them?"

47

THE COURT BAILIFF SPOKE. "ALL rise; court is now in session, the Honorable Judge Hammond presiding." Judge Hammond entered through a side door leading to the bench. Fixing his robe, he patted his head as if he still had hair and sat down looking into the courtroom over the top of his wire-rimmed glasses. Dadia looked to Johnny and caught his eye. He looked away from her. She contemplated his reaction.

Somehow, someone somewhere had decided Johnny was to be tried as an adult instead of a juvenile. Weeks away from his eighteenth birthday, he knew money had to play in this decision—money from the Foundation. His attorney gave him Hobson's choice: plead guilty, for if you plead innocent, you will still be proven guilty. He had the choice of taking the prosecutor's offer, a guilty plea giving him a lighter sentence, or nothing at all. *What were his odds of being deemed innocent?* He was the fall guy for someone. Only his friends and his father believed him. *His attorney, exactly whose side was he on?* Pleading guilty would only prove one thing—in death, Larry had the upper hand. There was only one thing to do.

So far, the prosecutor was in the lead with Grand Numen Jack Jones and the Foundation behind him with all their money and power. Johnny was going down for the murder of his son, Larry Jones. As the trial proceeded, Johnny feared the worst.

The prosecutor stood up and tightened the knot of his Oscar de la Renta tie, and sauntered over to the bench. His body swayed right to left while the eyelets on his jacket strained to hold the buttons in place.

"The court calls Mr. Robert Halley to the stand."

Mr. Halley came in from the outer hallway. Dadia gasped for air. She bent down, pretending to have dropped something, and quickly scurried out of the courtroom in hopes of being undetected. Brian waited and then quietly followed her out. Seth observed her strange response and exit of the courtroom, then honed in on Mr. Halley sitting on the witness stand with a curious intensity.

"Please tell the court, Mr. Halley, where you were on the night of October fifteenth."

"I left work around six thirty p.m. to run some errands with my wife. I came back around eleven forty-five p.m. and spent the rest of the evening in my office until Mike finished closing up."

"Mike?"

"Yes, yes, my employee, Mike Johnson."

With a questioning look from the onset of hearing his name aloud, Mike Johnson perked up and cleared his throat. *Did Mr. Halley just state he was in his office, working?*

Seth looked over to catch Mike's reaction to Mr. Halley's statement.

"Mr. Halley, have you ever seen this knife?" Mr. Halley looked carefully at the weapon.

"Yes, yes, I have," he stated, "when I hired the defendant." He pointed at Johnny. "In my office he pulled out papers from his back pocket, and they fell onto the floor. When he bent over to pick them up, the knife fell out of his jacket. I told him that no weapons were allowed in the store."

"And what was his reply?"

"He said he always carried a knife, but he would not bring it to work again. Um, yes, yes, I was satisfied with that."

Seth looked to Johnny. Johnny sat there, shaking his head back and forth, talking to himself under his breath.

"Your honor, please put into evidence Exhibit A, this knife, the one Johnny Styvers fingerprints are on—the same knife Mr. Halley, his boss, saw in Johnny's possession the day he interviewed him for a job at the Fast N Easy Convenience Store." The prosecutor looked to the jury. "No further questions, your honor."

Johnny's attorney, dressed as if he were on the cover of *GQ*, pushed his chair back and walked over to where Mr. Halley sat on the stand. Putting his index finger over his lips, pointing to his nose, he hesitated, in deep contemplation.

"Mr. Halley, now how can you be sure this particular knife is the one Johnny Styvers dropped in your office at the Fast N Easy?"

"See the wood grain of the handle? It's unique, looks like an eye, and the tiny chip at the end of the blade? Yes, yes, his knife had the same exact wood grain and chip, sir."

"No further questions, your honor."

Johnny looked at him with disbelief. "Yo, he's a frickin' liar!" he yelled, pointing to Mr. Halley. "Anyone could say that!"

Judge Hammond cracked his gavel sternly, looking over his glasses at Johnny. "Order in the court! Keep your client under control, or I will put you in contempt!" He looked to Mr. Halley and smiled, "You may step down, Mr. Halley."

Getting up, Mr. Halley fidgeted with his glasses, walking toward the courtroom doors, while he pulled out of his pocket a piece of gum. Fumbling it, the wrapper dropped to the ground. The sweet scent of cotton candy seeped into the air. Seth watched Mr. Halley bend down to pick up the wrapper. There behind the man's right ear, Seth saw a tat, just like the one Larry, Rob at Ashley's party, and for that matter, Ashley Wentworth herself, had. He watched him drop the paper into the garbage can next to the door and then push through the courtroom doors. Seth scanned the courtroom.

Mike Johnson caught on to Seth's intensity as Seth nonchalantly pulled out of his pocket a tissue and made his way over to the garbage can by the door—the same one Mr. Halley just used. Missing the tissue into the garbage can, he bent down to pick it up. Seth gently placed his hand in the can, holding a tissue to disguise the fact he was picking up the wrapper and slid out the courtroom doors.

Seth hastened down the hallowed hallway of the courthouse, looking to find Mr. Manteria. They were going to burry Johnny and leave him to rot in jail. Seth needed to do more detective work on his own. His father always said, "You want something done right, do it yourself." Behind him, Mike Johnson followed.

"Hey, Seth Kogan, wait up. I think I might be able to help you."

Seth turned, "You're Mike, Mike Johnson?" Mike nodded yes. "Actually Mike, I think you can. Johnny told me you live in Harrier, right?"

"Yeah, I do."

"I bet you know Harrier like the back of your hand."

"Ask, and I'll take you wherever you want to go."

48

JOHNNY FIDGETED IN HIS SEAT. The trial continued to progress, and they were going to pin this on him—he just knew it. His fate would be sealed in Larry's blood. The juror's faces believed every twist of words and statements made by the prosecutor against him. Larry was being made out to be some sort of hero—A+ student, lacrosse team captain, goody two shoes—and he, Johnny Styvers, a school truant, criminal with a long list of dirty deeds with an alcoholic father and an absent mother.

The prosecutor stood up. "Your honor, the court calls Ashley Wentworth to the stand."

Larry's grandfather, Darius Jones, and his son, Grand Numen Jones, smiled watching Ashley pledge her oath of truth. She was a loyal vassal. She and Larry had a thing for each other. She would seal Johnny's fate with her testimony and relinquish their grandson/son to heaven, and God's justice would be done.

"Ms. Wentworth, how long have you known the deceased, Larry Jones?"

"Well, I met him about a year ago, at the mall one night."

"And what type of relationship would you say you shared with him?"

Ashley looked first at Mr. Halley, Grand Numen Jones, and then to Johnny. *That was it,* Johnny thought. *This was the prosecutor's silver bullet, wooden stake. Ashley was part of the Foundation. It was her party that night, and she was a servant of the club. She was going to protect Larry. She was going to protect the organization.*

"Larry and I were instant friends. He invited me to his father Grand Numen Jones's center over in Rolling Hills. Before ya knew it, I was hooked and became a member. We did everything together."

"What type of person would you say Larry was?"

"A kind, outgoing guy." She paused, and a tear ran down her cheek. "I loved him dearly."

"No more questions, your honor."

Johnny's attorney stood up to cross-examine. "Ms. Wentworth, please, state what transpired the night of October fifteenth, the night Larry Jones was murdered."

"The night Larry died, my parents were away, and I opted to allow the Foundation to come into my home and host a recruiting party."

"A recruiting party? The court would like you to please elaborate, Ms. Wentworth."

"Well, the Foundation Club is for young adults, ages sixteen to twenty-eight. I met Larry at the mall one day, and we hit it off. He told me all about the Foundation his father ran, and he invited me to become a member of the club. After going through the initiation and swearing oath to the club, I received the coveted mark."

"A mark?"

"Yes, it's like a small tat—tattoo—behind your ear. It binds ya to the club and all other members for life. You become family." Ashley hesitated, "It's always been a loving club." Tears welled up in her eyes. "But recently, these things they make you do…I realized are not always good or loving things."

"Objection!"

"Council," Judge Hammond stated, "get to the point."

"Ms. Wentworth, please state your encounter with Larry Jones the night of October fifteenth.

Ashley continued, not listening, "I have come to realize that it is a manipulative club to do the dirty work of the elders and has nothing to do with the 'love one another' they preach."

"Objection, your honor! We are getting away from the facts of this case," shrieked the prosecutor.

"Strike that from the records," Judge Hammond instructed the court stenographer, a silver-haired woman who typed every word said. He looked to the jury. "Strike the last statement of Ms. Wentworth from your ears."

Larry's dad, Grand Numen Jack Jones, appeared agitated as he tensed in his seat. Mr. Halley grabbed a handkerchief from his pocket to clean his glasses.

"Ms. Wentworth, please, back to the night of October fifteenth and Larry Jones."

"I have video evidence that Mr. Halley, also known at the Foundation as GP drugged my best friend, Dadia Paola, with intent to harm her. Seth Kogan helped get Dadia out of my house away from him to take her home."

"Objection!" the prosecutor shouted.

"Overruled." The judge looked at him hard. "Continue on, dear; now I am intrigued."

"I found GP, I mean Mr. Halley, and told him to get the hell out of my house. I was going back to the cabana to tell Johnny, the accused, that the party was over, but he was gone. I heard a commotion from the woods and got my pistol from the cabana and went to investigate."

"You own a gun, Ms. Wentworth?"

"Yes, well, not exactly, it's in my dad's name, but it's mine. I've had it since I was young. My dad and I use to go to the shooting range over in Park View. I've won many shooting contests in my time," she said smugly. Her head stayed perfectly still, while her eyes meandered to Johnny. Johnny's mouth opened in excitement. She smiled then quickly focused back to the court. "So I go to see what the commotion is about."

"Were you scared?"

"Of course I was, but then again, I love the adrenaline that comes with it like when you're a little kid and you're getting ready to fall asleep and you hear a noise. Ya just know it came from under your bed, but you lay there stiff, telling yourself nothing's down there. You're scared out of your mind that if you look, it will mutilate ya. But something pushes at your brain, and you finally can't take it any longer. Ya brain is ready to burst, and ya stick ya head in harm's way." Ashley shrugged. "Only to find harmless little dust bunnies."

"Anyways, I heard a shot go off. I climb up the ridge to see a body lying on the ground, but can't make out who it is. Larry and Johnny are there. Larry was flicking a whip and, Johnny had a knife. They're both lookin' at each other in shock after hearing the shot. Johnny drops the knife, and they both bolt in opposite directions. I don't make a move. I stay hidden. All of a sudden, Larry is walking back with GP and Robert from the Foundation. They go over to the body lying on the ground. It's Frank Halley, GP's son."

"GP, as in Mr. Halley, and on the ground his son, Frank Halley." Johnny's attorney stated for clarity.

"Yes. GP, Mr. Halley, tells Robert to pick up Frank. In the meantime, out of his pocket, GP gets one of those old-fashioned tissues—ya know, the kind ya grandpa blows his nose in and then puts back in his pocket," she said with a wince.

"Ms. Wentworth, what does Mr. Halley do with this cloth?"

"He goes over and picks up the knife with it."

"Then what happened?"

Ashley looked to the back of the courtroom. In the shadows against the wall, her father gave her an approving nod. "GP, Mr. Halley, leaves with Larry, and Robert picks up Frank and carries him away. Before I can get back to the hedgerow of my property, I get the feeling someone or something is there and watching me. I turn, hoping it's my cat Pumpkin. Pumpkin is always sneaking up on me, sometimes scaring me to death! But it wasn't. But whom do I see in the distance? Elgin," she said with a smile.

"And who is Elgin, Ms. Wentworth?"

"He's a Mountain Crag, who lives up on the ridge. He nodded to me, and I nodded back. I kinda thought he was the one who fired the shot. He had his rifle in his hand."

"Do you know this Mountain Crag personally?"

"Well, sort of. They have lived up in the mountains for as long as we have lived in our house. They are a quiet people, never bothering anyone. When I was little, I would go play in the woods. He would be there, and we'd play hide-and-seek. He spelled his name in the dirt for me once. He never spoke a word, at least not to me. Maybe they're not allowed to talk to girls." She gave Johnny a look.

"So you are saying that Larry Jones did not leave with Johnny Styvers, but he left with Mr. Halley? And Robert left with Mr. Halley's son Frank?"

"Yes. That's all I know. I went back to the house, and everyone was leaving or left. I then called my daddy, knowing I should never have had a party to begin with."

"No more questions." The defense attorney looked to the jury, gave a small nod, and proceeded back to his seat.

The prosecutor now stood up. "Your honor, I have a few more questions for Ms. Wentworth."

"You may proceed," said Judge Hammond.

The prosecutor walked over to the jury stand and scanned each juror with his eyes. He then turned to Ashley, "Ms. Wentworth, now what time was it when you found yourself in the woods with a gun? And are you sure the gunfire was not from your gun? If you and your father were in a gun club, would you not have more than one gun?"

"Objection!" the defense attorney blurted out.

"Objection overruled," stated Judge Hammond. "Just answer the questions, Ms. Wentworth."

Ashley looked over to the jurors and scanned the

courtroom. "As a matter of fact, yes, my father and I have a collection of guns ranging from Beretta pistols, like the 3032 Tomcat to a Ruger 10 22 auto-loading rifle and of course my all-time favorite, a 1965 Charles Daly side-by-side shotgun. But on the night of question, it was a Smith and Wesson Model 41 pistol that was in my possession. Now the Smith and Wesson when discharged throws out a sound of a short crack, or ya could say, a loud pop, like a firecracker. Small and stylish, I might add. But that night a shotgun was heard."

"And how can you be so certain of this, young lady?" the prosecutor questioned.

"Well, a shotgun has a distinctive sound; it's a deeper, fuller sound. The sound that night—definitely a shotgun. Yeah, I'm sure because I could hear the pellets fall through the leaves of the trees." Ashley looked down to the right. "And since we're asking questions, I have one. Why are we worried about the sound of a gun going off? Wasn't Larry killed with a knife?"

"Are we done with this witness?" Judge Hammond asked. The prosecutor conceded. "You may step down, dear."

Ashley walked past her friends. They were all smiling. She looked to where Grand Numen Jones and Mr. Halley sat. Her father now stood in front of them, protecting her from their evil eyes. She walked through the courtroom doors to hesitate ever so slightly with a cock of her head, sending Johnny a small d grin.

Judge Hammond announced, "Court is adjourned. We will reconvene tomorrow morning at nine a.m."

49

"YOUR HONOR," JOHNNY'S ATTORNEY SAID, "I call to the stand, Elgin Von Craig."

From the back of the courtroom, Seth held the door. Elgin Von Craig entered dressed in a jacket two sizes his width and height. With each step Elgin bounced his upper torso in a slow and rhythmic pace.

"So, Elgin, where do you live?" Johnny's attorney asked.

"I live up the mountain in Rolling Hills, sir."

"Up the mountain?"

"Yup, with my pops, Myron, and our families."

"So, you live up the mountain. Directly behind the Wentworth property?"

"Yes um, sir."

"Elgin, please tell the jury what you were doing on the night of October fifteenth."

"Well, sir, I was curious that night, seein' light down by the Wentworth house. As I walked down, I start hearin' lots a noise and commotion. It was rather odd, sir, it's a quiet place. But that night it was lit up like a beacon!"

"And what did you do when you got closer?"

"Welp, bubby waz wit me, and we walked down closer toward the house, makin' sure my friend Ashley was OK."

"Your friend, Ashley? As in Wentworth?" Elgin nodded yes. "And your bubby? Who might that be?"

"Oh bubby, yup, that's my protector up the mountain, for huntin' an' such. It's my Winchester side by side. Best bubby a guy could ever have. Sleep wit her, I do."

"So you went to investigate the Wentworth home with a rifle," stated the defense attorney.

"Yup, an' as I waz walkin' down the hill I see a dim glow an' hear a chanting, like somethin' just ain't right. Soz I go in nice an' easy. What'da I see? Two guys hoverin' over a third, tauntin' him. I hold up, waitin' to see what they're up ta. Like a deer spooked, a fourth guy comes jumping outta the trees! I recognize him by his silhouette. I'm good at that, sightin' things, my pop's always said, and it's the guy sittin' over there." Elgin pointed to Johnny. "He grabs one guy and gets his knife away from em. Crazy crap, I'd say. This jumpa guy gets things under control an' frees the poor fella on the ground and screams to the fella, 'Run! Run!' That's when I decided to let bubby take over. One loud burst an' bubby got em *all* runnin', I'd say."

"No more questions, your honor."

The prosecutor jumped up. "Mr. Von Craig, how do you know for certain the person in the woods that night who jumped out from the trees was, in fact, the man sitting over there?" He pointed to Johnny.

"Yup, now most folk ain't very friendly toward me or my clan, but I sees I already met him, down in Harrier, sir. Over at the deli. We'da had some nice conversation about carvin' n such. I can tell bout peoples, sir, an' he'da trustin' fella."

"So, you had conversations with Johnny Styvers over at a deli in Harrier. How do we know you were not in on this, a coconspirator?" the prosecutor accused.

"A co what?" Elgin looked with question, "Sir, did ya say his last name is Styvers?

"Yes, son," Judge Hammond injected.

Elgin started to flail his hands as he reached for something in his jacket. His eyes started to well up with tears. "Ya honor, sir," he said, "May I ask him, 'how is ya momma? Momma Styvers? Is she all right?'" He looked to Johnny as a tear rolled down his cheek.

Johnny looked at him holding back the tears.

50

"ORDER! ORDER IN THE COURT!" The Honorable Judge Hammond demanded.

Elgin wasn't sure what just happened. He nervously pulled out of his jacket the ornate box he was protecting.

"Ya honor, sir," he said, "sir, this, this box, ya see. Momma Styvers talked in her sleep when she first came to us. An I'ma good listen a soz I found it, dug it up one night. I has been protectin' it eva since; hid it up the mountain, I did." Elgin handed Judge Hammond the box.

"Objection, your honor, what does this have to do with the case?" the prosecutor balked.

"Overruled!"

"Let the boy speak, councilman; let him speak." Judge Hammond was intrigued. He never dreamed a Craig from the mountain would ever step foot in a court of law. They had their own society that ran back to the 1800s. He had no jurisdiction on their property, and now this young man, here, in his courtroom, wanting to talk. He wanted to hear what this boy had to say.

"Do you know what is inside this box?" Judge Hammond studied the intricate woodwork.

Elgin looked at Johnny. "Well, ya honor, sir, this box belongs to the Styvers's kinfolk. She said it possessed treasure, sir—freein' treasure. And being I just met kinfolk of hers here in this courtroom, I figured it be safe to bring it out, an' you'd make sure it got to her kin, sir."

"So, son, do you or do you not know what is inside the box?"

"Objection!" the prosecutor balked.

"Overruled."

"Well, no, sir, I wouldn't dream of openin' it and don't rightly have the key, but this box, my pops sez, he made for this gal, Stella Thesdus. She came to him one day, many years ago, when he was a young'un, little older than me now, sir, with Ms. Rosemary, she's one of our heroes up the mountain. Ms. Rosemary owned an Antique store in Harrier where we use to sell stuff. Ya know, Ms. Rosemary said the gal wanted two boxes, identical like the gal's baby daughters, pops said, and swan fobs, identical ones, too, for all. He told me she was very young an' scared. Soz he made the boxes carved out a wood an' etched the swans out a Lucite from scraps from the DuPont plant. My pops, he taught me, too." Elgin pulled out of his pocket a Lucite square, etched with a bear in the forest, and handed it to Judge Hammond.

Judge Hammond eyed the box, the Lucite bear, and then looked out to the courtroom. Darius Jones seemed on edge, Grand Numen Jones, too.

"Well," Judge Hammond summoned Johnny's attorney to approach the bench. "Councilman, please secure this box on your clients behalf."

"So son, how did Mrs. Styvers get a hold of this box?"

"Well, sir, I found her in the woods, left for dead. Brought her back to our kinfolk, and we took care of her."

"How long ago was that?"

"Bout five years, I think. She was real bad and only recently did she remember even who she was." Elgin held his head low and closed his eyes. "Sir, may I go home now?"

"You may step down; thank you, Mr. Von Craig."

The prosecutor declined a cross-examination.

As Elgin started to exit the courtroom, Johnny stood

up, grabbed, and hugged him tightly. He whispered in Elgin's ear, "Yo, thanks, man, for lookin' out for my mom; you're my blood, foreva." His attorney pried him away and escorted him back to his seat.

Dressed in police blues, Mr. Manteria came through the courtroom doors, walked right up to Johnny's attorney, and handed him two envelopes.

"Council, let us now continue on," Judge Hammond said.

Johnny's attorney stood up. "The court calls back Mr. Robert Halley."

Mr. Halley, looking not as confident to be returning to the stand, was reminded he was still under oath and sat down.

"Mr. Halley," the defense attorney said, "you said previously that on the night Larry Jones was stabbed, you left work around six thirty p.m. to run some errands with your wife. You came back to the Fast N Easy around eleven forty-five p.m. and spent the rest of the evening in your office until Mike Johnson, your employee, finished closing up."

"Um, yes, yes," Mr. Halley stated. He eyed Grand Numen Jones and Darius.

"Mr. Halley, I see you are a big gum chewer," the attorney said, noticing the man's jaw moving, chewing something. "May I ask what type of gum you chew?"

"Bubble gum," he replied.

"Bubble gum," the defense attorney restated.

"Objection, your honor, this is irrelevant to this case," the prosecutor injected.

"Council, get to the point," Judge Hammond warned.

"Yes, your honor. Mr. Halley, is there one flavor you chew? Or several?"

Mr. Halley looked at Johnny's attorney. "Um, cotton-candy flavor, yes, yes." He spoke in a slow, low voice.

"Mr. Halley, your son is Frank Halley, correct?" Mr. Halley nodded yes. "And he works for the Foundation over in Rolling Hills, correct?" Mr. Halley nodded yes again. "And isn't Frank, your son, the same age as Larry Jones? Isn't he friends with Larry Jones, and worked under Larry Jones at the Foundation? And you, Mr. Halley, sit on the board of directors over at the Foundation?"

"Yes, yes." Mr. Halley looked to him with question.

Johnny's attorney went back to his table and picked up one of the envelopes. "Your honor, in this envelope is the knife, Exhibit A, which was previously put into evidence. Now, Mr. Halley, please look again at this knife. Is this the knife you saw in Johnny Styvers possession?"

"Um, yes, yes, most definitely it was."

"Your honor, I would like to put into evidence, Exhibit B, the chip to this knife blade, which has recently been recovered inside the body of a woman. You can see by the forensic photograph the chip completes the blade." He handed Judge Hammond the photo who, in turn, gave it to the prosecutor to examine.

"Your honor and the jury of the court, Mr. Halley's actions the night of Larry Jones's death came out of jealousy of Larry's position within the Foundation. Mr. Halley felt his son, Frank, should have that position. Mr. Halley was with his wife the night of the Larry's death, and, in fact, Mr. and Mrs. Halley were both at the Wentworth house that same night. Larry Jones went to that party with Frank Halley and had an altercation in the woods. It was Mr. Halley that cleaned up Larry and Frank's bad behavior, as stated by Ms. Wentworth in a previous statement. And the knife, Exhibit A, was, in fact, first owned by Grand Numen Jones and then owned by Mr. Halley!"

"Objection! All hearsay! Where is this proof?"

"Councilman, you are treading on thin ice; please get to the point."

"Mr. Halley went to the woods to clean up Larry and Frank's altercation as stated previously by Ms. Wentworth's statement. He then picked up the knife lying on the ground, the knife that *he* had given to *his* son, Frank, the knife that *he* was seen holding up as a trophy in this picture with Grand Numen Jones of the Foundation many years ago. I would like to place into evidence, Exhibit C, a picture of Mr. Halley at a Foundation party, receiving this knife from Grand Numen Jones. Please note, if you look hard enough, you can see the wood grain in the handle and a chip in the tip of the blade—the same markings as Exhibit A, the murder weapon.

"Mr. Halley had the deliberate intention of framing Johnny Styvers with a murder that would take place later that night. The murder he would mastermind of none other than the one person in the way of his son, Frank, from becoming a leader at the Foundation: Larry Jones.

"*Objection!* And where did this image miraculously appear from, and who's to say it is his knife?" the prosecutor yelled.

"Overruled. Council, I hope you have complete proof of all your accusations."

"Oh, I do, your honor. Mr. Halley would have gotten away with this murder if he didn't have one of many obsessions, an obsession for gum. I would like to put into evidence these two wrappers of bubble gum that I have just received as Exhibit D. Forensics has placed Mr. Halley at two different points during the crime with his fingerprint on two different wrappers of bubble gum— both cotton candy flavored—one found behind the strip mall on Russell Avenue near the murder weapon *and* at the origin of the altercation in the woods at the Wentworth Estate." The defense attorney continued, "Not only was Larry Jones killed with this knife, but the chip that fits its blade was found in the body of a woman in an attempted murder five years ago—the attempted murder of Hanna Styvers, by none other than Grand Numen Jones, who left her up the mountain five years ago to die! A witness to that night has just come forward, your honor."

Darius Jones looked to his son Jack, then to Halley.

In a rage, he yelled, shaking his feeble hands and lunged toward them. "You no good son of a bitch! How dare you kill my grandson, Larry, only to blame it on my other grandson, Johnny! And you…" He spit in rage as he held his son, Grand Numen Jones, in contempt. "So it was you? How could you kill my daughter, Hanna, one of your stepsisters? And what about my Stella's death? An accident? Did you kill her too?"

Johnny quickly twisted around. *What did he say?*

Grand Numen Jones stood tall over his father in a rage of fire. "How dare you, Father! To do that to my mother and me? I was only fifteen then; Stella was barely twenty. It was no secret; we all knew! Mother and I took your bad judgment into our own hands and took care of it for the protection of the Foundation!"

"Order! Order!" Judge Hammond cracked his gavel. The bailiff and two security guards immediately grabbed Darius Jones, handcuffed his son and Mr. Halley, and took all three out of the courtroom.

Seth looked over to Johnny with a priggish grin.

51

STELLA'S BLOG - by KATIE PAOLA

"I ONCE KNEW THIS GUY who had a heart big as a mountain, that if you stood on top of it, you could feel the heavens above. Whenever asked for his assistance, he (through his giving heart) helped all. Even those whom he'd happen upon—he could see their strife and lend a hand unconditionally. I so admired him. When asked why he always extended his heart, he said it just felt good inside, to see something better for another. To me, he possessed a perfect heart—though, he was not perfect.

I never played with his heart. I only spoke to it as anyone who cared would. I assume he felt I had deceived him in some way by not revealing my true being. I am truly sorry for that, but in the same breath, would he have opened up to me the way he did? For I think I helped, instead of harmed.

Fear is something that makes humans do strange things. Maybe my fear came from my past that crept into my future. But now I have realized that the only way to deal with fear is to face it head on and to conquer it. I never wanted things to end the way they did.

I too wanted to know the truth and to find a family I never knew. I'm afraid I've lost my only hope of family ties by my means of finding it.

I know this guy, who still has a heart big as a mountain, that if u stood on top of it, you could feel the heavens above. May his heart one day realize that sometimes things must be kept hidden until the moment in time they may be revealed.

In finding forgiveness for others, we find our greatest strength. I hope you can forgive me."

Keep thy heart with all diligence, for out of it are the issues of life ~
Proverbs 4:23

52

BRIAN SAT ON A PARK BENCH, watching the night air sparkle the water on the pond, borrowing the light of the moon's beam. It was a nice park with a nice little swimming pond. Recently, he had made this pilgrimage many times from Park View. Walking was something new to him, and each day seemed to bring him more energy than the last. Actually walking with his mp3 player had become very therapeutic. It helped clear his thoughts and put things into perspective. He grew two inches over the span of a few months, and his keg had shrunk to a small beer ball, slowly showing signs of a one pack.

Balance, he realized, was the key to life, especially between the physical and inactive. Many things had changed. Stella (Mrs. Paola) stopped writing her blog. And he missed it, for writing made it easier to share thoughts and feelings than face to face, at least for him. However, now he spent more time off the computer than on. The kids at school found a new outlook for Brian Kogan. He was now some sort of hero that wielded a pen instead of a sword, and a few kids forming bands wanted him to write lyrics for them. He looked forward to that endeavor.

Looking out in the darkness, he closed his eyes to concentrate on reliving the good parts of that night so long ago in the park—the parts where he held her, watched over her, and imagined their first real kiss. It was a good feeling, especially the one he knew only in his dreams. He wanted it again and wondered if it were better to have loved and lost or only to dream of love and never find it. For the pain of having it, then never to partake in it again, seemed so much more oppressive to live with.

When the night turned, he felt a chill up his spine as fall was coming back from its hiatus. Time had gone by quickly, and he bumped into her occasionally, here and there after the trial, with never more than the short, expected, "Hello, how are you?"

Looking up to the heavens, the sky tried to hide its deep darkness against the bright white of the stars. *There, the Big Dipper.* He smiled. That and the Little Dipper were the only two constellations he could find, and he was in awe each time he connected with them. Even the nights where darkness blanketed the sky, his faith in the Big and Little Dippers told him differently. Maybe that was what Einstein saw when he had looked to the heavens, for the more he studied the universe, the more he believed in a greater power.

As the night fell into perfection, he found himself enjoying the tranquility of it as he sat and pondered. Feeling the air kick up and rustle the leaves above, they motioned it was time to start getting back home. Enjoying the last few minutes of serenity a voice from behind seemed to whisper "hey" to him. He dismissed it until he thought he heard it again. Turning, he saw her.

"Hey," he said, hoping his thoughts wouldn't betray him. The whole girl thing still perplexed him.

"I'm surprised to see you here. Did you come in a car?" Dadia looked through the barren parking lot.

"Nah, I walked. It was a nice night.

She gave a look of approval.

"And what are you doing here? You shouldn't be out in the park alone at night," he said.

"I came with a friend."

He scanned around with question.

Out of her pocket, she pulled out a container of mace

and smiled. "Recently, I started walking here a lot. It just makes me feel better since Ashley went away."

He nodded understanding her feelings. "Any word on when she'll be back?"

"No, seems she's studying over in Japan now while her dad is there."

"What about her house?"

"Oh, I'm sure they will keep it for the day they return to Mountain Crest."

"Oh," he said, finding himself rhythmically swaying his legs back and forth as he sat on the bench. She sat beside him and followed his lead. He eyed her hand on the bench, palm side down, supporting her weight as she swayed, looking into the darkness of the night. He fought his own hand itching to move near hers. He copied her stance and decided to allow his hand to be in a slight proximity to hers, which was close enough.

"How's your mom doing? You know, if it matters at all, I still think she's great. You're lucky to have her," he said.

"She's doing all right. She has her moments. It hurts her that Johnny wants nothing to do with us. We have no other family." She paused and bit her lower lip. "It would have been nice if things were different. She really thought she was doing something good, helping. You know, like Mother Teresa's saying, 'Do small things with great love'? Well, that's my mom."

"Dadia, she did. She helped me so much. I love her for that."

"I think she knows. She loves you too. All's I have to do is mention your name, and she smiles. But— you know."

"Yeah," he said. *Wait*, he thought, *what did she say? She talked about him?* He felt a pinhead's chance of hope deep within then discarded it.

"So, can you say what happened with your grandmother's urn? The day she opened it up, what did your mom find?"

Dadia looked at him. "Oh, my God, there was a note from Stella—her mom—inside the urn. She told her about Ms. Rosemary Little and she had a sister Hanna and how scared she was. It was quite disconcerting."

"Why's that?"

"Because if she had really read Ms. Rosemary's note that told her to find her comfort within her mother's urn, if she had then opened it up, she could have found her sister years ago."

"She can't blame herself for that."

"I know—but sometimes you can't help the way you feel, no matter how hard you try." She bit her lip. "I think time will help heal a lot of things for her. Like it has with me."

Her legs stopped swaying, and she became very still. She looked out to the pond.

"I see Seth has been talking to your friend Stephanie,"
he mentioned.

"Yes, I could see them making a great couple," she replied. "Brian, I need to tell you something. This is difficult for me."

Brian knew what was coming. How she could only be friends with him. She could never think of him that way. He sat quietly waiting for the New Year's Eve ball to drop.

"A few years ago, before we moved here, something bad happened to me. It made me always on guard and very confused." She knew once he knew the truth, well, damaged goods never sold. She took in a deep breath. The night air was crisp and fresh.

"There was this boy I really liked. He worked at one of those restaurants that when you left work, your clothing smelled like food. I hate that smell."

"Dadia, look at me." He waited. She slowly turned back toward him. He looked at her with those eyes that put her in a trance so long ago. "You don't have to continue if you don't "want to."

"No one knows but me and my mom," she said as she looked away.

"Some things are hard for me. Sometimes I push people, guys—especially the one I like—away." She couldn't look at him. She stared out into space as her eyes started to feel puffy. She swallowed feeling a giant marble in her throat.

"You mean you're not disgusted with the way I look?" he blurted out, wishing he could retract that statement. Or at least hoped she'd get a good laugh.

Her demeanor lightened, and she questioned, "What are you talking about? You're perfect, just the way you are. Actually, it was those green eyes that captured me the first time I saw you at the mall." *Damn,* she said to herself. *Stupid! I can't believe I just said that!* She stood up, wanting to run home but walked toward the pond, stopping at the water's edge. He followed behind her, making sure he left just enough space as she seemed to be transfixed to another place in time.

"If it was warmer, I'd go night swimming," she said.

"Ah, night swimming," he replied with a nod as he stood beside her.

As if the universe gently nudged their arms like a puppy's nose wanting attention, he felt her hand slip into his. It was the championship game, and he was running across the goal line, football high in the air. He felt lifted ten feet high, and the roar of the stadium echoed out and down into the streets below.

53

IT WAS HARD TO BELIEVE HOW much happened in just a few, short months. Here he was again, but for the last time, to stand upon the steps of 284 Ewing Avenue. Today the sun did not shine, only lingering clouds that filled a gray-swept sky.

Johnny looked out into the neighborhood that held his youth. The vibrant, colorful place he had remembered now looked old and worn out. Back in the day, the lawns all had a military manicure and flowerbeds abound with rainbows of color and the crisp smell of flowers in the air. Up and down the street were the sounds of manly power tools in the hands of manly dads, early Saturday morning mowing, clipping, and weed whacking their prized possessions. But now the only the sounds were in the hands of lawn services with riding machines that could clean up the yard and be gone before you could take out the trash.

He looked hard and long at the only place he ever called home. The siding had grown out of its skin, while the wood around the windows and sills cracked like the hands of an old seafarer. He didn't want to leave, but they couldn't keep the house. Dad was in rehab. He opted to go full time, like sleep-away camp. They needed the money, and his father needed to get well. The buyer they said, a very generous person paid full price, cash no less, for the house. Johnny was allowed to live there free of charge until he had found another place to stay. He was grateful for the offer. It didn't take long, and he found a little place in Harrier, a studio apartment to call his own. It was small, but it would suffice. His night fears dissipated, and he finally started to sleep with the lights off. It made him believe that maybe there was something out there in the universe watching, wanting to help in some capacity.

Mr. Manteria got him and Mike Johnson a job over at the courthouse in Harrier. Mike believed in him for some reason and helped Seth find Ms. Rosemary, who told them about Elgin. He liked Mike and hoped that his work ethic would rub off on him. Mr. Halley was now in jail, waiting for arraignment for Larry's murder. Larry's father, Jack, was also waiting for arraignment for the attempted murder of his mother and possibly his grandmother, Stella Thestus. The so-called religious compound of the Foundation was crumbling and he felt a small vindication in that fact. He just knew his mother and grandmother were in heaven and justice was being served here on earth.

Seth was off to college, though he still had big shoes to fill, but Johnny knew he would succeed in whatever he put his mind to. His unique memory helped save his sorry ass by finding and placing all of the missing pieces together with his keen eye for details. The bubble gum wrapper from Mr. Halley ultimately put him at the scene of the crime. Brilliant. Seth connecting Ms. Rosemary with Elgin and his father Myron, unequaled. Only Seth could slither into Crag territory and get them to come out and talk.

Brian was back at Park View High School with a newly found respect, one he truly deserved. And then there was Ashley. She could have buried Johnny alive, but she didn't. Maybe one day Johnny would meet her again, in the future. Maybe, now that he had made it to the eighteenth floor of his blueprint, he would continue upward to finish each story as planned. He hoped that he would bump into her for the third time, maybe around the twenty-third floor, when his life would be more in order.

Maybe that old saying would come true, "third time's a charm." He smiled one last time upon the steps of what he called home for the last eighteen years.

He didn't care that Darius Jones was his biological grandfather and that, in some twisted way, Darius loved his grandmother, Stella. Brian and Seth were his real family, his Brothers of the Domain, and now he had Elgin. No one would ever take that away from him, no matter how far they each traveled in life. Nevertheless, as he stood there one last time on the porch of his childhood home, he still hungered.

Expanding his chest with a big sigh, thoughts of his mom appeared. She really wanted to know her blood family, the sister she never knew she had. He felt sad for that fact, but it didn't change anything between him and Mrs. Paola. She misled him. Brian told him it shouldn't matter; love is something that takes on many levels. He tried to convince Johnny she actually helped him, was there for him, and cared about him before knowing there was a bloodline. Maybe she was scared to reach out too. But she did, and he should just embrace that fact. But inside, he couldn't let it go.

There was only one way to get rid of mixed feelings he couldn't understand—leave them here in this house. Only time might change how he felt—maybe, maybe not.

Pieces of bark from the sycamore fell to the ground as the leaves on the tree took flight, being held by invisible strings. A ladybug, riding on the wings of air, landed on his forearm. He smiled, feeling a presence of the unknown. With it came an aroma of roses. He was a child again, sitting next to his mother on the front steps, eating chocolate chip cookies with Hershey kisses in the middle, talking about saving the environment. He was surrounded by the sweet smell of roses, the scent she always wore and wondered if somehow, in some way, she was trying to tell him something.

The End.